Alice & Henry

Alice & Henry

A Novel

Anne Eldridge

iUniverse, Inc.
New York Bloomington

Alice & Henry
A Novel

Copyright © 2009 by Anne Eldridge

All rights reserved. No part of this book may be used or reproduced by any means, graphic, electronic, or mechanical, including photocopying, recording, taping or by any information storage retrieval system without the written permission of the publisher except in the case of brief quotations embodied in critical articles and reviews.

iUniverse books may be ordered through booksellers or by contacting:
iUniverse
1663 Liberty Drive
Bloomington, IN 47403
www.iuniverse.com
1-800-Authors (1-800-288-4677)

Because of the dynamic nature of the Internet, any Web addresses or links contained in this book may have changed since publication and may no longer be valid. This is a work of fiction. All of the characters, names, incidents, organizations, and dialogue in this novel are either the products of the author's imagination or are used fictitiously.

ISBN: 978-1-4401-9086-5 (pbk)
ISBN: 978-1-4401-9087-2 (ebk)

Printed in the United States of America

iUniverse rev. date: 12/17/09

Acknowledgements

I would like to thank the members of the Compuserve Litforum Writer's workshop for the last four years of invaluable advice, teaching, and critique while I learned the craft.

I am grateful to my parents for believing in me and all their encouragement to pursue this dream. I love you both.

And speaking of love, a special heartfelt hug and warm smile of appreciation goes out to the readers who have followed me since *Olivia's Story*, the many who have joined me along my twisted path through *Precognition* (that journey has not yet concluded), all the way to *Alice & Henry*. You have motivated me through lazy times, chased me to the finish line as the drafts came and went, and every day proved to be a validation that I am on the path designed for me. Without you, I could not have come this far.

The individual names would likely fill several pages, and since all are equally important to me, I cannot name just a few and leave out the rest. You know who you are and I love you.

On with the story…

This book is dedicated to my daughter, Rhiannon, who is my real life Branwen. Daughter, sister, mother, best friend. I cannot imagine my life without you.

One:
Alice 2033

I sensed death in the dimly lit hall and supposed that was as it should be. This was the last stop for old folks like Henry and me—well, Henry mostly, as rumor had it, but at sixty-seven, I likely wasn't all that far behind him. A long rest didn't sound so bad. My feet hurt as did the rest of me. Getting old really sucked the big one, as we used to say.

My high heels clicked and echoed along the quiet corridor—a sexy, lively sound at complete odds with the utter hopeless hush of the place. The antiseptic air and shiny floors seemed to require rubber soles and quiet movement. I sighed, feeling more displaced and uncertain.

Nearly all the doors were open, allowing the subdued beeps of heart monitors to drift out. I nodded to the aides at the nurse's station and continued on my way to the end of the hall. Mine was a familiar face in this nursing home, though I'm sure they didn't understand why. I'd never travelled this particular hall and the visitor's tag clipped to my collar was one I'd cadged a long time ago. More than forty years had passed since I'd last seen Henry. Glimpses and glimmers here and there—nothing more.

The doubts increased with every step, and the rhythmic tap of my heels on the tiles became less determined. *Last chance to turn around and forget this foolishness*, I thought and nearly came to a halt. My fate, as I understood it, was likely already sealed, whether I wished it or not. I continued my echoing march down the hall, watching the room numbers get smaller with my progress, knowing I'd crossed the fabled point of no return.

Last night around midnight, Henry's fetch appeared at the foot of my bed. Dressed in pajamas, he swayed unsteadily, looking sad, old, and very sick. I knew him immediately though my eyes refused to believe the evidence before me.

The image seemed solid; I could not see the wall or furniture through him. For a long moment he stared into my eyes, arms outstretched, and a pleading look upon his face. He glowed in the dimness of my quiet room, energy radiating from him in visible bursts, like a bad electrical connection throwing sparks. He never took his eyes from mine as his mouth formed my name. The fetch disappeared. Gone.

A fetch is just a messenger, really—not like a ghost or walking the Paths, but a doppelganger that often appears shortly before a person's death. Henry would have no conscious awareness of it. That's just the way it is with fetches. It found me, like all unfinished business eventually will, and projected Henry's need of me. Because we are tied together at the soul level, it came like a homing pigeon bearing bad news.

I understood the meaning, knew that his time was upon him and the magnitude of what he asked—though I'd banished him from my life long ago in an act of sheer self-preservation. The fetch had gone without any assurance that I would come; I only stared as it delivered the message. After debating all the night and most of the day, I found myself unable to refuse him. I've never been very good at that.

His wife lay drooling on the Alzheimer's wing and it served her right, the psychotic bitch. Sarah had stolen Henry—or that was my take on it, and now she paid the price of forgetting him. That was one thing I could never, would never, allow myself to do.

Forgiveness came hard for me, as I tended to hold grudges, but then knowing what I knew, this was not the way to go. Stubbornly, I clung to my resentment and would likely go down with all flags flying. I wasn't ready to forgive her and you couldn't just say, "I forgive you, you sadistic whore," and be done with it. You had to mean it.

Maybe I would manage it on my own, before my final curtain call as Alice Keyes. Maybe I wouldn't. Who knew? I liked the unpredictability of never knowing what I would do until I did it. After all I'd suffered at that woman's hands I almost welcomed a chance to get even, a chance to come out on top for once. Henry hadn't done his part to make forgiveness possible and that only stoked the desire for vengeance. I shook the thought from my head. The battle within me had not yet been decided.

I paused at the room number I'd seen behind the fetch and peered around the doorframe. Private room. Alone. He still had money, then—a fringe benefit of his liaison with Sarah. The bump of his big feet tented the blanket near the footboard. A monitor recorded the beating of his heart, and marked every breath he took. I watched the spiking lines on the machine for a moment, then glanced at the acrylic sign on the door and saw the DNR order: Do Not Resuscitate. Those three letters said a lot about my timing. I'd always left it just a little too late, and this silly impulse to see him was no exception.

Feeling a bit foolish, I removed my shoes, pulled the pins holding up my hair, and glanced back down the hall to see if anyone noticed. What difference did it make now? He was dying and I was no spring chicken myself. The tears of another stupid goodbye, another wasted lifetime, stung my eyelids and nose.

I padded into the room, tossing my shoes on a chair by the door before closing it, then tiptoed the distance to the bed. His physical state hurt my eyes, but I looked anyway at the yellow-tinged, withered face seeking the Henry I'd known. Purplish-red gin blossoms splashed his cheeks and nose, a sickly contrast to the jaundice. Disbelief nearly turned me to the computer in search of a patient name, but then his mouth twitched in a smile beneath the oxygen cannula stuck up his nose. So brief, I'd almost missed it, but my heart jumped in my chest. How many times had I seen that innocent, little boy smile when he slept?

Too many times. Memories of the unparalleled, clandestine passion we'd shared riffled through my mind's eye like a stack of old photographs, each one an imprint that would remain with me into the next existence and thereafter. Forever is a very long time.

With gentle fingers, I reached out and touched his cheek. "Henry."

The little smile transformed him once more, but was quickly followed by a wince. The once generous lips had thinned over the years, and someone had cropped his hair. That angered me more than the fact that no one had bothered to shave him for what appeared to have been several days. I ran my hand along the flaccid, silver-stubbled skin of his jaw, tracing the bone and remembering how cleanly cut it had once been. He muttered something unintelligible.

"Henry. It's Alice." Gently, I took his hand.

I waited and hoped, while images of a younger Henry played through my head. God, he'd been beautiful. Not perfect, by any means, but damned near irresistible to me—to me and any other female with a pulse, my resentful mind added.

His eyelids fluttered, but remained closed. Long minutes passed and my eyes were drawn to the monitor. His heart rate rocketed when I spoke. An unwilling smile came to my lips. Yes, that would be Henry, and my own heart did a little trip-hammer ditty in answer. I couldn't help but remember how the very air would change in a room the moment he entered it. I leaned over and kissed the dry, sunken lips, not surprised at all when the monitor began to alarm and he gasped with a terrible choking sound.

"Damn you, Henry…" A strangled sob caught in my throat, but I buried my face in the junction between his neck and shoulder, murmuring against his skin. "I love you, and I forgive you, you old bastard. I won't be far behind you—I hope."

No promises on punctuality from me. He wouldn't believe it anyway. A wave of unexpected tenderness and conciliation swept over me. "Wait for me next time, darling," I whispered in his ear. Something he'd once said, a dirty remark that "he'd be rock-hard on his deathbed if I were within a mile of him," or something like that, came back to me. I ran my tongue along his earlobe and nipped at it, then paused to watch the wavy lines on the screen turn to leaping spikes.

I looked to the fork of his legs beneath the blanket, and wondered if his prediction would hold true in the literal sense. Unable to resist, my hand slid beneath the covers. I snorted with amusement as I yanked my hand from his pajama bottoms and straightened the blanket, satisfied that he'd recognized me.

I also knew he'd heard me, would maybe take the thought with him as he went. Maybe next time he'd do as I asked. Sometimes, he did, when it came to the important things. Leaving his wife had not been one of them. We'd paid a heavy penalty in this lifetime and more lay waiting in the next. I sighed at the thought. We'd fixed nothing this time around and the results of that would follow us—complicating an already knotted, jumbled karmic mess. Though I would remember it all, a solution to our difficulties just might elude me again. Four lifetimes down and who knew how many more in front of us, just waiting to be screwed up.

The rapid beep of the monitor turned into a harsh, braying squeal as the spiking lines turned into a disorganized squiggle and then fell straight. In a panic, I grabbed for my shoes, then a feather light caress brushed my cheek and I shuddered deliciously from the touch of the spirit that delivered it.

"You know I'll make you pay for this, Henry," I said with a smile through the veil of tears blurring my vision. I blew him a kiss and lurched for the door.

Two:
Henry 2033

Alice was lovely, even as a stubborn old broad who'd refused to have herself tidied up and rejuvenated by surgery and injections. I loved her—always had, though probably not the way she deserved. I looked down upon her as she bent to kiss me and noted that she'd taken down her hair. She'd done that for me. I knew it like I knew the sky was blue or that I was too weak to kiss her back. That hair, my god, could drive a man wild. I remember her merciless dark eyes by candlelight and her slim arms as she reached up to release that wonderful spill of golden-streaked brown. We were so young then—well, she was, and I should've known better.

I pulled away from the premature stroll down memory lane. Now that I was moving on, I understood that I'd be shown the whole miserable thing in great detail. I would not be allowed self-delusion in the space between this life and the next, so I admitted that much in advance. Practice for the real thing. You couldn't escape the Life Review portion of physical death, though you *can* skip out in the middle, if you've been around the block a few times. Of course, that usually just leads to more trouble. I had the vague sense that it had for me, more than once.

Yes, my dying, shriveled up, old man's heart still beat faster in her presence. I'd nearly cut the bonds that held me to the wreck in the bed, had been gnawing at them furiously like a wild dog tied to a stake as she'd entered the room and first held my hand and then my privates.

I knew it would be okay, then. She'd arrived and I severed the last tie holding me to this life. I could go. Maybe I'd waited for her. I can't remember now. That she'd turned up in the final minutes of my life didn't really surprise me; she had always known things that no mortal woman should know.

Though I was not completely in that body, still I smiled at her words and her actions. So appropriately inappropriate. So Alice. I *would* wait for her. I'd always done that, too—more or less.

Distantly, I heard the monitor announce the end of this last life and watched her lovely face as she took it all in. Though the urge to leave was strong, my urge to touch her was stronger. Her hand rose to her cheek as she grabbed the ridiculous high heels she still insisted on wearing, though I could tell they hurt her. I smiled at her threat and followed her to the hall, prolonging my journey for a last look. Alice passed the nurse's station and they didn't question her. There also didn't seem to be any rush to my bedside as one of the nurses frowned at the monitor on the desk, forked in another bite of her Healthy Time microwave meal, and pushed a button that silenced the alarm.

I'd put that DNR order on myself the day I transferred from the hospital to the nursing home. It didn't hurt my feelings that no one moved. They couldn't do anything for me but pull the sheet up over my face and call the funeral home. Big deal.

No one ran to my room, but Alice moved at a quick, stiff pace, an old woman's version of a gallop, away from it. Though she'd gone a bit soft around the edges, she was still slim and straight. Alice. I wondered what she would look like the next time. Achingly beautiful, at least to my eyes, and I would be drawn to her as I almost always am. That would likely not change either. Her eleventh hour confession had sealed it. I could put my foot in her lovely ass for that. Why couldn't she just let me go? I could ask myself that same question...

As she'd said, there would be a price to pay for her. That was nothing new, either.

"Time to go now, Henry," said the voice, and when the Being took my hand, I let it lead me away. All was done here.

Three:
Alice 1980

It's not as easy as you might think, growing up with knowledge of past existences. I wasn't born with full adult comprehension or anything, but I quickly grew into it.

Understanding who the players are in your life is not cheating—there are surprises, challenges, disappointments, lessons to be learned, and always lessons to be failed. The tricky part was figuring out how to avoid repeating the mistakes. Here on earth, distractions are everywhere. Shakespeare had it right when he said, "All the world's a stage..." We come and we go, returning to the footlights of our own little tragedies and comedies, donning our costumes and makeup, playing our parts and forgetting who we truly are. It doesn't matter what you know or what you remember, we are here to learn and most often, failure is the most effective teacher. Where Henry was concerned, I believe the odds were about 50/50. Stubborn beast.

I'd looked for Henry since I could talk, or so my mother said. At age three I demanded she tell me his whereabouts. She didn't know. I missed him terribly and chattered on about him so much that at first, my parents decided he must be my invisible friend and humored me by asking questions. I used to get angry when they asked stupid ones.

Years passed and when the chatter about Henry did not go the way of the diapers and the blankie, they considered I might have a screw loose. Three years ago, I overheard them talking about psychoanalysis and promptly shut up about the insider knowledge I possessed. They worried about me. I was their only child and there was a reason for that, which they didn't remember. I did.

They'd abandoned me on a hillside for the faeries to take the last time we'd been all together. Because they were so poor, he'd desperately wanted boys who would grow to help him in the fields. He bullied her into following him to the faerie mound, telling her I was a changeling, that he'd seen the boy child to whom she'd given life. Delirious and fevered, and unfortunately, as superstitious as the rest of her people, she couldn't be sure.

"The little folk have stolen our boy," he told her as she held me, unwilling to put me on the ground, shivering from exhaustion and the proximity to the ring of stones on the knoll. "They left this scrawny girl in his place! We only need to return her and the faeries will bring our boy back to us. The moon is right and all the portents are there."

She almost believed him. Almost. But his belief in the power of the faeries trumped her doubts. He held me no malice whatsoever, but truly believed that when they returned a boy child would be their prize.

Of course the plan backfired. When they returned to the mound, all that remained was a withered, animal ravaged little corpse in a ragged blanket. He told her not to grieve, for only the changeling had died. Their boy had been too good to be returned to them. Tears stained his homely face as reality overtook him and he realized what he'd done. He'd never been the same afterwards.

They'd had no more children in that lifetime and there would be no more to follow me in this one. If they treated me right, next life, if they chose to spend it together, they could have as many as they wanted.

Mom and Dad still held hands after twenty-nine years of marriage. They'd do it again. I didn't think I'd be a part of that one, though. This parent choice was a favor to them and something I did willingly. Had I been someone else, I could just as easily chosen to be their parent and abandon them, just so they'd know how it felt. I am not that kind of soul—though I have played my own fair share of unpleasant roles for the benefit of both myself and others. That's the Way It Works.

As the result of all the rounds I spent as a priestess, (or in later ages, the job description had been renamed: witch), I'd opened pathways in my mind through ritual and remembered all my past incarnations to flesh. My tendencies had sent me to the bone yard more than once, and every time the biggest contributing factor was my involvement with Henry.

I'd forgiven him. I always do, though his character defects have grown tiresome over so many years. I'd been so disappointed in him last time, I nearly took a pass on this go-round. But then, no doubt he'd have found me anyway whether I liked it or not—or the Universal Scorecard, who keeps tabs on these things would've thrown us together. Henry is like a hair shirt I keep in the closet and can't seem to stop putting on. I know I deserve better, but I rarely believe it when I meet him.

I laughed out loud at my first sight of him. August 29th, 1980. My first day of high school. As usual, the morons who set the school year schedule had placed the first day before Labor Day weekend. Dumb. Fourteen year's old and I'd spent all of that time searching strangers' faces for my Henry and never turning him up.

Half-pissed off and defiant at his seeming desertion, I let someone else bestow my first kiss upon me and went to the junior high dances with my little boyfriend, Allen, who dumped me for another girl before the Valentine's Ball. Great.

Allen was far from my thoughts as I looked at the room number and down at the crumpled schedule in my hand. American History 101. Instructor: Spears. When I walked into the room, he stood with his back to the class, writing his name on the chalkboard. I chose my usual position not too far to the rear and not so close to the front as to appear eager. I put my books in the rack under the chair, seated myself, and folded my hands on my desktop, waiting for the bell to ring. He turned around and scanned the room. I froze in my chair, eyes bulging at the name he'd scrawled on the blackboard: Henry Spears. And beneath it: *That's Mr. Spears to you.*

Oh haha, very funny. It had to be a joke, except it wasn't. There he stood in all his just-graduated-from-college glory and there I sat in the swamp of my fourteen year-old hormonal stew. Eyes so brown they were nearly black raked the room and came to rest on me. A frown notched the smooth skin between his silky black brows and I returned his stare. Dark hair, a little too long for respectability curled at his collar, and I knew he would sometimes let it grow to his shoulders, as he always had in the past, for that was his preference. He always came to flesh with an enviable mass of it, and usually kept it if he managed to live long enough to get old.

Truly, it was most likely my stare that drew his, for I was giving him the once over and considering the possibilities in the first seconds following the initial shock.

His frown deepened and he looked more disturbed, like a little boy just waking from a dream—the slightly pompous, self-congratulating expression fled as his eyes locked harder onto mine. He stared long past the time politeness or protocol would have dictated, his frown turning to puzzled concentration. Then I burst out laughing. He didn't remember. He never did and that was sometimes part of the challenge. I could already tell this was going to be one of those times.

I took my memories with me like Samsonite luggage or an American Express charge card I wouldn't leave home without. Henry was absent-minded and this time he was a *professor*—or close enough. Fred MacMurray's clueless, good-natured face flashed before my eyes; I'd just seen the damned rerun last Sunday on the Wonderful World of Disney. Hysterical giggles erupted from me and tears squirted from my eyes. I ran from the room, holding up an apologetic hand, hoping he wouldn't give me a detention.

The bell rang as I flung myself through the girls' bathroom door and fell in a heap next to the radiator, gasping and trying to pull myself together. In

Henry's defense, hardly anyone bothered to remember their lives. I learned the hard way that I was a rarity—narrowly avoiding my parents' misguided, but well meaning attempt to fix me.

But that's another story. *This* story had just turned interesting. Immediately the new song I'd heard on KZ93 this morning, *Don't Stand so Close to Me*, by the Police started playing in my head and I'd be lucky to remove it before I turned thirty. *Young teacher, the subject, of schoolgirl fantasy...* This was so tacky. I could walk right back into that classroom and brain him for doing this to us.

I would seduce him of course.

That would be the fun part. I chuckled darkly. Fourteen year-olds should not have access to past life memories. It was, I admitted, an unfair advantage in some cases. I was a virgin, but certainly not an innocent. I had memories that would singe the pages off my dad's *Penthouse* magazines and most of them centered on the man who was now my history teacher.

I splashed water onto a paper towel and blotted my overheated face, wiping away the faint brown mascara smears, snorting every now and then as the revelations came.

He did this on purpose. He deliberately got here before me and set this up, but he wouldn't remember that part, either. Sting's voice continued the soundtrack in my head. *Just like the... old man in... that-book-by-Nabokov.* I'd read that book, *Lolita*, and as I recalled, it ended badly, and no doubt this would, too. Hmm. I guess that's the way it would be. Good thing this was a public school and not a parochial one with uniforms—that would've been too clichéd for belief.

I ran my fingers through my hair, then yanked the bathroom door as Cathy Myers just started to push it open from the other side.

"Oh!" she exclaimed in that breathy, little girl voice of hers. "Mr. Spears sent me to check on you."

I'll just bet he did. And how many girls did you run over getting to his desk to volunteer, you little hooker?

"What was *that* all about, anyway?" Her tone and quick glance at her reflection in the mirror implied she didn't really care, but thought it was the thing to ask.

I put my best smile on and the not-so-nice thoughts away. "Oh nothing—you know how it is sometimes. I think I'm going to start my period. I was just heading back."

"Oh, *that*." Her mouth screwed up in a little twist as she smoothed her hair and eyed herself in the mirror. "I usually end up crying for no reason, not laughing. You're so weird, Alice..." Her china blue eyes met mine in the mirror, dancing as she thought of more insults, but then her cheeks bloomed carnation pink, and her eyes turned sly as she changed her mind in favor of a more diverting subject.

Transparent as a windowpane, was Cathy. She turned on me so fast I jumped a little. "So what do you think of Mr. Spears?" Before I could answer, she rushed on, already in the throes of a huge crush. "Oh my god, he's so adorable, so incredible, so…so…"

"Cathy!" I snapped my fingers in front of her nose.

Her eyes flew wide and startled. "*What?*"

"He's too old. You should know better." I flipped my hair smugly over my shoulder and felt pretty sure I would kill her if she laid one finger on him.

She giggled. "Who gives a shit? He's gorgeous!"

"Yeah, gorgeous," I grumbled as I paced her down the hallway.

"What? You don't think so?" Her silly, incredulous voice grated on my nerves. Though she'd been my friend through many lifetimes, she'd just as often been my rival and enemy. I hadn't decided which it would be, this time. My best friend hadn't arrived yet and likely wouldn't for some years. I didn't know it all, but some things, I certainly did.

I gave Cathy a withering look. "Sure I do, but he *knows* he's hot. That makes him completely un-hot."

"You're stupid."

"That makes two of us, then. But since you're already Village Idiot, I guess I'll have to find another job."

She barked an abrupt laugh, but cut it off as she paused at the classroom door, preening herself. "Do I look okay?"

I mimicked putting a finger down my throat and left her there. I knew she was simpering along in my wake, swinging her little butt in that too short, too tight skirt.

Henry fixed me with a teacher-look of disapproval. "Since I've already taken attendance, I've determined by process of elimination that you are Alice Keyes."

"Good work, professor," I replied in an acidic tone. Detention here I come.

He gaped at me, obviously expecting some sort of apology; a red rash of color stained the skin above his white shirt collar. I watched in fascination as it rapidly climbed the solid column of his neck and spilled onto his tanned cheeks. It was like watching the mercury in a thermometer held to a light bulb. "I'll see *you* after class, Ms. Keyes."

"I'm sure you will," I muttered under my breath, but loud enough that he heard. I darted a glance at him and caught the look on his face, which he quickly covered as he cleared his throat and addressed the class in a boring outline of what he would teach us this semester and what he expected from us.

I yawned behind my hand. American History was such a drag. Why couldn't he have chosen European history? We'd had more fun there... I winced. Except for that one time. I heard the flames crackling and felt the ropes cut into the tender flesh of my wrists. Better to not think of that one.

The bell buzzed its loud, jarring tones through the school, startling me from my daydream of our time in ancient Rome. Now there was some history for you! Hot nights. Olive groves. Togas. Mmm. We didn't always mess it up, only some times. The first day was a short one, the classes only twenty blessed minutes long.

I pulled my books from the metal rack beneath the chair and took my time as the other students raced on to sixth hour. I rolled my eyes as he wrote on a pad of what were probably detention slips, ignoring me. As if that were possible! Robby Felder tripped over his own feet on his bounding way out the door.

"Mr. Felder. Close the door behind you," Henry said in a tone that brooked no argument.

Robby shrugged and obeyed, throwing me a look of pseudo-sympathy. The door banged shut on the frame. Oh crap, here we go. I sauntered to the desk and stood near his elbow, my outward nonchalance masking a heart gone completely bonkers.

Without looking up from his scribbling, he said, "Ms. Keyes. I don't know what prompted that outburst, nor do I care, but you will respect..."

"Yeah, yeah," I held out my hand. "Give me the detention and get it over with already."

Again he flushed as he tore the slip from the pad. He pulled a little too hard and the thing ripped in half. He stared at it in naked disbelief, swept it off his desk with his forearm, and fumbled for his pen to start another.

I plucked up the pieces near my feet, tore a length of tape from the dispenser and neatly scotched the two halves together before he could retrieve his pen, which had rolled onto the floor and under the desk. I almost felt sorry for him. He was jazzed by this and didn't know why. With what little control I could muster, which at my age was admirable, yet not quite what it would eventually be, I concentrated on keeping the tremor from my voice. It wasn't easy.

"Don't bother. I'm sure this won't be the first torn detention slip the dean has seen. See you tomorrow...Henry." I couldn't resist and a nervous giggle slipped out. I hated being a teenager. I'd even screwed that up. Today was Friday and I was staring down a long weekend from hell. I wouldn't see him 'til Tuesday. Damn.

The pad of detention slips hit the wall behind me as I bolted through the door, pushing against the crowd of students milling in front of it. He might be a teacher and all grown up, but he was still pretty young. What? Twenty-four or five? Twenty-six, tops, I decided. He had no lines on his face and the lines that separated him from his students were almost non-existent, I reminded myself. He'd parked his butt on these high school seats just a few scant years before, I'd almost bet my lunch money on it.

I raced up the nearly-deserted stairs to the library for sixth hour, hoping I'd make it before the bell or I'd likely be racking up my second detention on the first day of school. A record? Maybe. It certainly would be for me. This was a first in that department. Thanks Henry, old buddy, old pal.

As soon as the assistant librarian finished her rules of conduct, I headed for the shelf holding the LCHS yearbooks I'd spied upon entry and began rifling. I was rewarded instantly with the class of '74. There he was, and I was right again. His dark hair curled on his shoulders and his brown eyes stared at me from the glossy black and white page. The long, almost girlish lashes drew sooty half crescents so perfect that I couldn't have forced that effect with a half a tube of mascara and a bottle of eyeliner. His sensual mouth curved into a cocky half-smile, the smooth shaven, silky cheeks just begging to be touched. I snapped the book shut and silently fumed. He'd been here all a long, just a few rungs too high on the ladder for me to see—until now.

Four:
Henry 2033

As Alice retreated down the long nursing home hallway, I fixed a questioning, almost pleading look upon the glowing, vaguely human shape next to me and he nodded his approval. He took my hand and...let me follow her. I couldn't believe my good luck. The gender of this Being was uncertain, but I figured they wouldn't trust me with a girl after this last wild ride. I flattered myself and enjoyed my joke. Just one of the guys, hanging out in the Afterlife, right? He seemed familiar to me and I think I knew his name. Something told me we'd been through this together more than once.

He sort of faded into the background and I thought he might be a teacher or a guide, if you will. I couldn't seem to think about him or care. I was still tripping on the non-physical—there was nothing on earth like it. No substance illegal or otherwise could induce the high I felt. Trapped in a dying old carcass as I had been for at least a year, I felt buoyant and downright cheerful to be free of it. I bounced here and there in Alice's wake, doing cartwheels on the air, back flips on the ceiling—which I could touch if I chose or ignore at will. I couldn't help it, the weightlessness and absolute absence of pain went to my head.

Alice slammed the door on her ancient car, one of those little green machines that saved Detroit after the stock market meltdown of '08. She'd had it modified, for the keyboard and command monitor were clearly not part of the original dash. All vehicle traffic operated on computerized grids now. No accidents. No deaths. No more Click It or Ticket! The steering wheel was a quaint reminder of the good old days and completely obsolete.

Alice stabbed the spacebar and a couple of other keys on the dash's keyboard and sat back in the seat as the car took her...home? I didn't know. Preset code, but I thought it a reasonable assumption. I sat in the passenger seat and drank in her loveliness as she stared through the front windshield into the night. The lines on her face hadn't dimmed the feisty spirit beneath even a tiny bit. She appeared to glow. Beautiful.

High cheekbones, a soft, thoughtful look in her bewitching dark eyes. I smiled. A witch she certainly was, I suddenly remembered. But then she covered her face with her hands and surprised me with a sob. Crying? Over me? What was this? I found myself peering at her, only inches from her face, when just seconds before the console between the front seats had separated us. Her pain crossed the flimsy veil between us and grabbed me right where it counted.

Her hair, unbound in its silver-streaked glory flowed over her narrow shoulders and I realized she was much thinner than I'd thought. I tended to see Alice in terms of how I wanted to see her, not necessarily as she is. Somehow, I'd expected her to celebrate my demise. God knows I probably deserved it.

"Damn it, Henry, why?" She said to no one in particular and thumped a delicate fist on the steering wheel as it turned itself down a dark side street. The car ignored the assault and continued on its course. Her fist had passed right through my chest and I shivered as fire and ice sang through my insubstantial core.

"Why what? Why not?" I asked, at a loss to understand. "You know the truth."

I felt the Being's hand on my shoulder and his rich voice flowed over me like sun-warmed honey. The second taste of that voice gave me to know that my assumption had been correct. I knew that voice like I knew my own name.

"You've always had a bit of trouble with that question, Henry. Look at her."

I looked and then turned to the voice, which now seemed to be in the back seat. His subdued golden glow shone softly on Alice's hair, competing with the silvery essence that was her soul's light. I lost myself in the sight for a moment. "She's beautiful and I love her. I can see her now as much as I want! She told me she wouldn't be far behind me and I can't wait to be with her again. What more is there?"

A long suffering sigh came from the backseat. "You have much to learn, little one."

I turned to Alice and did the only thing I knew how to do. As she leaned her head back on the headrest, wiping tears, I leaned into her and kissed her, melding spirit or whatever it was that is truly me, with her for the briefest of moments. Exhilarated, I glommed onto her bright essence and became drunk on it. Alice. Life. I wanted to merge with her and never part myself.

The next second found me floating a foot above the wet pavement of Lincoln Avenue, the taillights of her car moving sedately away from me. My angel friend held my hand in a firm grip and he chuckled. It was then that I remembered that I'd forgotten Sarah, my so-called wife.

Alice had sighed when I kissed her.

Five:
Alice 1980

O*h thunder only happens when it's rainin'…Players only love you when they're playin'…* You can say that again, sister, I thought. The windshield wipers kept dreary time with Stevie singing on the radio and I tried to ignore the indignity of being driven to school by my Mom.

"You're quiet this morning," she said, breaking away suddenly from her non-stop stream of consciousness chatter. Truly, I was surprised she noticed. My mother's mouth ran all the time. Thoughts passed through her blonde head and out her pie hole with barely a fare-thee-well. She was a surface dweller, always chattering and almost always upbeat, whereas I'd always seemed compelled to swim the murky depths of life, never satisfied until my toes touched the very bottom. Though I loved her, she often was the target of my impatience and irritation these days.

"Mm hm," I mumbled and cursed the rain that had put me in this car. I liked to walk. The high school was much further from our house than the junior high, but I'd intended to continue my morning constitutionals—which were more often morning sprints because I rarely made it out the front door on time. I liked to think and I couldn't do that with her rattling on over there about…a soap opera? Aunt Josie's bad back? I hadn't been paying attention. I rarely did. I just couldn't, regardless of how I tried.

Evil thought alert. I dropped the bomb just to see what would happen. "I found Henry."

At first I didn't think she heard, because she continued speaking right on over the top of me, like a cheery, pink steamroller smashing my words to a flat, vaporous gray line. "Huh?"

I caught her darting glance from the corner of my eye as she turned onto Wyatt Avenue. Almost there, the timing was perfect. "That's the good news. The bad news is that he's my new history teacher and the dumbass is like eleven years older than me, maybe twelve, I don't know. Do you suppose he'll go to jail?"

Mom's mouth popped open in a round, little 'o'. "Alice!"

I watched as she struggled with this juicy tidbit. Mom didn't like reality. She liked platitudes and clichés that fixed everything, and if not, there was clinical help for whatever ailed a person nowadays. I made a side bet with myself that she would speak those very words or some variation of it before I exited the car. Or, she'd change the subject and pretend I'd never said it.

She pulled into the front drive of the school and parked in the bus loading zone, which was mostly deserted, because I was way early this morning. Thoughts of Henry had kept me awake far into the night and then came restless dreams of him and wham-bam! there I was, grouchy as hell and ready to hurt somebody. Poor Mom.

Her eyes were frightened and the ever ready supply of tears already filling the well of her lower lids. For all that she was the most determinedly cheerful person I knew, she was also easily hurt. Her greenish-blue eyes swam in glossy pools. She tucked a wayward strand of fading blonde hair behind her ear—a sure sign of distress.

I'd just sprouted three heads and confirmed her worst fears, in other words. Her lower lip quivered. "I thought…well you haven't said anything about him in years … I told Daddy we should've… There's medication now and I saw this story on Phil Donahue …"

Ding! Ding! Ding! We have a winner. I reached for the door handle. "God, where's that faerie hill when you need one?"

"What?" A huge tear spilled over and splashed down her cheek.

"Don't cry, Mom. I was just kidding. I'm sorry, so never mind, okay?" I forced a smile. "If it stops raining, I'll walk home tonight."

I smiled again and waved, cutting off her words as I slammed the door. We were two strangers from two separate worlds speaking two separate languages. She was the concerned parent from Planet Happy Life and I was the disgruntled teenager from Planet Strange.

The very second my foot hit the front steps I remembered the detention. I cast a frantic glance at the clock on the wall. Shit. I thought I was early and I was nearly late after all. I had exactly fifteen seconds to make it to the other end of the school. I ran clonking and tripping in my high heeled boots, a selection I'd made based on the rainy-day ride, an overdose of Fleetwood Mac, and an irritating desire to flaunt myself in front of Henry.

My skirt, long and filmy, floated around my calves. The black lace shirt tied snugly at my waist and the flesh-colored camisole made people look twice when I wore it. I looked like Stevie Nicks' little sister right down to the wild, blonde-streaked light brown hair. I had been more than once. In the sisterhood. I don't know if she remembered, though judging from her songs, she remembered a *lot*. I hadn't met her this time yet.

The bell rang as I fell through the doorway. Henry sat as presiding jailor at the head of the classroom. He fixed me with a disapproving glare and made a check on the book in front of him with an exaggerated flourish. Great. Could this day get any better?

I melted into the nearest seat and watched him from beneath my lashes as he made a big show of shuffling the papers around on the desk in front of him. Suddenly, I became aware of the utter silence of the room and to my horror, realized I was the only one there. Except for Henry. My hands were empty and there was nothing to do but sit there and try not to look at him or feel his eyes upon me. Hyperawareness caused my skin to tingle, every nerve ending almost painfully alive and near the surface.

Adrenaline flooded my system and my heart did a sick little somersault. An internal fire bloomed in my cheeks and a pulse pounded thickly in my ears with a meaty thud-*thud*, thud-*thud*. Somehow, I could hear the clock on the wall behind me. It kept counterpoint to my heartbeat.

"Alice, come here, please." His voice echoed off the empty walls.

I jumped and looked at him, stricken. Strangely enough I felt tears prick my eyelids. What? No. The sound of his voice brought them.

Trying and failing to control my breathing, which had just now nearly hit the panting stage, I pushed out of the desk and dragged myself to the front of the room, willing self control. I'd missed him so much and yet…

In front of the desk, I finally stood and raised my eyes to the dark pools of bright obsidian that belonged to Henry. He opened his mouth to speak and then closed it. He cleared his throat and tried again. "Alice."

He made a strangled sound of frustration.

"Yes?"

"I…well, you…" His eyes rolled heavenward and he muttered, "What the hell is wrong with me?"

I could've told him, but I wasn't in the mood. The emotions ripping along my central nervous system pissed me off. He stared at me in consternation and his Adam's apple rose and fell as he swallowed several times. "Listen. We got off on the wrong foot Friday. I'm new at this and overreacted, I think. I took your permanent school files home with me over the weekend. I barely got through all the glowing reports from all your teachers from kindergarten right on up. I know you're not a trouble maker."

"No. I'm not." I paused, thinking of my mom. "Usually."

One silky eyebrow climbed his forehead and I found myself wishing there wasn't a desk between us. I suddenly wanted nothing more than to crawl in his lap and tell him everything. This sucked. I had to get a grip on myself. I stared at him and kept my face straight, pretending I was forty-five and he was fourteen and had just farted in public. Attitude. I reached for it.

"What I'm trying to say is that I'd like to keep this between us, okay? I'm sorry for overreacting, but if I can't control my class, I won't be much of a teacher."

I smiled tightly. "So you're sorry, but you don't want me to tell anyone that you have a heart beating underneath that suit? Is that it? You want to be the tough guy."

He looked at me sidelong and my heart turned over—the internal acrobatics were wearing me the hell out, and I stifled an unexpected, nerve-induced yawn. I simply wasn't used to this sort of emotional rollercoaster.

"Yes. You've guessed it. The Tin Man has a heart. Things happen. Giggles happen. It happened to me at a funeral once." He fussed with his tie as though it were too tight. "I understand that, but I couldn't let you out of the detention. There are rules."

"So you are the detention teacher, too, then?" I asked innocently and thought about changing my prissy ways. The dark side had its upside if Henry was the prize. Oh wait, I'd already decided on Lolita, so I guess the good girl was on her way out anyway.

He looked away. "No. I volunteered for it. You were the only student on the list and I put you here."

I made a decision then to let nature take its course. He was a goner and I think we both knew it, though again, it couldn't be spoken of. Not now anyway. "Okay, Henry. Your secret is safe with me." I gave him a smile and put all the force of my personality behind it. The effect was astonishing.

He looked at me with something like terror in his eyes. Again, he swallowed and I heard it. I held his gaze a little too long. The fifteen minute warning bell rang and startled us both.

"See you fifth hour," I chirped.

He stood and hastily buttoned his jacket and I wondered what he was hiding behind those seersucker flaps. I spared him some dignity and didn't look where I wanted to. I grinned though, as I clomped my way from the room.

Six:
Henry 1980

I passed out in front of the TV with a beer stuck in my crotch. The girl, Alice, had me totally freaked. Three nights of bar crawling hadn't driven her from my head. Monday night after a long weekend and work tomorrow. I groaned out loud and popped open the last of a six-pack of Bud, hair of the dog, while Johnny Carson told jokes I didn't hear.

She stalked my dreams. Those dark, luminous eyes watching me, that sweetly shaped mouth whispering to me, telling me of things I'd rather not know. A bright, golden light shone at her shoulder and I turned away. These were things I had to forget. Must forget!

I woke with a gasp to the dying notes of the Star Spangled Banner and dumped the beer between my legs. Jesus. This was not right. Not right at all.

I dragged myself to bed and stared at the ceiling. The alarm clock jarred me from *another* dream of her. I threw it across the room where it knocked a hole in the plaster. Damn. I'd have to fix that...

With a groan, I hauled myself upright, feeling like shit, wishing this was college and I could just blow it off. But no, I was a teacher now—a grown up, and grown ups had to suffer for the sake of responsibility. What a complete load of crap.

My underwear held the predictable morning tent as I stepped to the window and looked down on Logan Street. Rain sheeted against the window. I noticed that the sill needed paint and I needed to get laid. In a bad way. That would fix it.

Sarah...what was her last name anyway? Thomas? Thompson? I'd met her, of all places, at the Watering Hole. Hole it was, too. Didn't matter. I had her phone number somewhere. I searched the cluttered top of my dresser and the pockets of the dirty clothes piled in the corner, which yielded nothing but crumpled receipts, some spare change, and pocket lint. Oh well, I shrugged. She'd turn up again. They always do.

Seven:
Alice 2033

"And so we commit the body of Henry Andrew Spears into God's keeping. Ashes to ashes, dust to dust. From dust you came and to dust you will return. Amen. Let us pray," ordered the minister in melancholy tones.

I stood on the outer fringe of the mourners, glad for the dismal clouds and October mist in which to hide myself. Sarah sat in her wheelchair at the front, as was her due, being his wife and all. She was having a Good Day, which meant she was behaving herself for the most part. She hadn't tried to strip to her underwear, nor had she shrieked nonsense about demons trying to claw their way out of her ass.

Leave it to Sarah to blame gas on the devil's minions. I found her choice of self torment interesting and had observed her at this dramatic behavior more than once in the Alzheimer's wing day room, where I occasionally went to, well, watch the horror that she'd become. I'd struggled for years with the concept of forgiveness for this evil creature, and had never once come close to doing it. Many times I'd sat in a quiet corner, watching or reading, trying to find forgiveness in my heart, but finding instead only disgust and unabated resentment. Henry had never known I'd done this and neither did Sarah—or at least I didn't think so. With a visitor badge on my chest, I passed unnoticed, just one more old lady in a whole damned ocean of them.

Perhaps in this demented state, Sarah occasionally relived our ancient history. Today, she didn't appear to have a clue as to what was going on here, but seemed entranced by the buttons on her coat. Still I was careful to stay out of her sight. Hard telling what seeing me might start with her, though she'd never paid the slightest bit of attention at the home. Maybe I'd changed too much or she was too far gone to recognize me. Maybe I'd just been an uninteresting bug she'd flicked off her life screen and she'd never taken much notice of me at all.

A cloud had settled over the lonely knoll of Irish Grove cemetery and caused it to do its best impression of a faerie mound. Although I knew well the glamorous shroud concealed not heather outside its borders, but good old Illinois corn. Harvest would come late this year and the musky scent of dried husks and golden stalks competed with that of wet dirt and rain.

It should always be this way for funerals. Death should creep about in the earthbound clouds and farewells said in the relative privacy it afforded. Mist curled in ghostly tendrils around the grave markers and droplets fell from the branches of the tree overhead.

Over the preacher's droning exhortation for Henry's soul and his deliverance into Jesus' loving arms, Sarah cackled to herself, lending a sinister quality to the already surreal setting.

"Bastard… tie me up! Tie me *up*!" Sarah shrieked, her voice a rusty nail shredding the muffled stillness of the knoll. Her nurse tried to shush her and the preacher stumbled in his prayer, then pitched his voice louder. Bowed heads came up in startled jerks and quickly returned to their former positions. Sarah mumbled and began to weakly jerk at the restraints holding her to the wheelchair. Her head fell back and I could clearly see that she'd yanked up her dress. The nurse tried to pull it down to cover the grotesque, varicose vein-threaded white blobs that were Sarah's legs.

"Noooooo! I said, tie me up, you stupid fucking loser!" Her hand wormed its way under the dress's hemline and she moaned. The preacher's long, pale face turned whiter and his eyes flew wide, obviously horrified by the obscene display in front of him. He lowered his gaze, cheeks suddenly painted with hectic red patches and fumbled with the bible in his hands. He continued, loudly reciting the prayer over Sarah's yelled obscenities.

The dull glint of a needle, a small spurt of fluid from the tip as the nurse depressed the plunger and within seconds, Sarah quieted, her head lolling to the left side of the high-backed chair. She hastily straightened Sarah's dress and shoved her legs together in a more demure position and I would've bet my last pair of Gucci boots that I was the only one who'd understood those remarks. Amazing that those words still had the power to anger me, set unhealed wounds on fire, and renew the hatred I felt for her a hundredfold. Forgiveness? How in the hell could you forgive that? How?

A playful, misplaced breeze lifted the veil on the hat I'd chosen and I glanced around, surprised when the pins fell from my hair and it suddenly spilled loose upon my shoulders and back.

"Amen," said the mourners in response to the minister.

An unseen hand tickled my ear and tugged a lock of my hair.

"There will be a lunch served immediately after this service given by the ladies of the…"

"Henry!" I exclaimed in a frustrated whisper. "Go away. Go to the Light. You know how it works, dammit. Go on!" I turned and hurried to the car with mincing steps, the wet ground sucking my stilettos into it with every awkward stride, locks of my hair floated in an unnatural manner in front of my face, tickling my nose. My knee gave a painful twinge as I nearly lost my shoe and then pulled the heel from the swampy ground. When would I learn?

With a jerk, I yanked open the car door and felt a playful tweak to my bottom. "Damn it, Henry. Why are you doing this?" I fell into the seat and slammed the door on my ankle. My eyes filled with tears of pain and aggravation as I punched the code that would take me home.

Nothing stirred in the car. He had gone. For the moment.

At the visitation, in the hour before the funeral, I'd come in late and stood alone at his open casket. Sarah, incapacitated and wheelchair-bound, sat cluelessly off to the side, her head cocked at a querying angle as people tried to comfort her; her vague eyes and bizarre remarks showing it unnecessary. He'd had no children with her, so I'd been spared a receiving line. Small knots of people just sort of wandered around informally and when they'd cleared from the front of the viewing room, I took my turn.

It was a small funeral. Henry had not really gone along with Sarah's plans for him. Not at all. Instead of the role of a capable, popular public figure she'd envisioned and tried to force him into, he'd withdrawn from people and life, crawling into the empty comfort of a whiskey bottle, keeping up only the minimal appearances. This much I knew. The evidence showed on his poor face and the lack of real grief in anyone in the room backed up my theories.

He looked freaking awful. Why do people always claim the contrary when looking at a dolled up corpse? With a quick hand, I filched a rose from the casket spray with the red ribbon declaring Beloved Husband in glittery script. That reminder of circumstance pissed me off, knowing that he hadn't been my husband, nor had he been a beloved one, either—the contradiction brought angry tears to my eyes. Had he left her and married me, those words would've been true, not the lie they most certainly were at the moment.

I didn't look at him again, but made my way out the front door, returning to my car, which sat lined up with the others that would be going to the cemetery. I would see this thing through, but I didn't have to stay for the bullshit.

I'd thrown the rose on the passenger seat, a bit disgusted with myself for giving in to those hard feelings. Realizing Sarah's mental deterioration, it came clear that someone else had ordered it for her, someone with a well-meaning assumption and a kind heart. That expensive rose-filled casket blanket was evidence of sympathy for a seemingly loving wife incapacitated by a terrible disease and her devoted husband of over fifty years who had died. No one alive knew the truth of the marriage that had been to Henry nothing more than a prison sentence. No one but me.

Prison might've been kinder…and it had been a very real option for him at one time. As my little car took me home down winding country roads, I picked up the flower and studied its synthetically-produced perfection, running my fingers along the rose's stem, feeling the bumps where the thorns should be through my lace gloves. I held it to my nose. Nothing. It was an over-wrought, manufactured hybrid and its visual flawlessness had robbed it of its scent and thorns and substance. Perhaps the person who'd ordered it understood more than they'd realized. The rose, to my mind, stood as a perfect metaphor describing Henry's life with Sarah.

I lowered the window a fraction and slowly tore away the crimson petals, letting them fly through the crack as the car negotiated the curves on Fifth Street Road. *He loves me. He loves me not,* played through my head.

The outline of the old corncrib, the one that had buckled and curved crazily crooked on uneven ground, appeared through the mist. It had always reminded me of a ship riding a wave on rough seas. It stood, as it had since before I'd been born. Always amazed by it, I stopped my destruction of the rose and stabbed a key that slowed the car to a crawl, noting that the roof was still not broken, though boards were missing—the same ones that had always been missing. The building didn't look like it should still be standing, but there it was, defying gravity and Illinois weather just as it always had. I wondered how it could. Rusting, ancient farm machinery still sheltered, forgotten and abandoned, beneath its inadequate and wavy roof beams.

I pushed the space bar and the car reaccelerated, but only a little as it traveled the remaining dog-leg curves in the road, then returned to a sedate fifty-five miles per hour as the blacktop straightened out once more. I missed real driving sometimes. I'd taken these very curves at a hair-raising speed more than once, just for the hell of it… but that was long ago. Now, I could stomp the accelerator to the floorboard, put the pedal to the metal as we used to say, or take a suicidal turn on the wheel and nothing would or could happen. It almost seemed too safe.

My ankle sang with pain and the rest of my body tuned up for the concert, bringing me back to my small task of taking the rose apart, petal by petal. At last, the rose's core lay exposed on its too-green stem, revealing a useless stamen and pistil, all dry, sterile and free of life-giving pollen—another sad and bitter truth concealed within the outer illusion.

Eight:
Henry 1980

5th Hour, American History 101
First Assignment:
Essay

Tell me about your favorite era of American History.

*Minimum: 3 pages
*Ideas: Favorite Personage (Does not have to be famous, but there must be recorded evidence of this person's impact on history)
*Favorite Event or some historical happening you find interesting.

Meet me in the Library! Find your reference materials and then seat yourselves in the group area—we won't have to be so quiet there!

Assignment Due: Friday, Sept. 12

***

I scrawled the instructions upon the board before the bell rang and took the stairs to the library two at a time, though there was no hurry whatsoever. As I bounded up the steps, I wondered if they would follow, or if I'd have to come back and get them. Alice's face popped into my head. No worry there. She'd bring them. I knew that like I knew my own name. I really couldn't wait to see what she'd turn in on this one. Her essays were perfect, as were her test scores. To catch her off-guard seemed like a challenge I couldn't refuse.

***

I held the neatly printed pages with steady hands, though I did seem to be holding my breath. She'd turned in far more than the minimum requirement and the packet I held was substantial. I smiled, thinking I should've known better than to think I would throw that girl off her track.

So I settled back at my desk on a Friday afternoon, unwilling to wait until I got home to read it, knowing that it would be the best of the class, and anticipating the chance to give my red pen a breather. I saved hers for last. It arrived in my pigeonhole the day after I'd made the assignment along with a mysterious velvet bag, which I immediately stuffed in my desk drawer. I refused to give in to curiosity until the rest of the papers were turned in.

Alice Keyes
5th Hour American History 101

"First, because Witchcraft is a rife and common sinne in these our daies, and very many are intangled with it, beeing either practitioners thereof in their owne persons, or at the least, yielding to seeke for helpe and counsell of such as practise it." A Discovrse of the Damned Art of Witchcraft, PERKINS, 1610.

Thou shalt not suffer a witch to live.
Exodus 22:18 King James Version

Alys Prudence Kerr
b.1645 – d.1662
Hanged for the Crime of Witchcraft

From the moment Henry Sayre cast his eyes upon Alys Kerr, she was doomed. Seventeen year old Henry, betrothed to Sarah Holbert since age three and none too happy about it, had lost his head at the first sight of her.

Alys possessed the fair complexion and burnished hair of many of the Welsh people from which she was descended, not unlike King Henry VIII and his daughter, Good Queen Bess. There the resemblance stopped, for Alys and her mother still covertly practiced the Old Religion as their female ancestors had in Wales since the beginning of time. Branwen Kerr passed her knowledge of the Goddess to a daughter who only had to remember.

With dark, flashing eyes and an endearing smile, Alys's face haunted Henry's dreams from the moment the new Apothecary and his small family moved to Camden in 1660. Henry's words, spoken a few weeks later in confidence to his best friend Samuel Hayes would be the ones that ultimately condemned her. The sentences uttered by a lovesick boy in the throes of his first love? "Samuel, I am bewitched. I live for the sight of her!"

And so Henry did what most besotted young men did: he snuck around and contrived to meet Alys "by accident," becoming more entangled with every word they exchanged. One night in mid-summer, he'd sat on the woodpile upwind from the privy, staring at the stars and thinking of her. His nights, for all of the winter and spring had been wakeful, tortured with sinful thoughts of her. When he slept at all, the erotic dreams often caused him to spill his seed, which led to more sinning on his part. The Church frowned on self-abuse, but he'd counted that as far less a transgression than what he'd like to do with her—and him a nearly married man. Their stolen kisses had inflamed his passion and his imagination. The small, rounded breast beneath the white apron and dark clothing drove him mad with lust. He reached for himself again beneath those glittering stars, unable to help it. He was seventeen. What could else he do?

So often had he memorized her every line that he immediately recognized the figure moving down the wooded path behind his house by the light of a full moon. Of course, he followed. What else could he have done?

It never occurred to him that when she pulled off her cloak and stood clad only in harvest moonlight, offering herself to him, that he should refuse her. He ran to her and took her joyously on the fragrant meadow grass and crunching leaves, groaning as her white limbs enveloped him.

He had been a virgin until that moment, as had she; the blood of her lost maidenhead a dark stain upon grass bleached nearly white beneath the moon. He stared shame-faced and guilt-ridden upon the sight, but Alys looked upon him with eyes full of gladness and told him they had pleased the Goddess, and thanked him for honoring her with his body. She was a strange girl, but he only loved her more because of it. He never wanted to touch Sarah. The very idea repulsed him. But this? This was ecstasy!

Henry's father, William, was the magistrate of Camden and Sarah's father, Charles, was the head of the village's church—two powerful men with a plan for an alliance between their families. Henry's course seemed set.

Sarah Holbert, though only fifteen, knew with inborn woman's intuition that what little affection Henry had felt for her had been taken elsewhere. Her mother, Abigail, had a keener sight than her daughter and while Henry's eyes followed Alys, her eyes followed Henry. Her predatory mind began to stalk the possibilities of bringing down Alys. She knew the girl was odd and it was only a matter of time before she landed upon the way to finish the affair once and for all.

Then, a great, hysterical tide broke upon the shores of New England. Satan was loose among mankind and his handmaidens were everywhere. News of witch outbreaks reached them and eventually infected the population of Camden, just as it had other villages up and down the coast. Sarah Holbert found the answer to her problem on a tattered broadsheet from upriver Saybrook. She took it to her mother with her complaints against the Apothecary's daughter. Alys Kerr was definitely a witch and proving it would not be difficult. Abigail soothed Sarah with reassurances and swore that she would have the Magistrate's son for her daughter, whatever the cost.

Alone in her bed, Alys dreamed of Henry. She lay sated in his arms, a vivid recollection of their many trysts in the clearing and knew that he was her mate, the other half of herself. She wondered if he'd started a babe inside her, for that was a natural consequence of what they'd done. She smiled in her sleep.

He had only to break the betrothal contract with Sarah Holbert. Often she'd wondered why he seemed to hesitate in doing it, for that was his right. The elders would agree if he told them truthfully that he would never get children upon her, that they were not compatible. His father was the Magistrate and would surely be able to sway any resistance from the Holbert's.

Incompatibility had not been an issue with the two of them. She rose up from the long meadow grass to gaze upon his beloved face and instead saw herself swinging from the branch of the great oak in the town square. Horrified, she cried out at the sight of her blackening face and purple, swollen tongue, the sound of the rope creaking as her legs kicked weakly and she slowly strangled to death. What did these god-fearing colonists know about the art of execution? Not enough, for she died slowly and horribly while Sarah Holbert's earsplitting laugh, the laugh that had sent chills down Alys's spine wherever she chanced to hear, echoed through the strangely deserted square.

She sat up with a gasp, surprised to find herself safe in her bed, but she knew the dream for the omen it certainly was. Henry's love would cause her death as it had before—though she'd tried to forget. It was so easy to forget! And so dangerous.

Alys jumped from her bed, snatched her cloak from its peg, and climbed out her window. Breathless, she ran down the footpath to Henry's house, frantic to wake him without waking the household. She tossed pebbles at his window and finally, he came and raised the sash, his white nightshirt billowing in the breeze. His eyes widened at the sight of her and when she opened her mouth, he shook his head violently and put a finger to his lips as he closed the window. Minutes later he held her in his arms as she trembled and told him of the dream.

"Henry, we must fly from this place. Now. Tonight!"

"My love, we cannot. Not yet," he said and cast a fearful look over his shoulder. He pulled her to the sheltering darkness of the trees near the path.

"What say you? Henry! We must. Mistress Holbert…she will accuse me and Sarah will condemn me! We have to go. Tonight!"

He pulled back and looked at her, frowning. "How can thy know this will happen? 'Twas nothing but a dream, sweeting."

"No!" Alys's voice hissed through the darkness and the wind caught her cloak and nightgown, sending it swirling around her legs. "'Twas a *sending*, Henry. I am doomed if we stay. We must leave this night. I know it."

He shivered with desire in the unseasonably warm November night. The half moon gilded the leaves still clinging to the trees and turned all to silver. He reached out a finger and pushed back her hood, wanting to see the bounty of her burnished tresses by moonlight. Overcome, he pulled her to him again, his hardness trapped between their bodies. She was so soft against him and he clasped her little bottom through the thin material of her nightdress, fitting her closer still to him. "Oh God in Heaven thou art so lovely!"

"Henry!" She shoved him away. "We must think!"

He shook his head as though awakening from a dream. "Truly, we must, but first I must get you home. We cannot be seen out here in our night clothes."

"But…"

"We cannot leave, my dearest. Not yet. We have no way or means to go. I own not even the clothes upon my back until I reach my majority at age eighteen—in just a month from now. Then I shall have part of my inheritance for… Well, that has changed. We must be careful from now on and I will talk to my father about breaking my betrothal to Sarah. All will be well. You shall see."

She squeaked in terror. "Henry, you mustn't tell your father. Not now! The time has passed for that and he won't do it once I'm accused. He shall think I've ensorcelled you. He won't let me live."

"Hush, my love. Hush. We will speak of this on the morrow. I shall meet you in the grove after nightfall and we shall plot our future."

"There will *be* no future if we stay!" she exclaimed, near tears but could tell by the maddening expression of superiority on his face that he did not believe her, nor would he run away with her tonight.

"You are barefoot and in your nightdress, Alys. We cannot go away like this. We will be stopped and returned here against our will. Or robbers will take us. Or…" he paused. "We cannot do this without more thought."

She let him pull her down the path and when they at last stood at her gate, she whispered. "Henry, a life fraught with hardship is better than no life at all. Think on it. I will be dead and you will be sentenced to a life of misery tied to Sarah—a living death. We have been given a chance to right the wrongs of the past," she gazed up at him, watching the emotions play upon his face.

"Lifetimes are not to be thrown away lightly, Henry. We might never…" she paused, for she knew in all likelihood this would not finish it for them, but it would certainly affect all that followed. He'd grown used to her views and mostly ignored them, she knew, for he was certain that her heart be true and good. She followed the rules of the Church as well as any, it was only that she couldn't let go of her Goddess or her memories of having lived before. He knew that. He did! "…I do not know that we would be allowed another chance. I love you, Henry! Tomorrow we must go from this place. No later than tomorrow."

She flung herself into his arms and then darted away, feeling his eyes upon her as she clambered through her window. She stood watching him while he stood watching her. Finally, he disappeared into the shadows.

The pounding upon the front door at dawn the next morning sent Alys's heart into a terrified hammering. She sat bolt upright, eyes wide with fear, frozen and unable to move. They had come. There would be no chance to flee.

She endured the stocks for days on end, suffering from the brutal chill wind that had chased away the long, warm autumn. She endured the taunts of the townsfolk, their insults, spittle, and the occasional rotten vegetable. She knew well that death would be welcome when it came, for it would come. There was nothing to do but wait and suffer. Her seventeen year old heart and young body cried out in despair and was unwilling to depart, but she'd been here before. It was not so hard this time. Harder than anything she'd ever done, but it was easier to give up hope when she'd once known the flames.

The trial passed in a nightmarish sequence of lies and wild flights of fanciful fear. Many times she had confessed to the crime of which she had been accused, for they would take no other answer—though she had no more to do with Goody Butler's baby dying or the birthing of the Browne's two-headed calf, than she had with the sudden fits that Sarah Holbert threw, frothing at the mouth and screaming of demons tormenting her.

She had heard of pardons given in other places to confessed and repentant witches, but knew none would be forthcoming here. Their eyes held her doom.

Henry's testimony, though a brave defense of her and a proclamation of love had only been twisted into more evidence—his unguarded mention of bewitchment used against her as proof of her sorcery. His father and Sarah's protected him from accusation, and though they used him mercilessly, he was held as a victim, not a participant.

Mistress Abigail Holbert perched on the spectator's benches and gave testimony in a smug, almost triumphant manner, her small glittering eyes flitting across the fearful faces as she spoke of the ghastly things she had seen the Apothecary's daughter do when she thought she was alone. Sarah took her cue and threw herself into a seizure on the floor, pointing her fat finger at Alys and begging her to stop.

When at last it was over and the sentence of death by hanging had been passed for the safety of the community, they led her to the tree and she did not fight, nor did she struggle, but only did what she was told. She felt grateful that she had managed to turn the attention from her poor mother, who could easily have been standing here beside her.

She stood upon the makeshift scaffold, a roughly hewn crate that once held chickens, and dully searched the crowd for Henry. She did not blame him that he could not make himself witness this. Another foretelling had come to her. Henry would pass this lifetime in the arms of Bacchus. He would fling himself from this place, deserting Sarah, and drag himself from tavern to tavern until he would die penniless, drunk, and miserable in a gutter a few months from now. He'd never been able to withstand guilt or tragedy.

Reverend Holbert said a prayer for her soul as she waited for the crate to be kicked out from under her. She did her best to forgive Henry and hoped their next life would be better.

***

Henry,

I have tried to change the archaic language to modern for ease of reading, though I know it slipped through in some places. In the velvet bag beneath this paper are copies of the Saybrook County records of Alys's trial and her death certificate. Henry's is beneath that. And lastly, the diaries which belonged to them.

I found the books in the house where Alys lived on a trip to Camden where I visited the Office of Records and other significant places. (I pestered my parents until they took me there). The Apothecary still stands to this day, is an historical site, and it was nothing to slip down to the root cellar and find the loose brick where Branwen, (Alys's mother) hid the diaries. Never mind how she knew to do that or how I knew they would be there. Inside joke, okay?

Hope you enjoyed the story. You don't have to read the diaries, as the language is so full of thee's and thou's and archaic phrasing, it would be a total pain to try to read. I only included them as supportive documentation. Alys's death and Henry's downfall may not have impacted the future of the nation, but it certainly changed the lives of the ones left behind. There is a monument in the town square, beneath the oak tree to the lives lost during the madness of the witch hunts. Alys was pardoned posthumously. Henry's father, William Sayre, Magistrate of Camden, wrote it himself twenty years after her death. That document is under glass and I could not take it.

Alice

***

I held the black velvet bag in my hands for a long time, lost in thought and truthfully, more freaked out than I had been before. My heart pounded an uneven beat and I wiped my eyes with the back of my hand, searching my mind for a reason I might feel as I had reading this paper, and came up blank. A short, brutal stab of fear had hit me when they'd pounded upon the Apothecary's door, followed by a sadness so overwhelming, tears had sprung to my eyes. I read the paper twice, from start to finish and felt the same way both times. Incredible.

A long, shuddering breath escaped me and I pinched the bridge of my nose between my fingers. I felt as I had when my mother died. Grief is an emotion that once experienced, you never forget. How could I possibly feel this way, at this moment, about this paper? Human history held endless tales of the injustices it had committed upon itself. I'd been immersed in it nearly all my college career and had never been affected like this.

The velvet prickled soft and then rough as I stroked it both with and then against the material's grain. The small sound of a plastic lining crinkled beneath the bristly softness. Held closed by a silken cord, the bag also contained a Velcro closure further down inside, holding the books and documents snug within it; the rigid strip raising an edge along the velvet. It was a strange little contraption and I wondered where she'd found it. The pouch looked as though it had been made for the purpose she'd given it. Maybe it had.

The old desktop upon which I leaned was not level and the red pen I used for grading papers had fallen on the floor again. From a distance I heard the approach of the janitor's floor buffer along the hallway. I groped for the pen and laid the velvet pouch aside, uncertain that I wanted to open it, but feeling that I would, regardless.

My eyes returned to the bag and I fingered the tassels at the end of the cord. What had possessed her to write such a thing? Questions of how she knew the intimate details of these peoples' lives now three hundred years gone buzzed through my head. Diaries or no, there were things written here that she couldn't have known. A vivid imagination, then. That must be it. She'd filled in the blanks...to entertain me.

Entertain was not the word I should have chosen. It felt wrong, even as I thought it, but my mind insisted upon it, so there it stayed. The red pen hovered at the upper margin of the neatly printed page.

I didn't ask for fiction.

I glanced at the bag and my own voice said in my head, "You know it's not. Give her what she deserves, idiot."

My hand scribbled the A+ and then trembled as I shuffled the pages to the last one. Beneath her neat calligraphy, I scrawled:

Alice,
Please see me after school in my classroom.
Thank you,
Henry

Why did I thank her? Why did I sign it with my first name and not Mr. Spears? I threw the pen against the far wall and pulled my hair. It was too long, but so what? Why did I write that at all? I didn't want to see her. Didn't want to hear what craziness had prompted this paper. Did I?

The answer was yes. Tomorrow she would come to me, alone in this classroom. I shifted uneasily on the seat. Time alone with Alice caused strange things to happen to me. I half-feared and half-anticipated it. What could I say? The course was set.

Nine:
Alice 1980

Cool didn't begin to describe me as Henry chose Cathy, his Number One Fan, to hand out the essays—but that was on the outside. Inside, I was a seething bundle of exposed nerve endings. All the long days remaining in the school week, I'd watched for some sign from him, but only saw a deliberate sort of indifference. I thought he'd not read it yet, then I thought he had and refused to believe me. Giving me an "F" was not beneath him.

The lifetime I'd written about was not the only one and there was far more, and admittedly, far less to Henry Sayre than what I'd revealed in the essay. But I didn't want him to think... that is, I didn't want to be *too* obvious. After all, if he identified too closely with that Henry, he'd only think it some fantasy one of his little teeny-bopper crushes had written with him in the starring role. I didn't want that. Not at all. It's why I gave him the diaries. I only wanted to nudge him a little further awake. The weekend had been eternal. Would he read the diaries?

Though my heart pounded and heat flooded my cheeks, I faked indifference as I waited the seeming hours it took for Cathy to get to my paper. Of course it would be the last in her hand.

It wasn't the grade I was about to receive that turned me hot one moment and then clammy cold the next. It was the mystery of not knowing how the reading of one of his many lifetimes would affect him. Had it hit home? Did he think I was rubber room material like my folks? What would it be?

I watched with increasing irritation as Cathy sauntered down the desk rows bestowing papers and resolved that if she didn't get her ass in gear and quit showing off, I would happily kick it for her. Finally she got to mine, peeked at the grade beneath the turned down upper corner, (a little respectful habit of his when he let students pass out papers), and with a wink, made to lay it on the desk. I snatched it from her hand, nearly ready to explode. She rolled her eyes and whispered, "Geez, Alice, cool down. It's an A+."

Well, now, that was a surprise. I smoothed out the folded corner, wanting to see it for myself, then noticed that he'd not returned the velvet pouch. I forced my gaze to remain on the paper and willed my hands to stop shaking as I flipped each stapled page. My eyes froze on the red-inked scribble at the bottom of the last and I swear my heart stopped. It's what I'd wanted, wasn't it?

Suddenly I knew he was staring at me—knew it like I knew my palms were sweating or that my panties had become wedged in my butt-crack *again*. Annoyance flared and I briefly renewed my vow to never wear them after I'd moved out of my parents' house. I'd quit now, but Mom would blow a gasket. She lived in fear of the dreaded accident and dirty underwear scenario. A daughter sans undergarments pried from a car with the Jaws of Life would probably kill her.

I squirmed in my seat a bit, knowing it wouldn't help but did it anyway, and then forced my attention back to the essay. I slowly folded the paper and tucked it inside my History folder, then raised my eyes to the front of the room. Dark pools of ebony burned into mine, the skin beneath them shadowed with what looked to be exhaustion. I thought he might have been losing sleep since school started.

Henry stood, thrust his hands in his pants pockets, and said, "Not bad, class, not bad at all—though truthfully the grammar and spelling could use major work in some cases." He lifted a comically cynical brow and scanned the guilty faces, bringing laughs. "Lucky for you, I'm not a member of the English Department. Please open your textbooks to page thirty-one. Today we will discuss the…"

I opened my book, but didn't really hear him anymore. His voice droned far away and I drifted forward in time imagining what he might say to me after school. Not after class, so what he had to say would probably take more than a minute or two. The next two hours and ten minutes would be a living hell of anticipation.

***

I shoved my books into my locker and looked at myself in the mirror stuck to the inside of the door. The last owner had put it there, or maybe the one before, though this hallway was so dim even at noon that it didn't do much good for makeup checks. But then, I didn't wear much makeup as a rule. My eyes looked huge and frightened in my pale face. I fluffed up my already tousled hair—no matter what I did, the slight natural curl made it look that way. With a clang, I slammed the locker shut and jostled my way through the crowded hall, catching a slight chemical odor from the open door of a science lab, then moved on down the student-clogged back stairs. A door was open somewhere down there and the temperature cooled a bit as I descended. Still too warm, but maybe that was just me.

Every step I took increased my heart rate and I felt nervous almost to the point of nausea. I ducked into the girls' bathroom and leaned against the wall for a moment, resting my forehead on the cool tiled surface. The smell of stale cigarette smoke and disinfectant were somehow soothing, a distraction of sorts. Smoking was forbidden on school grounds and the rule cheerfully ignored by everybody. It gave the gym teachers something to do.

All the disadvantages and downright unfairness of being fourteen and in this predicament had me demoralized and a little scared—and that, as usual, pissed me off. I'd laughed at first sight of him, but as the days went by I began to understand just how awful it was to know he stood only a few feet from me and so far out of my reach as to have been ten thousand miles.

Truthfully, I hadn't seen it coming, and if I hadn't seen this, then what else was on its way? There were times when thinking you understood most of how it all worked backfired and left you swinging ass in the breeze without answers or simple means to get them. This might just be one of those times.

Outside the girls' restroom, the frenetic boisterous sounds of teenagers just released from their day-long captivity gradually receded. The time grew between slamming locker doors, reminding me of Jiffy-Pop popcorn in the final seconds between pops. When five minutes had passed in relative silence after the last clang! I opened the door, ready to face him.

Henry jumped when I entered the room, though surely he had expected me to obey? And surely he had to have heard my boot heels on the tiles of the deserted hallway? He held the velvet bag in his hands, gingerly, like it might be a time bomb ready to explode. I could almost hear it ticking... maybe it was a bomb, in more ways than I knew.

"Alice."

"Henry," I parroted. The irreverence returned on sight of him. I *knew* him, damn it. It didn't matter if he was in a different body, my history teacher, and older than me. That was an illusion. Immaterial.

A weak smile twitched his mouth and fled. "Your paper was the only A+ work in the class, though you came pretty close to an F."

"Heaven or Hell and no space in between, then?" I moved closer to him and sat on the edge of his desk in a deliberate, non-student way. I refused to be in awe of him or subordinate to him in private.

"I didn't ask for historical fiction. I asked for facts." He handed me the black velvet bag, his face arranged in stern lines and I thought he'd rehearsed this speech—it had that sound—along with a slight undertone of doubt, as though he didn't quite believe what he was saying. "Though your rendering of these events was nothing short of marvelous and your creative writing is to be commended, there is no possible way you could've known these things."

"Did you read the diaries?"

He flushed and loosened his tie. "I read most of hers. No time for his. You were right. The language is...difficult. Not a quick read."

"Is that why you have circles under your eyes?"

"That's none of your business."

I smiled. "You're right. How rude of me to point out that you look tired, and maybe the reason might be that you stayed up all night reading Alys's diary. You must not have finished it, because if you did, you'd know what happened."

I untied the knot holding the bag closed; the interior Velcro strip's ripping sound somehow vulgar against the quiet tension filling the room. Carefully, I pulled Henry's cracked leather-bound volume from it. I would soon have to put it in its box, away in the dark again or it would fall apart. "Here. He wrote part of it. I only narrated both sides into the essay and perhaps that is the cause of the confusion."

He shook his head. "No. I'm thinking of Alys's thoughts as she waited on the scaffold. Henry couldn't have known what she was thinking—he wasn't there. No one could've unless she spoke the words. And I don't think she did, did she?"

I threw him a look of surprise. He'd actually read my paper and given it a great deal of thought. Dismay followed quickly on the heels of astonishment. He was right, I couldn't have known, except for the fact that I was there, and I wondered what he'd make of that if I told him. I decided against it. He'd only think I was crazy. And why not? It *did* sound crazy without the memories for a frame of reference. I knew he didn't have access to those—at least not yet.

"Well, you see, William Sayre, Henry's father and Camden's Magistrate, took mercy on Alys's mother and let her stay with her the night before she faced the rope. She held her daughter all night long and only let go when they pulled Alys from her arms at the tree."

A wince crossed his fine features as he pulled his tie completely loose from the knot, and fumbled with the top button of his shirt. Then he slumped, his hands gripping the chair arms, his eyes focused on the desktop.

"Alys told her everything that had happened, everything that *would* happen, and Branwen knew who her daughter was looking for at the last. I took a little creative license, there, true. But that's who Alys was. She would've forgiven him."

He raised his eyes but only stared into space, his gaze distant and thoughtful. Suddenly frustrated, I thrust the book beneath his nose, opened to the final passage. "Henry was there. He watched the whole thing from behind a barn. It's not rocket science, professor."

He stared at the journal, but I know he wasn't reading it; his eyes weren't moving. His voice, almost a whisper, caused me to lean closer. "Why did she need to forgive him? He'd done nothing wrong."

I breathed a gusty sigh. "He didn't listen to her. He dragged his feet breaking his betrothal to Sarah, and because he played footsy with Alys and didn't marry her, Sarah had all the ammunition she needed to launch the accusation and make it stick."

He looked confused, as though he didn't quite follow me.

"It's one thing to accuse the Apothecary's weird daughter; it's another to accuse the Magistrate's daughter-in-law. There's a world of difference there, in status. Besides, had Sarah done that after he dumped her, then it would've been clear that it was her hard feelings that were the cause. See?"

His eyes returned to the desktop, but he gave a barely perceptible nod.

"His guilt drove him to the booze and the sight of Sarah made him want to puke or put his hands around her fat neck and squeeze until she turned..." I almost said 'black' but stopped myself at the memory of Alys's face, my face only different, as she swung on the rope. "Branwen, Alys's mother, wrote the last entries and told of how he ended his life, dead in the gutter at eighteen. He froze..."

He uttered a strangled noise and twisted both hands through his hair. "Stop. For God's sake, stop!"

"Okay." I waited as a part of me watched from a distance, amazed at my own vehemence and his response to it. If he wasn't crying, he was damned close to it. I think I was still angry with him for all that, as well as the current stupidity. No, I *know* I was. We'd been in love and perfect for each other and he had screwed it all up. Now we were in this mess and not because of that mess, but because of another one in between. Stupid.

Henry took a long shuddering breath and lifted his head. "All right. I'll give you that. I didn't read it all. I'm sorry. I should've known you'd have your act together and not turn in something that wasn't..."

"Real?"

He turned a suffering look on me. "Yes, real."

This had to be one of the oddest conversations I'd ever had. We were supposedly talking about two strangers three hundred years in the past but our emotional reactions were as though... I knew the reason, but poor Henry didn't; he only had strong feelings with no explanation for them. I wanted to be easy on him, but I just couldn't seem to do that.

Outside our little circle of angst, a storm broke with a shrieking wind we heard in the insulated, windowless walls of the classroom followed by a wall-shaking clap of thunder. A few moments later, we were plunged in darkness.

The storms had come and gone all day. This one slammed into the school with a vengeance.

"Shit," he said in the darkness and I heard jingling sounds. Keys and spare change in a trouser pocket, maybe. Then the scratch of a Bic lighter and a small flame lit his tired face. "I'll walk you to the office so you can call a ride."

"My dad is an over-the-road semi-driver and my mom's not home. She took my grandmother to the doctor out of town this afternoon." I shrugged. "I walk most of the time. I'm not afraid of the rain. I've done it before."

Another sigh. "I bet you have. You don't look like you're afraid of much. But no need. I'll give you a ride." He smiled weakly. "It's the least I can do for keeping you after class for an A paper."

In my head, Sting wailed, *Wet bus stop, she's waiting. His car is warm and dry.*

Will you just shut up? I told the voice in my head. *I know! I know!*

He stood and the lighter went out. He tried to flick it again and burnt his thumb. "Shit. That's hot. It's pitch black in here."

"I know," I said, stupidly, my cheeks suddenly on fire. The urge to throw myself into his arms and kiss him washed over me like a giddy wave. After a few seconds, he tried to light the lighter again, but it seemed to be out of fluid. Damn the luck. I stayed seated on the desk while he repeatedly flicked the Bic. With the journal tucked safely back in its bag, I could feel him standing only inches away in darkness punctuated by fitful sparks from the empty lighter. Energy radiated off him like a tangible field of static electricity. It went straight to my head.

He gave up and said, "Well, give me your hand; the hallway is dark, too."

"I can't see you."

He chuckled. "Right. Put your hand on the desk and I'll find it."

Instead I slid from the desk, threw myself into his arms, and caught him by surprise. I knew I had, because he stumbled, grabbed onto me, and pulled me close. Only a heartbeat or two had passed before he remembered himself, and jumped back to arms' length, firmly taking my hand and dragging me behind him. As soon as the dim light of the main hallway appeared, he dropped my hand as though it were hot.

Maybe it was.

I shouldn't have done it. But I did. We ran to his car in a downpour and dripped in awkward silence as he drove me home, only breaking it when I had to tell him where to turn.

He pulled up to the curb in front of my house and stared out the front windshield with a miserable look on his face.

"Well, thanks for the ride…" I shivered a little, soaked to the skin and the air had cooled with the rain.

"No problem." He waved a dismissive hand, but his eyes slid over to me. "You shouldn't have done that, you know."

I pursed my lips and looked around as though searching for an answer. "Hm. Don't think so, Henry. In fact, that's exactly what I should've done if only to show you what this is and what it's not."

"But I didn't… I never… You," he stammered, outraged. But I could tell he was shamming. That false note had crept back into his voice.

"Really? Then what's that mean?" I glanced down at the lingering bulge in his trousers and he blushed to his hairline. "*Action* speaks way louder than words." I'd felt him, hard and ready, the moment I crushed my body to his. I tore open the pouch and thrust Henry's diary at him. "You read the wrong one, Henry, as usual. Take it."

He didn't move, but his knuckles whitened from the death grip he had on the steering wheel. I picked up a towel that lay on the hump between the floorboards and dried off the briefcase that sat like a shield on the seat between us. I placed the ancient book upon it, hoping that the long bench seat would put it out of the reach of the rain as I opened the door. The pouch was plastic lined. I wouldn't have taken it from home had it not been.

Without another word, I left him and knew that his eyes followed me as I bolted through drenching rain. From inside the house, I dripped on the hardwood and stared through the sheers at the old Buick idling at the curb. Long minutes passed and I wondered if he would come after me.

He didn't.

Ten:
Henry 2033

The Being told me I'd had enough of Alice for the moment. Azriel was his name, I finally remembered. I think I was supposed to follow him to the Light, which was only symbolic of the transition from physical to pure Spirit.

That was how the human mind processed the incomprehensible. When something is too huge to be conceived or understood, we grope with our insufficient brains for a reference point. Light was the closest we could come for a visual description of what awaited us in Spirit, and people returning after a brush with death had no alternative but to use what their brains offered up: a simplistic, inadequate term. I knew that because this was no dress rehearsal, but the real thing.

It's probably why we needed angels, too. We were like little kids in Playland at times like these. Too small and scared, or too easily distracted by all the rides and pretty lights to find our way alone.

I supposed I might be in a bit of trouble for not seeking that Light. I couldn't remember refusing Azriel outright, but the result seemed to be that I still roamed the earth plane. He hadn't asked me to go and seemed content to let me wander—though he *had* pulled me off Alice. Maybe I'd enjoyed that just a little too much?

Admittedly, I was in no hurry whatsoever for the play-by-play review of the good and bad of this lifetime just past. I knew it already, didn't I? Why dwell on it? Free will was totally where it's at—and as Warren Beatty proved in 1980, Heaven could certainly wait.

In a word, you had to want it. I didn't want it. Not just yet.

Sarah. The mere thought of her had taken me to her. I hovered above her bed, looking down on her and trying to decide how that made me feel. Somewhere on the other side of this nursing home, they were carting my body away to the morgue.

Unlike Alice's pure silver-white radiance, Sarah projected something I'd walk a mile to avoid if a puddle of it had lain in my path. Was this what mental illness looked like? I came closer. No. The longer I stared the more I realized this was Sarah at her most essential. This is was what she'd built for herself here in this life. I wondered what shape my own stuff had been in before I died. I couldn't imagine it being this bad.

Colors shifted around her. Murky olive and ochre shot with streaks of angry red and sickly chartreuse, reminding me of a gangrenous wound. Here and there a bit of healthy gold and blue surfaced, only to be swallowed by the ugliness that I could now see in living color. I hadn't considered Sarah for years and years. Maybe not ever, but seeing her in this way brought her into sharp focus. The bitter soul sickness she'd hidden beneath the mask of feigned respectability was now fully revealed.

The twisting, cloudy aura gave up an image and I recoiled, bouncing against the ceiling, having forgotten for a moment that it wasn't there. This plane was mostly about belief, when you get right down to it.

There stood a young girl in a long-sleeved black dress. A snowy white apron draped her from chest to hemline. She gazed up at me and I descended for a closer look.

A white lace-trimmed cap covered her dull brown hair. Her pale almost lashless eyes stared balefully at me from a round, putty-colored face. Her best feature was her mouth, a ridiculous bow-shaped little thing that was ruined by what appeared to be a perpetual pout. The beginning of a double chin rested above the high neckline of the dress.

She pointed a pudgy finger at me. "Mother said you belonged to me. She sent the witch to the hangman. I hate you. You ruined my life. You didn't do what you were supposed to do and I followed you. Did you know that?"

I bristled, suddenly angry. "That commitment wasn't your Mother's to make. I wasn't hers to give you, little girl." I gaped as she turned into Sarah circa 1983. Her lank hair was permed, teased, and sprayed into a ridiculous mass of layered snarls. A giant wave of bangs rolled backwards in a curl that looked like an ocean wave just before it breaks on the shore. The sides were slicked back with gel. Large cotton candy pink disks hung at her ears and the pouty little mouth and rounded cheeks were painted to match. Pale blue eyes stared at me from spiky, spider legs of black mascara and layers of metallic eye shadow.

Shoulder pads jutted beneath a long garishly striped shirt. Unbuttoned to the waist, the shirt revealed a black bustier shoving up her large breasts and showed a deep shadow of cleavage. A wide belt nipped painfully at an ever-expanding and contracting waistline. Leggings encased plump thighs and high-heeled shiny patent leather ankle boots adorned her feet.

The hard neon-plastic version of Sarah—another futile attempt to make me notice her. She swung her pink-lacquered, pointing fingernail from me to the woman on the bed, the multitude of Lucite bracelets on her wrist clicked together and a cloud of Poison perfume enveloped me. I remembered the squat purple-black bottle with the crystal stopper that had held court on her vanity table. The fragrance repulsed me nearly as much as she did. I hated it. She wore it to spite me, I think.

"You did that to me. This is your fault."

I shook my head. "No Sarah, I'll take responsibility for my part of this. And that part was in giving in to your blackmail and letting you trick me. But you did that to yourself, sweetheart. Only you."

"No! You're wrong! I did it for you, Henry, and you failed."

"I think not."

She melted back into herself and I looked down at her ravaged face and bloated body tied with restraints to the bed. I shuddered at the sight, remembering her particular kink, the obsession which had caused my downfall. The irony of seeing her this way now was not lost on me—not at all. *Be careful what you wish for* came unbidden to my mind. The thought was callous, I knew, but very much deserved in this case. I'd never managed to get what I wanted, but she, this demented, cruel bitch, had tied me to her as securely as she was now tied to her bed. I glanced around, waiting for some sort of heavenly rebuke from my Guide, but none came. He seemed to be elsewhere.

Alice had been a water sprite dancing on the foam, while this one had been a mad sea cow wallowing in the waves with her legs open. Images flitted through my mind, ones that were Sarah's alone, for they'd happened before I met her—or at least remembered having met her.

Sarah had targeted me like a guided missile from the moment she'd laid eyes on me. After that, she remolded and redesigned herself to meet what she thought might catch my eye. Three months in a row she'd put her finger down her throat to get herself to a size she thought might snag me and I cursed the drunken idiocy that eventually caused me to climb between those flabby thighs.

I saw all of it now and understood the constant gum chewing and breath mints, though she didn't smoke in the beginning. They masked the odor of vomit. I saw a great deal now. Was I supposed to? I looked for Azriel and he was nowhere to be found.

***

Alice pulled the hat from her head and with a flick of her wrist sailed it into a chair across the foyer. She hobbled on black stocking-clad feet through her living room, having kicked off her version of funeral shoes the minute she stepped inside. With a groan, she turned and limped back to the doormat, snatched up the wicked-sexy shoes then continued her painful-looking progress. She dropped the stiletto heels into the kitchen waste can as she passed it, then came to rest against the kitchen counter. Harsh whooping sobs erupted from her and tears ran down her face.

Pity and grief gripped my heart, her sorrow a sharp dagger tearing through my soul, surprising me with the force of the feeling. I didn't want—had *never* wanted to be the source of such pain, though undeniably, it was me that had caused those tears. As I watched her suffering, I realized that death had been nothing for me but a much-welcomed release. I'd felt nothing but relief and joy that my misery had finally ended. Ditto for Sarah and her sorry state—nothing but a sort of detached relief that I no longer had to deal with her.

Alice's tears turned a key in the locked door to my heart. All through the funeral I'd watched her, then gave into the temptation to play with her—the reason for her being there had been lost on me. I'd barely noticed the casket or the human train wreck it held. But this? This hurt me and sadness took me over as I stood there in her kitchen and for the first time truly understood that I'd left both her and my body behind. The pain and misery had gone, but with it had gone any chance of reconciliation.

It was over. My life as Henry Spears was over and could never be reclaimed.

That knowledge racked me up, but good. I was on the outside looking in now and nothing could change it. But hadn't it always been that way, really?

It could've been so different. *Should've* been. But I'd done what I had to do; made the only choice I could've made for the two of us. Sarah had left me no alternative. We both knew that, had always known it. This knowledge did not change the way I felt.

After a time, Alice's tears subsided and another emotion seemed to take her over. Her hand shot out and she snatched a wine bottle from the rack, then threw open an upper cabinet door with enough force to bang it against its neighbor. Dread washed over me as I glimpsed the full bottle of prescription painkillers, which she abruptly slammed onto the counter. The bottle bounced and rolled into the empty sink. I watched in alarm as she fought with the corkscrew. Alice wouldn't. She couldn't! She'd be forever with a guardian trying to sort out a suicide!

"Azriel!" I shouted and searched frantically for my angel. Could he do anything about this? No answer. Angels. Never around when you need them.

Alice went dead still. Her hair lay in untidy, beautiful disarray on her shoulders, a silvery cloud of ringlets and curls. She squared her shoulders and turned formidable, the lines framing her mouth and the webbing around her eyes like the veins and fissures on an ancient Grecian statue. With a hiccupping sob, she sloshed wine into the glass and uncapped the pill bottle. Desperately, I tried to take it from her. For all that I could touch it, my hands passed right through the brown plastic.

With a deliberateness that scared the shit out of me, she stared at the pills for a long moment and swiped at her face with the sleeve of her dress. Her hands trembled as she shook out a single tablet into her palm and then washed it down with the wine.

Relief nearly dissolved me where I stood as she put the bottle back in the cabinet and softly closed the door. Alice was too smart. She knew too much to do that, however badly she felt.

I followed her to the bathroom, watching as she turned on the faucets to her hot tub and steam began to fill the bathroom, reminding me of the mists of Irish Grove cemetery where my body now lay the prescribed six feet under. I couldn't have cared less. It was a disgusting, revolting thing, not connected to me at all now and I simply could not want it back, even though I understood exactly what that meant now. Slow learner, I supposed, but then there were so many distractions in the afterlife.

Like Alice stripping unselfconsciously, right at this present moment.

She peeled off her clothes and sat on the edge of the tub to remove her stockings. When she stood, she sagged in all the customary places, but I admired her anyway. She'd held together very well. Desire surprised me. I had no true physical body, but I wanted her as though I did. Badly.

Whatever her form, I was crazy for her and I knew right then that if I were twenty, I would still jump on her, though she was pushing seventy. I supposed the space I currently occupied made age irrelevant.

Alice picked up a remote and the *Somewhere in Time* soundtrack flooded the room. Abruptly my emotions shifted again and melancholy took the place of lust. She'd loved that movie, which we'd seen together in a stolen afternoon out of town. I'd given her the album for Christmas in 1980, the only Christmas we'd been together. And even then, it really wasn't legit. She'd snuck out, through the snow and damned near a blizzard to be with me. The gift she'd given me that night had been far more precious.

The memories seemed destined to come, whether I wanted them or not. I couldn't seem to *not* be here with her. It's all I wanted. All I'd ever really wanted.

"Now perhaps, Henry, you can understand how weak the excuse you used to deny Alice truly was. You see her clearly and yet, you know that you would want her if as many as fifty years separated you in earth time."

I turned around to find Azriel standing behind me, and realized he could read me like a book. He'd taken on some features in his absence, looking more masculine, a little more human. Maybe earth time wasn't such a good idea for him, either. He still looked ethereal, though, so I didn't worry too much about it. "About time you got here. I thought she was going to off herself."

Azriel laughed "This one? No. But I want you to think, Henry, about how it was when she came to you at fourteen. What you did to her and yourself was unnecessary."

"I wanted her and almost went to jail for it."

"And if you had, she would've been waiting for you. Do you deny then, that she is worth the wait?"

Alice threw a handful of fragrant salts into her bathwater and began lighting candles. She turned off the overhead lights and with a stifled moan, slid into the water, her long silver-white hair trailing upon the surface. She punched a button that turned on the jets, then raised the wineglass and peered through the rich, red depths.

Soon the sweet, overlapping scents of her bath and candle wax filled the steamy room. The candlelight flickered and caressed her face, taking years away from it as she leaned back and closed her eyes. Regret washed over me as I imaged myself with her in the water, old and wrinkled, but a healthy, hale septuagenarian—not the cirrhotic, dialysis-dependent, cancerous ruin I had been. Could I have withstood what Azriel suggested?

An unexpected vise of guilt clamped down on my heart and squeezed 'til I nearly cried out. It made me angry.

I turned to Azriel. "You don't understand. I didn't know what she knew! In that time, it was wrong for a grown man to…to… Later, she told me to leave and not come back!"

The feathery sketch of a golden eyebrow rose on Azriel's still as of yet, undefined face. "She told you to leave because you still refused to end your marriage to Sarah, though she'd brutalized…"

I threw up my hand. "Stop! I'm not ready to think about that."

Azriel bowed his head. "As you wish. But you did resist the truth, long before—though you set the conditions for this lifetime, not her. Think back. You married her once when she was twelve and you were thirty."

Amazed, I watched as a hole opened in the steam cloud beside Alice's tub, revealing a panoramic scene of a Welsh landscape. Fascinated, I took in the soaring towers and battlements of a Norman castle which stood gray and solid against a fiery sunset-streaked sky. A battle-hardened warrior with my eyes rode toward it, his weary heart lifting and the word 'home' upon his lips.

I sighed as tender emotion flooded my being. This lifetime had been one of my favorites, though brutal in many ways. Alice—Carys in this place.

The name, Welsh of course, meant 'love' and I couldn't have chosen a better description for her myself. She married me, a spoil of war, a peace offering from her father Llewellyn, the local chieftain. I was conqueror of her small country, but she willingly, even joyfully, came to me. I counted myself among the blessed.

I spied her now as I clattered across the sturdy oak planks of the bridge and onward beneath the sharp spikes of the portcullis, spurring my weary horse to a gallop and leaving my small company to trail behind me. My love stood high upon the northern battlement, a tiny figure dancing upon a crenel and my heart clenched with fear. If she should fall… but no, she leapt backwards, waved once, and disappeared.

Joyful shouts of welcome and the chaos of homecoming ensued. I slid from the horse and with impatient hands, stripped off gauntlets, greaves, and helmet, pitching them carelessly to one of the man servants milling about me. Voices shouted over each other in a senseless babble as a colorful flood of women tumbled from the arched entrance, adding their high-pitched shrieks and giggles to the cacophony.

I waited with eyes on the door for my darling. Then she came, flying on winged feet, her honey-colored hair loose and streaming behind her as she ran to me. Her cheeks were the velvet pink of rose petals, her luminous, dark eyes fastened on mine. She hurled herself into my arms and covered my dirty, sweat-streaked face with sweet kisses. She was fragrant as a flower. I breathed in her scent and wanted nothing more than to drown myself in it.

The steam abruptly closed the window through which I looked and I spun around to Azriel, dismayed. Alice lifted the wineglass from the side of the tub and sipped.

"Don't take it away! I want to stay there for awhile! I was happy then."

"Yes. You took joy from her and she from you. Mutual bliss is a gift and never wrong. You spent no time worrying that she was a child, then, but lived for her. Every heroic act you performed, every love song you composed… all for her." The dulcet tones of a lute played somewhere just out of sight and a tenor voice rose in song, and I knew it had been my very own, raised in a love song I'd written for her during a long, peaceful winter between the seemingly endless warring. Quickly, the dramatic tones of the room's sound system drowned it out. Or maybe Azriel had.

I stared at him in outrage. "It was a different time."

"It does not matter," he said.

"Oh well, thanks for telling me *now*. Am I the only one who doesn't know the rules?"

He laughed and began to fade. "You always knew, Henry."

Eleven:
Henry 1980

I threw my briefcase and keys on the table and grabbed a beer from the mostly empty fridge, then paced the kitchen. What was this girl doing to me? My sopping clothes dripped on the ancient linoleum. I turned and stared at the briefcase. The diary.

The wind howled and rattled the ancient windowpanes. Rain blasted against them in sheets and I vaguely wondered if this dump had a basement. Maybe if I read Henry Sayre's book, more of this would make sense? No, nothing about this made sense and reading it would only make it worse. Alice had woven a spell around me. I laughed. The whole witch thing had gotten to me. The next thing I knew I'd be seeing ghosts in the corners or boogeymen under my bed. Ridiculous.

"You read the wrong one, Henry, as usual." What the hell did she mean by that? From the beginning she'd acted as though she knew me, refused to call me Mr. Spears except when we were in class, but I'd never set eyes on her before the first day of school. Why would I have? She was only fourteen. Self-revulsion overcame me. I'd gotten a boner twice in front of her. What was wrong with me? I couldn't believe this was happening.

I stomped to the bathroom and grabbed a towel, then stripped out of my dripping clothes. Another future dry cleaning bill lay in a wet, wrinkled puddle on the floor. Shit. I'd never fix that suit without it. Shivering, I dried myself and pulled on the sweats I'd left next to the tub that morning.

Suddenly exhausted, I fell onto the couch and stared out the window. The phone ringing startled me. I let the machine pick it up.

"Hi Henry. This is Sarah Thurmond. I met you at the Watering Hole a few weeks ago and..." The voice was bit shrill, nervous? *"And well, I just wanted to tell you there's going to be a live rock band there Friday night, and um, maybe you could meet me uptown? My number, in case you lost it, is 8-5888. Talk to you soon. Bye."*

I had lost it. Probably went through the washing machine with the rest of the bits of paper and crap I never remembered to empty from my pockets. My head fell back on the couch and I realized I couldn't remember what she looked like. I was a little drunk. Well, really drunk, I guess. I shrugged. Why did the name Thurmond sound familiar to me?

A few seconds later, I had it. Charles Thurmond was the big cheese over at the college. I'd taught classes there over the summer while waiting for the position at the high school to open up. I'd never meant to come back here to Lincoln, but my dad wanted me to. He was the Superintendant of Schools and had given me the heads up on the retirement party for John Ryan—my old history teacher. It was something to do, until I decided what it was I really wanted to be when I grew up. Marking time. I had the credentials. It seemed better than moving home and depending on my dad until something came clear. None of the feelers I'd put out turned up anything. Why not? It was the mantra of my life.

I'd met Thurmond and his wife attending a state-wide education fundraiser with my dad last spring. He'd called me just before break and insisted I go because, "you can never make too many connections in this business." Dad was also on the city council and a member of the Rotary Club and he'd have a good old-fashioned heart attack if he knew what had happened today, right after he kicked my ass into the next county. I'd kick it myself, if I could.

I turned on the television and flipped the dial to a rerun of Gilligan's Island, belched and returned to the kitchen for another brewsky. My eyes landed on the briefcase again. The damned book called to me and I couldn't understand why I felt the way I did about it. Upset and half-scared about people I didn't know, who'd drawn their last breath over three hundred years ago. Stupid. But when Alice had talked about them, it was like… She was so damned intense and I felt myself slipping into something not quite myself when she talked. That whole conversation blew my mind. It was almost like I knew what she was saying without knowing what she was talking about.

I shook my head and gulped my beer. It was a tragic story and it moved me. What could I say? The cracked leather of the old book felt warm in my hands and I opened it. The language was horrendous, the spelling worse, though giving Henry Sayre a break, they all seemed to spell words anyway they wished back then—kinda like my freshman class. I yawned and turned pages until I saw the name Sarah.

The jarring ring of the phone startled me and I stared at it. Four rings, then five, six. The stupid machine refused to hold the four-ring setting. I heard my muffled voice on the machine. The beep. Long pause. Click. I looked down at the yellowed page, my eyes returning to the name, Sarah. Interesting.

I closed the journal. After all, Alice had hit the high points and I didn't need to read it. I didn't want to think about it or her anymore—it wasn't healthy and the whole thing disturbed me. The rewind button on the answering machine worked just fine. I wrote down the number and called Sarah Thurmond.

Twelve:
Alice 1980

I nearly tore the pages from the phonebook looking for Henry's address, feeling a little guilty, but doing a great job of ignoring it as I scanned the S's for him. There! 122 Logan Street, Apt B. Oh not good. Not good at all. Why couldn't he have lived in Beason or Middletown, somewhere too far to walk to? I could probably see his place from here. He hadn't said a word about that in the car and I guessed I couldn't blame him there. *I* wouldn't have told me that. I smiled. Sometimes a small town had its advantages.

The rain stopped, though the low hanging clouds threatened more, but I was too keyed up to behave myself. I pulled on a hooded sweatshirt, some jeans and tennis shoes, and tore out down the front steps. With the hood yanked up, just in case, I trotted down to the end of the block where Pekin and Logan intersected. The old brick apartment building sat on the corner across the street. An oversized 122 announced the address in bold white numbers. There were four doors on the bottom and only windows up top. No letters hung on the bare doors and I thought maybe they weren't used. The one on the far right looked painted shut.

I scanned both ways for traffic, crossed the street and turned around. I could see my yard and most of the front porch from here. If ever I needed proof that souls are drawn together lifetime to lifetime, this was it. There sat his car, an elderly, but nice old Buick. I strolled down the walk and paused for the rearview of the building. Two doors on the bottom, two on the top, and outside stairs led to them. Upstairs there were barbeque grills sitting on each side of a balcony type porch that was identical to the one on the lower level. I couldn't make out the letters through the screen doors without walking into the little graveled drive that ran behind. A car pulled into it and I walked on, circled the block, and went home.

***

Of course I couldn't sleep knowing he lived only a block away. My mom left for work at eleven and I slipped down the stairs and out the door nearly right behind her. My father's snores almost shook the pictures off the walls—he'd come home this morning from a weeklong run. I felt a twinge of conscience, but I'd only told him my dad was an over the road truck driver, not that he'd been on the road…

I sat on the porch of a dentist's office across the street from Henry's building. Dark clothes, dark shadows, perfect. I had a fairly good view of the back of the building. The lights were on in both upstairs apartments.

After a few minutes, I gathered my courage and slipped across the street to crouch behind the car in the drive. I tiptoed onto the wooden porch and peered at the first door. "A". Okay, one down, three to go. Halfway across, the right upstairs door opened and banged shut. A guy bounced down the steps with a garbage bag in his hand. Holy shit. I froze behind the open stairs and he passed not six inches in front of me whistling the refrain from The Stones' *Miss You*. Frantically I looked around and there was no place but here, behind the stairwell, to hide. I crouched into a ball and prayed. Thank god all the lights were off downstairs. The bag hit the trashcan with a loud thud and thump of his feet on the wooden porch vibrated under me.

"I been hangin' on the phone, sleepin' all alone, I wanna kiss you. Ooh, ooh ooh ooh… His feet on the stairwell did a little shuffle and the weathered wood swayed beneath him, vibrating against my curled up body. The idiotic urge to giggle nearly made me wet my pants. Jeez. The things people do when they're alone…or so they think.

"Well I've been haunted in my sleep. Da-da da-da da-da dum …" Patter, patter, he did a little switch step and I nearly bit the palm right off my hand. "…four rings, it's just some bitch who's comin' roun' to say, Hey! what's a matta man? Won't you come down t' the Hole cuz I'm jus' dyin' to meet choo!"

I looked up and between the risers, saw Henry doing a little bump and grind, climbing one step at a time, Mick Jagger-style, whoo-hooing in a falsetto that should've cracked glass. My shoulders shook from the silent giggles and a little trickle of wetness hit the cotton crotch of my panties. I squeezed my legs together harder. Would this never end? At last, his voice trailed off and the door slammed. I bolted from under the steps, tore down my jeans in the dark space between the buildings by the trash cans and peed, laughing and snorting all the while. Then I realized what he'd been singing— the changes he'd made to the lyrics.

Oh my.

Thirteen:
Henry 1980

"...and my dad's the president of the college!" Sarah Thurmond shouted over the crowd noise and the rock band.

"That's cool!" I yelled, and hoped the band would play louder. I already had that part figured out anyway—there weren't any other Thurmond's in town. She was all right, I guess, but not really my type. Too much makeup. Too much perfume. She cracked her gum in between gulps of some foo-foo flavored wine cooler—and worse, she had her hands on me all the time, touching, grabbing, and plucking at my sleeve. She'd be trashed in a hurry, the way she slammed her drinks. That's what I was thinking at nine o'clock. I'd met her at seven. Way too early, if my boredom gauge was still working, and judging by the yawn I'd just stifled, it was.

"...and then Sherry said, "Oh my god, Sarah, I can't believe you just did that!"" Sarah laughed until tears ran down her face. Her laugh was a shrill scream that only Jack Daniels could take the edge off—lots of it. I downed my drink in four long swallows. It would take more than this to exorcise a certain little blonde enigma from my head. Why couldn't this girl just shut up?

"Oh-my-god I love this song! Let's dance!" She grabbed my hand and hauled me to my feet. I signaled the barkeep for another jack and coke just before she yanked me out of his line of vision. The band was on break and the jukebox was turned up to ear-splitting volume. Air Supply. I could barely listen to them and not want to throw up. It figured that she would love that kind of lameness.

A miniature disco ball suspended over the bandstand threw multi-colored shards of light over the dark walls and the swaying couples shuffling around the smoky dance floor. The next thing I knew she had her pelvis grinding against my crotch and her tongue in my mouth. Hm. That was eleven o'clock and I kinda noticed that she had some pretty nice tatas...and wasn't shy about showing them off. I can't say I remember much after that, but we shut the place down, I think.

7:00 a.m. I woke up certain my brain had morphed into an unexploded grenade that would detonate if I moved. I cracked an eyelid and immediately shut it, dismayed, slightly disgusted, and more than a little pissed off that I was not where I should've been.

I had to take a leak and I didn't have the first clue where to find the bathroom. The room spun crazily, but the situation had turned critical. I sat up, refusing to look at the lump in the bed next to me. No. Wouldn't do it. Not yet. I stumbled around until I found the john, did my business, then ransacked the medicine cabinet, hitting the jackpot with a bottle of Tylenol #3. I doubted that would take the edge off. Killing myself just might be more effective—except I didn't have the energy. I swallowed two pills and palmed two more. No pockets. Shit. Naked as the day I was born.

God, please let me have been too drunk. Please let me have been too drunk. Maybe saying it could make it so. I tried to think back, but it hurt too much. I struggled to remember how I came to be here and couldn't; that was the least of my worries.

I crept back through the dim room, dropped on all fours and began the frantic, quiet hunt for my clothes. I had to get out of here. Not very nice, I knew, but that's all I could think about doing, and hopefully, without waking her up. I'd gone from 'not very nice' to 'giant shit' in less time than it took to yank on my pants and button my shirt.

Dressed, I tiptoed to the nearest door. With it safely closed behind me, I then stood looking around, hoping some hazy memory would surface. Nope. Nada. Complete dead zone. I climbed carpeted stairs, opened another door into a huge kitchen, spotted what I hoped was the back door and ran, well, lurched for it. If this was her parent's house, her father's was the last face I wanted to see hung over at seven-fifteen in the morning, leaving his daughter's bedroom.

My car failed to materialize in the driveway. Damn, it must still be uptown. Without breaking stride, I picked a direction I thought was right and kept walking. Home, to my relief was not all that far, only a couple of streets over, then a long walk down Logan. I might make it without puking. Maybe.

When I opened the apartment door, the phone was ringing and the dread I felt at that sound nearly drowned my relief at getting away without a scene. The stupid, psycho answering machine had reset itself again.

I shuddered in remembrance of other mornings where I'd not been so lucky, and sent up a silent prayer of gratitude for what I'd just avoided; only that wasn't enough. I wished I could hit rewind and save myself the trouble.

Scenes. I just hated them, and there always was one, if you got caught trying to sneak away from the mistake you just made. First came the *look*, always and without fail. It's the hurt one that said you surely didn't use me? Oh, no… most enduring relationships begin with sex between complete strangers. Right, I forgot that. And then, because you really *are* a big shit, but you don't like to admit that outright, you pretend you want to stay and you end up banging her again. She'll make you, to prove it was some big love at first sight chapter from a romance novel so she doesn't have to feel like a slut. You curse yourself for being an idiot and getting yourself into it in the first place.

So, just when you think you can safely put on your clothes and shag your sorry ass outta there, she offers to cook breakfast. That's when you know you're in deep shit. You start to give an excuse, one you've already thought of because you know what's coming, but then your empty, whisky-rotted gut rumbles loud enough to rattle her earrings, which are still on her because she was too drunk to take them off before she passed out. The right side of her face is dented from sleeping on the damned thing. Oh yeah, she slept through that, but a little change in your pocket jingling as you try to put on your pants wakes her.

So, that's how it works most of the time. You endure runny eggs, burnt toast, and bacon that might squeal if you touch it, and hope to hell your next escape plan isn't foiled and you won't have to chew off your leg to get out of the trap she's set for you.

Welcome to the eighties—where men are the only ones who have one night stands. Maybe I'd been drinking in the wrong places, but I'd never seen it turn out any other way. Just once, it would be nice to have a woman wave you out the door, just as relieved to have you gone as you were to be going. If these women existed outside of the realm of prostitutes, porn movies, and male fantasy, I had yet to meet one.

I am a gentleman for the most part and have a great deal of respect for women. I *like* women. Hell, I could respect one who just wanted sex with no strings. That's an honest thing. It was this messy stuff that happens when a woman clings to the idea that she's a good girl and can't face the reality of what she's done, did, doing all the time. Desperation maybe, but that's not my problem. Believe me, I don't think, or well, I'm pretty sure that bad girls can be good and that's just fine. People can change. You only end up in trouble when the good ones wanna be bad and can't admit it.

Maybe I was wrong about Sarah. Maybe she's a hard partier and just takes it where she finds it. Something tells me she's not. She's a fucked up little princess who thinks the world owes her something. And now, I, Henry Spears had just made it to the top of that long list of debtors. I had a bad feeling she was used to getting her way and wouldn't let go of this.

I tore my wallet from my back pocket and checked the flap where I keep… The shiny foil wrapper shone like an accusation. Henry, you stupid shit. Things just turned a whole lot darker in my world. I could only hope that Sarah took her pills when she should—or that the whiskey dick had finally failed. Son of a bitch! How could I be this stupid? That's what I was thinking at eight a.m.

On the answering machine, the caller hung up with an angry wallop that missed severing the connection. A muffled "Fuck!" and the second try got it. Sarah? Probably. That was what is known as A Close Call.

Fourteen:
Alice 1980

I put the pieces together from the clues I'd been given. Henry'd been losing sleep over me, probably wanted to kiss me, and some girl wanted his body. Great.

Knowing what I knew about him from our long history, I also guessed he'd probably made the date with her in a lame attempt to get me out of his head. We'd been down that road before, but this time he had more than a good reason: I was jailbait. It made a stupid kind of sense and I wanted to beat him senseless for *that*.

'Some bitch' wanted to meet him at "The Hole." There were plenty of holes in Lincoln, but only one with the bad taste to put the word in its name—I tried to be nice and exclude at least twenty girls I knew at school who would accurately fit that description.

I'd waited all my life for him and I wasn't about to leave this alone, even if a sane person might think it none of my business. My sanity could be questioned only because I couldn't seem to let him go and somewhere deep inside, I thought him worth the effort.

After school the next day, instead of crossing the diagonal walks of the courthouse square on my usual path home, I walked two blocks further and sauntered past the Watering Hole, just to see what I could see. What I saw plastered on the front windows were the predictable posters announcing that Nebula! The Ultimate Rock Experience! Playing Here Friday Night! Four scruffy guys trying to look cool in spandex, (and mostly failing), gave their best smoldering, sexy glares from a glossy neon-enhanced reproduction of the Milky Way. Way too cool for me, thanks.

***

Mid-September sunsets are incredible. Fiery shades of pink and gold painted a pale blue sky just turning to mauve and plum. A warm, fading summer breeze still played among the trees; the leaves only beginning to get that dull, tired look that signaled the blazing changes to come.

I wheedled permission to go to the movie, to walk there all by myself and meet my friends like a big girl. Four and a half gloriously free hours lay open before me, more than enough time to stake out the Watering Hole and see what was up. If nothing was, then I'd go late to the show and sit by myself or maybe find someone to sit with if I was in the mood for socializing by then. I'd read the movie review of Flash Gordon (it sucked monkey-butt, but that's all right), and could fake it through a parental inquisition. Our group always went for pizza and cokes after, so I didn't have to be home until eleven. No probs.

The Watering Hole is across from the downtown train tracks. There are no buildings across from it, but along the tracks runs a grassy swatch the length of the block with slightly sick-looking dwarf trees and park benches placed here and there. I'd never seen anyone sitting in them and never noticed them much until now. The benches were placed far enough from the street that I believed I might be able to sit on one and remain unnoticed, especially if there were cars parked along that side.

I half hoped he would see me, figuring it would freak him out enough to make him behave himself or ruin him for his date. He'd returned the journal and practiced ignoring me the rest of the week. Such was the magnetism between us, that every sense I possessed seemed trained upon him. He stole glances at me when he thought I wasn't paying attention and then looked at everyone *but* me while teaching history at the front of the class. Dead giveaway.

At six-forty, I passed his building and noted that his car was still there. At six-fifty, I sat camped on the park bench across from the bar in full regalia. I hadn't tried to disguise myself, but wore my black lace handkerchief skirt, platform boots and white gypsy shirt with the long, gauzy pointed sleeves. I'd tied my red shawl around my waist. The nights were cooler now.

Three times a bright blue Mazda RX7 zipped down the street. On the fourth pass, the driver, a woman, parked it in front of the Watering Hole. I watched as she checked herself out in the rearview mirror, primping. Less than thirty seconds later, Henry's Buick turned the corner and parked next to it. She wiggled her fingers at him. He nodded.

When she stepped from the car, my heart dropped to the ground. My great and holy Goddess, it was Sarah. Yes, *that* Sarah, the one he'd abandoned in the seventeenth century, the one who'd sent me to the gallows—a homemade, makeshift one that barely qualified, but the result had been the same. I stood slowly, torn three or four different directions as my mind whirled over this new development.

The feminine part of me gloated as I looked her over from head to toe. Too much makeup, too much hair, and a skirt short enough to put her nearly in the Dominion of Whore. In all, it looked like a colossal effort to doll up dishwater. Some things did *not* change—only the camouflage had improved in 1980. Puritans were so *boring*—which is probably why I ended that lifetime at the end of a rope.

On looks, I'd slammed that one out of the park this time around, but boys my age were intimidated by them. They looked, but didn't touch, or so it seemed to me. After Allen, my dating career had stalled. Their eyes followed me, they whistled from cars as they drove by me walking, but no one asked me out or wanted to go steady. It would've been a waste of time, at least from my point of view. Maybe they sensed that, who knows?

My appearance didn't matter; Sarah was in the driver's seat this time. I glanced down at myself and said every curse word I could think of. *Fourteen.* Fifteen next month, but I might as well have been five. I could just kill him. He had no idea of what he was getting himself into!

Before I could move or think, they walked quickly to the front door and disappeared inside. I collapsed onto the bench. Night fell and I sent gratitude to the juvenile delinquent who'd shot out the streetlight above my head. I thought backward and tried to trace the threads in the karmic tapestry we had woven and realized that this had been coming for a very long time.

He and I had met in a failed attempt to work things out between the colonial lifetime and this one. Truthfully, Henry was not solely responsible for why things were the way they were between us now. I hurt him. He pissed me off and I dealt him an unintentional blow that ended up killing him. That's life. This age difference was his revenge for that and I probably deserved it. Henry had an unpredictable streak in him and never had I known or could foresee his next move. Guess that's what kept life interesting, and likely what kept me coming back for more of him.

Sarah had taken a pass on the 1920s. She would've had plenty to think over during those three centuries. But then, time had no relevance in Spirit. It only mattered here, as I'd just been reminded. Three stupid years and a lousy month had nearly set him out of my reach. It seemed ridiculous when put in the context of the thousands of years we'd spent together elsewhere.

Henry and I almost always choose each other when we come to flesh. We might be soul mates, but that rosy concept of blissful reunions without strife is a complete lie. Humans can only learn through conflict, adversity, and disappointment. Sad to say, but that's the only way we can appreciate harmony. He and I had learned more through our battles than we ever did from our quiet, peaceful existences—though we'd had those, too. Everyone needs a rest every now and then.

Personally, I didn't think Henry owed Sarah shit. I mean that. But that's my opinion. Clearly, Sarah believed he did owe her something and was here to get it—or barring that, forgive him for the perceived injury. Judging by her appearance, I thought the latter highly unlikely.

She worried me for a whole array of reasons. Henry Sayre had despised her and thought her evil. She'd proven him right when she and her mother accused Alys of malicious sorcery and had her hanged. Sarah was dangerous then and might still be now.

But what could I do?

I comforted myself with the fact that they'd arrived here tonight separately. He hadn't kissed her in greeting or taken her hand when they went inside, so this had probably just started. She didn't have a betrothal or her parents behind her—though admittedly, that hadn't worked so well the first time.

Maybe it would just be a fleeting thing and never develop? I could wait it out. Eighteen wasn't that far...

No, I wouldn't wait. Couldn't wait. *He* wouldn't wait that long. He was too damned good-looking and yes, ignorant. He needed me. Now.

Muffled rock music and voices pitched over it came to me on my lonely park bench. Cars filled every space in little downtown Lincoln and people strolled in pairs, sometimes in mobs, up and down the sidewalk on the other side of the street, roving from bar to bar. The clock in the courthouse dome dementedly bonged ten times; it never kept the right time, but I knew that it was an hour and twenty minutes fast. Time flies when you're having fun or trying to save an idiot from himself.

I shivered in the shadows, glad for the shawl I'd thought to bring. No one paid the slightest bit of attention to me. I couldn't be seen at all now in the dark. The uneven ground of the grassy swatch made walking in platforms a little iffy, but I swished on through it, crossing Broadway at the tracks, stepping into the blue haze of the streetlights overhead. Nothing to do now but go home and tell my mom the movie sucked and Cathy was being a bitch. One true, the other false. Cathy was all right most of the time. She'd solemnly sworn to not call me between six and eleven tonight and didn't ask any questions. We always covered for each other. Perhaps that is what friends are for.

Sometimes I wonder what the hell is the point. We never seem to get anywhere at all.

Fifteen:
Henry 1980

Just as I prepared to throw the crispy-fried remains of my hung over, abused body upon the bed, I saw the note on the pillow in the blinds-darkened room. It had been torn from the pad next to the answering machine.

Henry—
You shouldn't have done that...you know.

In my mind, the wipers cleared the pounding rain and the defroster tried to undo the steam fogging the windshield. I'd looked over at her, still shocked at her boldness in the darkened classroom and ashamed at my response to her. Her dark, deep-set eyes looked right through me. That wild hair lay in damp ringlets on her shoulders and framed her sweet, narrow face. Her skin glowed creamy white against the rain-soaked, black silk and chiffon blouse clinging to her small, rounded breasts. She crackled with vitality and the space inside the car seemed inadequate to hold her. She was so... pretty and so very strange.

Her straight nose turned up a little at the tip, flaring a bit at the nostrils and fit her face really well, but it was her mouth that did me in. It curved easily into a seductive, yet somehow sunny, smile that most girls my own age couldn't have reliably pulled off. Ethereal. I felt completely alive in her presence, the absence of which I hadn't noticed until I looked upon her in my classroom and she'd burst out laughing at the sight of... me? Was that it?

In my own words, she'd given it back to me. Seven of them altogether and I didn't need to ask who'd left the note, though it could've been my own conscience. Sarah might argue that I had none, but damned if I didn't. Her name was Alice.

Too tired to think, I pushed the note to the other pillow and hoped I might never wake up, but knew I would.

***

I woke to the sound of the damned phone ringing around four pm. I rolled over, groping for the other pillow to put over my head and my hand landed on Alice's note. To my relief the caller hung up on ring number six. Scrubbing the sleep from my eyes, I studied the bold script on the white paper and tried to decide how I felt about it. Her list of violations was short, but incriminating. She'd spied on me, stalked me, invaded my privacy, and for some reason that didn't bother me at all—or not much anyway. I think it bothered me more that she knew what I'd done. How strange. I yawned and stretched, imagining what might have happened if she'd been here when I got home, my mind inevitably drifting straight back to the effect she had on me.

Alice held the promise of devastating beauty, even just shy of fifteen—I looked up her date of birth in her permanent record: October 24, 1965. Despite that first fit of hysterical giggles, she had shown not one shred of the shallow, teenaged girl silliness I witnessed five days a week. Mystery surrounded her as though she willed it, from the romantic clothes she wore to the lit from within glow of her warm brown eyes. Her tender lower lip nearly made me crazy, for it just begged to be kissed, bitten, sucked on…

Not to mention she had an ass that would make a Calvin Klein jeans model cry in envy. Her faded blue jeans hugged every willowy curve—when she wore them. My wayward dick gave a mighty twitch at the thought and I silently cringed. *Fourteen*, Henry. Out of reach. Way out of reach!

My mind, seemingly unfazed by this warning, returned to its increasingly familiar Alice-track. I couldn't seem to stay off it for very long and it only got worse as time and familiarity worked its magic upon me.

She unnerved me to the point of near speechlessness most of the time. Standing in that classroom droning on and on about American history, with that face looking back at me was a sweet, if awful kind of hell. If she'd been eighteen, I would've held her and never let her go.

Dust motes floated lazily in the shafts of late afternoon sunlight shining between the slats of the blinds, which rattled in the occasional gusts through the open window, scattering the particles. I justified my Alice-thoughts in the privacy of my bedroom, testing them, tired of denying how I felt about her and realized that my self-judgment was only a surface thing, only valid when the voice in my head asked what would your father say? Or what if someone found out? Or worse still, how would you like your name splashed across the front of the local newspaper when her parents had you arrested? I could lose my job and ruin my dad's good name and his fledgling career in local politics. On top of everything else, he'd just thrown his hat in the ring for mayor.

Admittedly, those age laws didn't mean much around here—more than a handful of the drunks at the bar last night were upper classmen or just graduated from high school and certainly under the legal drinking age. Had

I been anyone else, a gas station attendant or mechanic, no one would've thought twice about it.

A teacher though? One who was charged with responsibility for these loose-cannon teens? That was like painting a target on my back and begging somebody to bust me. No good.

After only a few weeks I knew which of my freshman girls were dating seniors, which ones had boyfriends who'd already graduated, and heard all about the dramas of those relationships. During study hall last Tuesday, Chatty Cathy had dished *all* the dirt on the Jackie Walker scandal, a freshman in my second hour class. She begged me to let her help grade quizzes, having finished her homework and claiming certain, imminent death from boredom. Knowing that idle hands are the devil's playground, I warily let her sit at the corner of my desk with the grading key and red ink pen.

Thus began the immediate chatter for which she is known. It seemed in no way to impede her grading ability, because she fairly flew through six separate class's papers. Before I knew it, I had been given the low-down on nearly every student of interest in the high school. Alice, curiously enough, was missing from the list.

Jackie Walker's boyfriend was an eye-popping twenty-five, according to Chatty, but he'd lied about his age. She fell in love and boinked him. By the time he confessed his age, it was too late! No heavy sigh from Chatty—oh no, an eager look of appraisal scraped my face for a reaction to the news.

I can't remember exactly what I'd said to this, except it doused that fire in her eye and replaced it with a dreamy version of defeat. The possibilities had been explored, rejected, and I'd been returned to crush status. Just the way it should be.

Strange how I could look upon virtually every other pretty student in that school and not feel anything more than a vague appreciation of their looks. No temptation and no wayward thoughts—or no more than the usual amount a guy would have.

And then there was Alice.

Only Alice had ignored the boundaries. I grasped onto her sweetness, her wit, her strangeness, and let thoughts of her drive the ugliness of what had happened with Sarah out of my mind. The irony of that was not lost on me.

"You're not right, Henry. Just not right," I said as I hauled myself from the bed and my fantasies and headed for the tub, feeling the sudden need to wash any lingering trace of Sarah off me.

I wondered how long it would take for Alice to show up here again. But more than that, I wondered what I would do when she did.

My thoughts were interrupted by the phone ringing. I ran to it, thumbed the switch back and forth on the machine until it landed on four rings and listened as it picked up the call. Long silence. "Henry, this is Sarah. I'm just calling to tell you what a great time I had last night." Long pause. "You left your jacket in my car. Please call me." Her voice, taut and strained, sounded anything but delighted over a great time. I could hardly believe she'd had the nerve to call. Surely she'd gotten the message when I snuck out on her this morning?

I stood staring at the machine, then looked for something to throw, punch or break. The bath could wait. I needed to move and blow off some aggravation. I shoved my feet into my shoes and let the screen door slam behind me as I headed over to get the Buick. A yellow parking ticket flapped beneath the wiper blade—another layer of frosting on this shit-flavored cupcake.

Four hours later, after I demolished a pizza and drank several beers, I took the other two pills I'd cadged and went back to bed. I turned on the radio to KZ93.

"*Rhiannon rings like a bell through the night and wouldn't you love to love her?*"

Stevie Nicks. Suddenly I made the connection between Alice's dreamy clothes and hair and Stevie—a woman who could stop traffic, even on a bad day. Totally hot. I smiled. Rhiannon. The witch. The Goddess. Alice.

Dreams unwind. Love's a state of mind…

It sure is, sweetheart.

I left the door unlocked. Sarah wouldn't dare. Alice would.

Sixteen:
Alice 1980

I hadn't planned to leave a note on his pillow, only intended to go home in defeat. But then I'd stood in front of his building just a little too long, thinking of all the things that needed saying between us. He might get bored with Sarah and his car could turn the corner any second. That hope trumped any fear of discovery by a possible roommate—I didn't know anything about Henry's living arrangements beyond his apartment number and location. I just couldn't let this happen without at least trying to save him from Sarah. I couldn't seem to stop myself. Honestly, I didn't want to. So that was that.

A dagger of disgust sliced my heart, along with a feeling of misplaced betrayal. Crazy, I know, since this seemed to be a crush gone terribly wrong from the viewpoint of a casual observer. I knew better. I kept a vigilant watch, thinking I'd see the Buick any second. But as the time dragged by, it occurred to me that maybe Sarah had learned a few tricks since the 17th century and he might not come home for hours.

From the dentist office's front step, I watched until my curfew time arrived, but he hadn't come yet. I ran for home at three minutes before I'd be looking at a week of solitary confinement and made it with a full sixty seconds to spare. Dad was back on the road and Mom left for work. I paced the floor of my room for exactly five minutes before running out the door to the safety of the dentist's surveillance porch.

I wanted, needed to talk to him. I had to tell him all I knew of Sarah, had to find the words that would pierce the veils shrouding his soul's memories. Maybe our lives might depend on it. That fear drove me as surely as the longing for him. My feelings were all over the place. I wanted him. But then I'd always wanted Henry. It seemed to be hardwired into me.

At ten minutes past two, Sarah's little Mazda rolled down Logan Street, its distinctive wind-up toy sound drawing my attention to the deserted intersection. It didn't slow down, but I heard the gears grind as she shifted going past.

I stared at the corner for a good ten minutes, willing the Buick to appear, which soon turned into half an hour. God, Henry. Don't. Just don't. He did.

I cried quietly and called upon the moon, the Goddess in her heavenly form, to help me. There she was, riding high on a corona of clouds as wispy as my skirt. A wide expanse of sky above Henry's building showed stars scattered like jewels on a black velvet cloth.

Four-thirty in the morning and the shadows I loved turned gray and nebulous. Birds trilled here and there, rousing me from the thoughts that had kept me outside all night. I'd been so still, wrapped in my shawl on the steps, that I almost expected dewdrops to shake from me as I stood. Chilled and a little stiff, I paused only to stretch and yawn before I ran across the street, bare feet flying up his back stairs, hesitating but for the briefest moment before I opened the door...

At twenty past seven, I waved to my mom from one of the wicker chairs on our front porch as she pulled into our driveway. Comfy in my p.j.'s and wrapped in an oversized sweater, I clutched a cup of coffee and forced a smile as she waved back and looked maternal askance upon me.

I was very tired, but couldn't sleep yet. The backdoor slammed and her weary, booted step sounded on the living room hardwood. She opened the screen door and finished up a jaw-cracking yawn in progress. Dressed in jeans and a t-shirt with a flannel shirt tied around her waist, she looked tired enough to drop where she stood.

"Hey baby, what are you doing up so early?"

"Couldn't sleep. I kept waking up for some reason. Finally, I just gave it up and here I am."

"Oh." She yawned again. "Well, I'd like to join you, but I can hardly keep my eyes open. Nighty-night."

"Night, Mom," I replied and felt relief that she'd taken a pass on the coffee. The screen door slammed and I heard her feet on the stairs. I wanted to be alone for this.

"Love you..." drifted to me out on the porch. She'd paused on her upward progress.

"Love you, too, Mom. Always." Tears sprang to my eyes. Too long a night. Love of any kind played upon my raw feelings. I rubbed my face with the fuzzy, sweater-clad back of my arm. Settle. Must settle in and wait.

With my feet up on the porch rail, I leaned back in the chair. It would be a blue car delivering him, or a tired, walking Henry, skulking from the scene of the crime. I hoped the morning would bring him and not the afternoon, or worse yet, tomorrow... that would mean big trouble. I thought about Sarah and didn't think she could hold him. Not yet.

I stirred creamer into my coffee and yawned, wiping the tears it wrung from the corners of my gritty eyes. Henry shuffled into sight, crossed Pekin Street and turned his back to me, waiting for cars to pass, his rumpled chambray shirttail fluttering over his wrinkled jeans. Tall and broad-shouldered, he swayed a little on his feet and I thought he must feel like crap right now. He deserved to feel that way, but the sight of him evoked a tenderness I hadn't felt before in this body. I loved him. His pain was my pain.

I slept a solid eight hours and felt like a new girl.

Barefoot in the dark, I skipped along the narrow concrete lip of the short landscaping wall next to the sidewalk, descending for the driveways and rising up, twirling on tiptoes, my long, sheer skirts floating on air. To the corner I came and watched my mother's taillights disappear around the curve where Logan Street turns into Fifth. The night sung through my very veins and I became one with it. Standing in the shadows of the house across from Henry's apartment building, I held up my arms to the sky, letting the wind love me, and listening to its song through the leaves above my head.

It didn't matter that I was only two or three blocks from downtown on a Saturday night. Just about anywhere outside that bubble of raucous liveliness, you could breathe in the stillness of a sleepy little town all tucked in for the evening. I sat on the concrete step of the elevated yard, wanting a minute or two to just enjoy the darkness. Cars passed by. A black cat streaked across the gray pavement and became one of the shadows on the other side of the street. Henry's bedroom window beckoned and he could've seen me clearly, had he glanced out of it. A little thrill passed through my body—a shiver of pure lust and longing.

His car sat in its customary place on the street—apparently he'd retrieved it. No blue Mazda's in sight. I could guess how that went. He walked out on her before she'd awakened. Tacky, but very revealing—he hadn't meant for it to happen and that made me happy.

I stood beneath his window and music drifted down to me, soft and low. Would I do it?

Yes, I think I would.

Seventeen:
Henry 1980

I opened my eyes to a room flooded with moonlight. It shone on her bright hair. An angel bathed in silver, a living dream stood at the foot of my bed. I didn't move, afraid I might awaken and she would be gone. She glided through moonbeams and shadows to the bedside. The sweet night air clung to her and I breathed deeply of it.

Plaintive notes of an old Emerson, Lake and Palmer song played on the radio, speaking for me as truly as if the words had been my own. *From the Beginning,* the soundtrack from a sweet dream, surreal and wonderful. Had she chosen it for me? Anything could happen in dreams. The codeine and Budweiser blanket around my brain provided a foggy cushion upon which I floated, miles away from the real world, and happy about it.

Whatever was done is done, I just can't recall. It doesn't matter at all…

Greg Lake's voice echoed through my skull, speaking directly to me. More words of mystery issued from the speaker, words of change and foolishness, and destiny. Some things, it seemed, were meant to be. It really didn't matter, did it? No. I wanted her and held out my arms. She came to me, her slim beauty swathed in diaphanous material, the glimmer of tears on her pale cheeks. Don't cry my darling, I thought, and knew she heard.

My angel sighed; lips cool against my neck, her fingers tracing my cheek and jaw. I gathered her in, melding our bodies together. She fit me like she'd been made for me. Lips soft as rose petals met mine.

Bright sunlight filled the room and I sat up blinking, alone in my bed. Alice! She'd been here. Or had she? The dream came back to me and I couldn't tell if it was real or just wishful thinking. I slid from beneath the covers and jumped to my feet, searching for proof and unsure that I wanted any. Angels didn't walk in the daylight and look up at you from the pages of a history textbook. I shook my head, confused, then slowly peeled the sheet and blanket all the way back. The end of a white satin ribbon glowed from between the pillows. Bit by bit I pulled, almost afraid it might disappear in my hand.

I held it to my lips. It smelled sweet. Just like Alice.

Eighteen:
Alice 2033

Rain pattered softly against my windows as I slid gratefully between cool sheets. The hot bath, wine, and pain pill knocked the edge off the physical agony—the dark partner with whom I danced almost every day now.

Henry had checked out and my fifty-five year love affair with high heels had just ended. The arthritis I'd denied—though my doctor had told me plainly years ago, made it impossible to continue my pretense of height. At 5'3" another three or four inches always felt pretty good and I felt a little sad to be saying goodbye. Trashing the shoes had been a symbolic, long overdue gesture. As always, I'd done something for Henry at a great expense to myself and now the time had come to pay. Well, I'd always paid, hadn't I?

It was long past time to admit many things about myself and one of them was that no almost sixty-eight year old woman should wear four-inch heels. As I'd embraced the first two faces of the Goddess—the Maiden and the Mother, so now must I fully become the Crone, though I was loathe to do it. My time in that role would be mercifully brief, because I refused to count it in real time. The Great Wheel turns and takes us along with it.

Dulled but jagged teeth of pain gnawed at my joints. My wrenched knee gave a muffled throb and my ankle joined in the chorus to remind me it wasn't over yet. I didn't think I'd have to wait much longer. I didn't know my exact departure date from this life, though I could call it pretty close, but the last reason to stay had just gone. The dark, unidentified stranger residing within my body did its silent, parasitic work upon me. Fortunately, the work of killing me was slow going. I'm a tough old bird, or so said my doctor—a fresh-faced kid who looked about twelve, but I knew was in his mid-30s. He'd not been wrong yet, and he wasn't wrong about this, either.

My daughter and best friend, for whom I'd not had to wait long at all, at least from the perspective of nearly seventy years, had left on her own quiet adventure with my blessing a long time ago. She'd found her Apothecary, his name was Arthur and he was a pharmacist, which always made me smile.

She'd earned a restful life and made one for herself. Mine had not been, but now I could relax. She'd be all right. Branwen, now Elyse, had always been wise. She remembered all and feared nothing. My sister. My mother. My daughter. She'd been with me always. Her dark, laughing eyes looked up at me from a chubby baby's face. Where had the time gone? I sent her a kiss on the invisible lines which held us together and she returned it, with love and understanding. We would meet again. Always. Tears spilled from my eyes. The pillow lay soft against the left side of my face and accepted the watery offering. The bridge of my nose held a tiny pool until the well filled, found a wrinkle to run along, and joined the others soaking into the pillow. I let them fall.

I lay on my side, my hair wrapped in a towel and my body wrapped in a satin gown, watching the billowing clouds that had settled decisively upon the earth and swathed my privacy-fenced backyard in mystery. Through the glass doors, I saw that puddles had formed on the paving stones of the small sitting area just outside. A bright-eyed sparrow alighted on the back of my chair, then took to the sky.

Unseen arms wrapped around me from behind and a whisper tickled my ear. "I love you."

I sighed and settled against the supposedly non-existent person who shared my bed. "I know Henry...I know."

Nineteen:
Henry 1980

I passed out the dismal results of a pop quiz I'd pulled on them when they'd walked through the door. Alice, of course, turned in a perfect score. I handed back the papers back myself, laying them face down on their desks as they reread the chapter and filled out the study pages in their workbooks. It shouldn't be this hard. It was.

Alice didn't look up from her reading when I paused at her desk, suddenly awkward and unsure of myself. She sat cocked back in the seat with her textbook propped on her non-existent belly; the spine of the book resting on the edge of the desk.

Immediately, I spied the paperback concealed within the history book and she didn't try to hide it, though I'm sure she knew I stood over her shoulder. I looked down on her hair and wondered if she put the blonde in it artificially. Truly, there was nothing fake about her. I guessed no. Without looking from the book, she held up her workbook pages, already done, then twitched her hand as if to say, "Go away, you're bothering me."

I stifled a grin, shaking my head as I placed the quiz on her desk. Then my eyes landed on the book title printed at the top of the page of the paperback. *The Sensuous Woman.*

"Amateurs," she muttered

I swallowed too fast and choked on my own spit. Alice didn't look up at first, but the tops of her cheeks rose in a smile. I sputtered and coughed, and knew my face was likely turning beet-red.

She turned innocent eyes upward and said loudly as I tried to draw breath, "Mr. Spears, you should really do something about that nasty cough." She peeked at the paper, read what I'd written there and… winked… at me.

I stumbled out of the classroom, still coughing, hearing the predictable chatter already starting up as I headed for the men's room.

***

I looked up from the workbook pages I graded as she poked her head around the classroom door. "Henry, we have to stop meeting like this."

She sauntered over the threshold, dressed in faded jeans, a lace-edged Fleetwood Mac Rumors tank top, and her signature, leather high-heeled boots clicking on the floor tiles. On Alice's shirt, Stevie Nicks draped herself over Mick Fleetwood's skinny knee. Her sleeves reminded me of Alice's black blouse… They could've been sisters, the resemblance was so strong.

"What will the neighbors say?"

I'd almost missed what she said. "Very funny. Close the door and get over here. We need to talk."

"I know."

I fixed her with my sternest 'dad' look. I'd seen it often enough. "Explain yourself, young lady."

Her mouth twitched. "My goodness, if you keep that up, I'll be going to bed without my supper."

"Stop."

She faltered. Her cheeks turned rosy and she looked away. "I… don't know what to say."

I could certainly understand that and felt the same. I wanted to bolt, but had to fix this. We had to get this straightened out and I wasn't sure what that meant, exactly. What I should do and what I wanted to do were opposite things.

"I don't need to tell you that I am almost exactly ten years older than you?"

"I'd guessed eleven, maybe twelve."

"Like you, I was one of the youngest in my class."

She nodded and an awkward silence sprung up between us as she waited for me to get to the point.

"I also don't need to tell you that what you did the other night could land me in jail, out of a job, and probably tarred and feathered?" Appeal to her sense of reason; that might work. "And that's just what the school board would do to me."

One delicate shoulder lifted in a shrug. "Doubtful. Unless you tell somebody, and I certainly won't."

"Alice, look at me."

She turned large, doe-eyes on me and looked every inch a frightened deer that had just winded danger. I thought she might sprint from the room any second.

"We can't…I … Damn it. It's not right!" My voice sounded desperate and pleading. "Don't you know that?"

Her dark eyes shone with unshed tears. "I know what I want."

"I'm trying to tell you that this can't happen." My dad's face rose up in my mind and I couldn't argue with the truth of that statement.

"You don't need to feel bad. I came to you, not the other way around. Stop painting yourself as some dirty old man, preying on a child. I'm not a child."

"You are." But then, not at all, my mind added. I had to make her believe me.

Her face crumpled and so did my resolve. "Why did you do this, Henry? I said I was sorry. I begged your forgiveness. I forgive you all the time. Why couldn't you give me a break, just once?"

"What?" I thought back over what she'd just said, couldn't make heads or tails of it, and thought maybe she meant the thing with Sarah. "If it makes you feel better, I agree with you about Friday night. I was drunk. But as stupid as that was, it won't get me a prison sentence."

She turned the saddest eyes I've ever seen on me. "I've gone to the flames for you. Felt them tie me to the stake. Smelled my skirts smoldering and waited for the fire to consume me. We have a habit of bad timing, but what you're saying doesn't mean much stacked against that. You're going to have to think of a better excuse."

I stared at her with a strange sensation creeping over my scalp. I smelled cloth burning, felt the heat and heard the whoosh of flames as though someone had thrown an accelerant on it. The black robes of Dominican priesthood brushed my legs as I started forward, trying to save her. Rough hands jerked me back, held me down, and made me watch. Ashes and smoke. Blackening flesh and horrific screams. I think they were my own as well as the girl tied to the stake. Red-hot irons pressed against my eyelids, sealing them forever.

The last thing I saw was my beloved burning before they took my sight away. I shook my head at her words, trying to clear the images from it, my heart shattering, fragile as the stained glass window above my head. I ran a shaking hand over my face, the colors of the glass a blurred kaleidoscope with the sun behind it. A cathedral, I thought. I blinked hard, bringing Alice's face back into focus. "What the hell are you talking about?"

She bit that wonderful lower lip, her eyes huge in her pale face, then whispered, "Never mind." She turned and bolted. I caught her with her hand on the doorknob. Frosted glass blocked any view from the hall, a happenstance for which I was grateful.

I turned her toward me, my arms shaking for reasons I couldn't comprehend. "I want to know, Alice. I'm not putting you down," I said gently, my voice trembling and strange to my ears. "What did you mean?"

She shook her head, her face wet with tears. "It's no use. You don't remember. Let me go."

I should have. That was probably the only chance I'd ever get and I knew it.

"No." I seemed to lose control of myself and nearly jerked her off her feet, crushed her body to mine, and buried my face in that wild hair, breathing deeply of her unique scent—sweet and green, like wildflowers in a meadow.

"Shh. Don't cry," I whispered. I'd never wanted anything or anyone like I wanted her at that moment. "Alice. I don't know what's wrong with me. I'm sorry." Helpless angry tears stung my nose and eyelids. I held them back with every ounce of strength I could summon, still not believing what was happening.

Her arms tightened around me and she whispered, "Don't be sorry, Henry. I do know. That's all that matters now. Trust me."

I just didn't think I could do that.

***

I nosed the car out onto Primm Road, but didn't turn toward town. Cornfields and anonymity were what we needed right now. Both times we'd slipped out of the school through a side door in the cafeteria that opened into the teacher's parking lot. That would have to stop. Sooner or later we'd meet someone and then it would begin: my worst nightmare.

Twenty:
Alice 1980

Henry drove a long time without speaking, turning down roads I didn't recognize, his eyes riveted to the blacktop stretching before us, but distant at the same time and I wondered what thoughts were taking him so far from me. Was it the witch fire? Something had happened to him when I'd said that. The memories might be closer to the surface than I realized.

I didn't know what to say to him that wouldn't sound crazy. I'd learned from my parents a long time ago that telling that kind of truth was not only unacceptable, but often landed me in my room, doing without something—or nearly on my way to a therapist's couch. Even if on some level they understood me, people always seemed to fear what I said and maybe that was the problem: they did understand me and it scared the shit out of them. I'd already said too much.

He pulled off onto a rutted dirt road so choked with trees and underbrush I wouldn't have noticed it. We got out of the car and I followed him down a narrow path to the banks of a creek. Sunlight sparkled on greenish-brown rushing water, dazzling the eye. The scent of water and living things, the Goddess's heady perfume, filled this peaceful grotto. Trees swayed in the breeze and between the gaps in their gnarled trunks, blue horizons embraced cornfields, row after golden row, nearly ready for the harvest. Samhain—summer's end approached. The Old Ways called to me, as I suspected they always would, though I'd left those things behind me long ago. Here with the natural things of the earth, I felt my confidence return. He'd brought me to my elements.

He stared at the creek and I stood on his left, slightly behind him and suddenly realized he'd begun dressing more casually. Today he wore brown corduroys and a beige pullover. He'd shoved the sleeves up to his elbows and the ever-present jacket had hung on his chair all day. In the weeks since school started, he'd grown comfortable with his new job and gradually, the suits had been abandoned. His skin glowed, tanned to healthy golden brown and I thought he looked good enough to eat.

"I don't understand any of this. I feel so strange when you speak of…" His shoulder twitched and he turned worried black eyes on me. "Your words hit my ears and this god-awful feeling passes over me. I don't know why, because I don't have the first clue of what you're talking about… but then, I do!" He shook his head and scraped a hand back through his hair. "I think I'm losing my mind."

I didn't say anything. Couldn't. It would be better if he worked some of this out for himself. Sarah could wait. Perhaps this was the path to his memories after all.

He fastened jet-black eyes upon my face, eyes that had turned speculative, and he continued his thought. "Or maybe *you* are, and you're pulling me right along with you."

"Insanity isn't supposed to be contagious." I smiled a little grimly, knowing that indeed it was. Contagious insanity is what killed innocent people when fear and intolerance took over. It had happened many times in human history. He knew all about that; history was probably his major.

"And then, there's what happened between us the other night…"

"Nothing happened. It was innocent."

"I didn't mean it that way." He smiled a little. "I thought you were an angel. Thought I was dreaming."

"Maybe you were."

He pulled the crumpled ribbon from the front pocket of his pants. "I don't think so." He stared at it for a long moment, then crammed it back inside. A keepsake?

"How did you feel about that?" I waited with my heart in my throat.

His gaze returned to the water. "The song. I couldn't figure out how that song came to be playing on the radio when I opened my eyes. *From the Beginning…*"

Disappointment caused me to sigh and I slipped into priestess with novitiate mode. "That song is esoteric and contains layer upon layer of truth, though most think it's just some sappy love song. Serendipity put it in the disc jockey's rotation that night. You were meant to hear those words. It had meaning for you, didn't it?"

He shot me a swift look. "There you go again. Saying things that make no sense. Sometimes, I think you're talking in code."

"Me?" I raised my eyebrows. "What about you? I asked how you felt. You replied with a question about coincidence. I answered it."

He shoved his hands in his pockets and kicked at a decent sized rock buried in the hard, uneven soil of the bank. "I felt very strange, but I'd taken codeine pills earlier to help with the hangover."

"I see." He didn't have to tell me how he felt. I'd seen his face in the moonlight, felt his heart beating and his warm, sleepy body awakening to mine—but that didn't mean I didn't *want* to hear it. "You're not on drugs today, are you?"

He smiled sheepishly and my heart did a flip-flop. "No."

A large flat rock jutted from the bank behind the charred remains of a small campfire. Empty beer cans and bait containers littered the ground around it. People take what they want from nature and leave trash as an offering to the Goddess. The whole world was out of sync—but then it had been that way for a very long time. I plucked an empty plastic bag caught on a bush and picked it all up while he watched. Then, I perched on the rock and patted the empty space next to me.

Reluctantly, he came, but hesitated in front of me with a wary look in his eyes. This was going to be more work than I'd realized. "Sit, Henry. I won't bite."

He rolled his eyes, but sat. "Okay. I'm sitting. Now what?"

"Close your eyes. I'm going to tell you a story."

"Huh?"

"Just do it. I want to see what happens."

He shook his head and the look on his face told me that he thought this was stupid. Finally, with the sunshine checkering his face beneath the canopy of turning leaves, he closed his eyes and I began leading him through a lifetime in Wales.

Twenty-One:
Henry 1980

Alice's voice filled my head, painting living landscapes on the back of my eyelids. I shivered when she touched me, but kept my eyes closed as that strange tingling passed in waves over my scalp. Invisible currents passed from her hand to mine and I held on for dear life as the images came.

Hawthorne branches. May bonfires glowing against a star-strewn Welsh sky. A small circle of standing stones and an entire village winding through them in a ritual dance. Lovers honored the Goddess, writhing naked in the fields and insuring another year of good harvests. Dark, smiling eyes met mine as we leapt a small blaze together and then held out our hands to be tied together by the priestess. Hand-fasting. Flowers in her hair. The birth of our first child, conceived at Beltane.

I never lay down with anyone else again—though it was expected and certainly allowed for festivals, but simply put, there was never another woman that could take my eyes from her. A happy, uncomplicated life passed through my mind. Hard work, sweet nights, and always my lovely girl by my side to face the best and worst that life could offer.

Death came to me as an old man, surrounded by my grown children and grandchildren. Hers was the last face I looked upon, but I knew we would meet again. Always. There was sadness in parting, but joy in it, too. We would be young again! Hurry, my darling. I can't wait...

Alice told a brief story woven from simple words, narrating scenes I somehow already knew. I opened my eyes when she ceased speaking and looked at her a little fearfully, her hand clasped tightly in my own. When I'd let go of life as that other man, another Henry long dead, I knew what it meant to die. Without fear, I felt myself let go and become effortlessly free. Remembering it seemed like the most natural thing in the world. Alice brought me back to the present before the next images fully materialized, but I glimpsed them there in the background. Another time. Another life. And another...Alice.

I swallowed hard and blinked. She seemed to have a golden halo somewhere behind her, though the sun was on the other side of us and the lighting was all wrong. The wind lifted her long hair, blowing a wayward lock across her face. She smiled and brushed it away.

"How in the hell do you do that? *Are* you a witch?" I knew exactly how ridiculous that sounded and how rational at the same time. Darrin couldn't have said it better to Samantha.

Alice's smile deepened and she demurely dropped her gaze. "I'm not doing it, *you* are. These are your memories; I'm only helping you reach them." She raised her eyes to me, and I thought I saw amusement in their shining depths. "I was there with you, if you missed that part."

She shifted slightly on the rock and let go of my hand. "To answer your second question, I guess I'd have to know what you mean by that. There're so many misconceptions." She picked up a crimson leaf from the ground and stroked it between her tapered, graceful fingers. The nail beds were a healthy pink and the tips white. She wore no polish on them. The wind rattled through the trees, bringing a sketchy shower of the first fallen leaves down around us.

"Maybe I was once, though priestess, wise woman, or healer might be more accurate. I don't fly around on a broom. I never worshipped the devil—there isn't one, except for the one that lives in men's hearts." She dropped the leaf, fixed me with a disconcerting look, and I wondered if she'd picked up my thoughts. "It's not like *Bewitched* and never was. Real magic has almost been driven from this world—I remember it, though, and it had nothing to do with any of those things, or crappy TV special effects. It's about the natural world and the illusions we create in it. That's all. Simple."

"I see. Simple." Squinting at the sun, which now shone in my eyes from the western horizon between the trees, I became aware of the amount of time that had passed since we'd been here. It had gone much too quickly. "So, you're saying…"

"I'm not saying anything." She stood and dusted off the seat of her jeans, then reached for the bag of garbage she'd collected. "I'm not telling you how it is. I'm not posing any theories. This is for you to determine, Henry. You have to decide for yourself what your version of reality is. I only know what yours used to be, not what it is now."

I frowned because I'd hoped to settle something out here, only to find it more complicated. The only thing I knew for sure was that I felt confused. She turned toward the path and I said, "I don't know what to think, Alice. I feel like I'm tripping on acid or something, this feels so unreal."

"It's real," she said over her shoulder and I watched that sweet ass, oh yes I did, as she climbed the trail. I just wanted to put my hands on it and squeeze. Just once, maybe twice?

I yanked myself out of that erotic thought, stopping just short of the kisses I'd like to plant on that gorgeous behind. "But…" I stepped up alongside her at the passenger side of the car, taking the garbage bag from her hand and tying the handles together. "Whatever it is, we can't change the fact that you're fourteen, I'm almost twenty-five, and your teacher."

The look on her face gave me to know that her natural retort would've been, *almost fifteen,* but her dignity would not allow it. She rearranged her expression to one of barely tethered anger and it took me aback. Alice planted her feet with both hands on her hips and said, "That's not *my* fault."

"I didn't say it was. It's only…"

She crossed her arms, eyes flashing, brows nearly meeting over her nose. "It's only? What? That you're a coward? You think I'd turn you in? Point a finger at you? What?"

I opened my mouth, but before I could say anything, she continued. "You weren't worried about that when I lay in your arms kissing you! Angel, my ass." She turned and reached for the Buick's door handle.

"Wait. Don't." I put my hand on her arm and turned her to face me. "Don't say that. It wasn't like that for me at all. I forget myself when I'm with you—like I'm not quite me, but *more* me somehow. I don't know." I took a deep breath. "Alice, that night was the truth. It's just that it's impossible. I'm too old for you."

Some of the tension left her at my words and she nearly smiled. "Close your eyes, Henry."

I stared a long moment at her, as mesmerized as I could be, wondering if she would take me on another trip, but did what she asked. She snaked her arms under mine and folded herself into me. Standing on tiptoes I imagine, her lips met mine in the sweetest of kisses. I stood trembling like a stone suddenly exposed to more heat than it could withstand, about to crack and dissolve into a molten puddle. As her mouth moved against mine and her body pressed hard against me in all the right places, I dropped the trash bag. The next thing I knew, I was kissing her back, parting her lips, my body answering hers. Jesus. I'd kissed a lot of girls, but it had never been like this. It was like being burned from the inside out.

With a gasp, I broke the kiss. Another second and I would've had her on the ground with her jeans around her ankles. She trailed kisses across my cheek

"You can't deny *that,* my love," she whispered in my ear. "You can try, but I don't think you'll manage it."

I pulled back from her and raised my hand to her satiny cheek. She was right. I couldn't. But somehow, I had to do that very thing. I wished myself luck with that as I opened the door for her. I looked down at myself and also wished for the jacket that would cover the most obvious of a multitude of sins. It still hung on my chair in the classroom.

We drove back to town in silence, until she told me to drop her off at the park; she'd walk the rest of the way home. I can't say I wasn't relieved at that, but when she closed the car door, it was like the golden autumn afternoon all around me had darkened somehow. It wasn't the first time I'd noticed that effect when she left me.

Twenty-Two:
Henry 2033

It's not that I needed to sleep in my current state—or could, really. No, but it was close. Curled up next to Alice, I rested for a time in her soothing presence, as near asleep as I could come. In those swirling, precious minutes, when the barriers came down and she began the descent, she could both hear and feel me though she'd not crossed the threshold yet to dreams. There in that space, we could meet for a little while and she could allow herself to be with me in her own place. It was good.

Better still, when Alice climbed a silver stairwell of her own making, I went with her. In her dreams, on the astral plane, she didn't suffer the pains or weariness of old age. She looked as she had at twenty, but then again, so much more than that. Here I could hold her, dance with her on moonbeams, merge with her in a rapture I could never put into words.

I hadn't realized how much I'd missed that. It seemed like such a long time… though I got the feeling that however far apart we'd been on earth, we'd met here often, slipping through the night like she used to do as a teenager. On the spiritual plane, nothing mattered and we could touch each other without fear, reprisals, or resentment. I realized that we'd never spoken a word in that sacred place. Didn't have to. Making love here didn't require a body and there were so many more ways to do it. Sex truly cannot compare, though it's an excellent substitute when one is earthbound.

There are so many layers of reality, so many ways of being, that it's hard to believe we forget all this when we're awake. Most people call them dreams. I call it heaven.

When her body called to her and she began to wake, she held my hand as she returned and I lay down with her once more on the bed, feeling her make the shift to consciousness. With a sigh, she turned over, opened her eyes, and looked right through me. A desolate tide drowned me in separation—a poignant sense of otherness made more devastating after our joining.

A golden presence lit up the wall in my peripheral vision. Alice rose with a little groan, pulled the towel from her hair, and limped to the bathroom.

She walked like she needed another pill. Maybe the pain had awakened her. She'd hurt herself today.

"How much longer must I wait for her, Azriel?" I spoke without looking at him, and traced the rumpled sheets where Alice had lain with my finger. Like walls and ceilings, I could perceive or disregard as I saw fit. The sheets were real to me, so therefore I could touch. I made no impression upon them. They made their impression on me. Alice's warmth still lingered in the folds.

"Time means nothing at all to me," Azriel said. "I do not know." The light on the wall moved, growing bigger as Azriel appeared in front of me. A movie star-square chin and chiseled jaw had defined themselves on his face, as well as blazing blue eyes. Blond hair curled upon his shoulders and he fixed me with a meaningful gaze. "Alice knows, though. She will come when she is ready. She is rare amongst your kind."

"I know." Strangely enough, when I said it that time, I knew it truly and understood what I'd thrown away. "I am sorry about so many things I've done or not done."

"Yes. You are. But not all is cause for regret."

I looked at him closer. "You're changing, Azriel. Is that all right?" I felt concern for him. After all he was my guardian. He'd always been there, I now knew. I didn't want him to harm himself looking after me. It wasn't his fault I'm an idiot who doesn't do what I'm supposed to do.

He smiled showing a row of perfect white teeth. "Yes. I'm fine. It's you who are changing, Henry. You are able to see me more clearly now, and what you see is your perception of me." He held up his hand and gazed at it for a moment. "It is not easy to explain. I am more than this and yes, less than this as well. But it matters not. It is the way of Spirit. I am what you need me to be."

"Am I endangering us both by staying here? Alice said I should go to the light. I don't remember refusing, but…" The toilet flushed down the hallway.

A soft expression came over his beautiful face. I say beautiful, because though he'd taken on masculine features, handsome ones, too, he was unearthly. No one would ever mistake him for human. "Henry, you are not in danger. Your life is in front of you, playing out in minute detail, as it should be, as it has been decreed. It matters not that you are with Alice—better that you are, for she has much to teach you."

I didn't answer. This didn't make any sense. How could I be here with her and not a ghost or trapped? How could that be okay?

Azriel knelt at the bedside and gazed, smiling, into my face. "What? Did you think you should be in a little dark room with a viewing screen?"

I thought about it for a moment and still didn't understand. "But isn't there supposed to be a light? I seem to remember something about that."

The angel's glowing, radiant nimbus gained in its scope and strength, enveloping me and everything else. He chuckled. "Do you see a light now, my child? You never refused. You took my hand. That is all that was required. Heaven is not a place; it's a state of being."

I'd never felt safer or more loved in all my lives.

Twenty-Three:
Henry 1980

My gut twisted into a tight knot as I parked the car next to the curb. A blue RX7 sat in the driveway behind the building. Not cool. That slot belonged to Mrs. Hawkins, the old lady who lived below me and owned the place. Upon giving her the check for the deposit and first month's rent, I'd told her not to put up with me if I was too loud at night.

She winked a creased eyelid over the wire-rimmed spectacles that always perched on the end of her short, pointy nose, reminding me of a wise old owl, and said, "Sometimes, being deaf as post isn't a bad thing. Out go the hearing aids, and off goes the noise. Mrs. Theobald, your neighbor across from me, is in the same shape, I'm afraid. The neighbor across from you isn't here much." She'd grinned and her cheeky, crevice-lined smile charmed me. "So, party on, young man. We won't hear a thing!"

That shiny little sports car parked in her space pissed me off. I felt protective of her. She'd been good to me, and for an old lady, was totally cool. I helped her out whenever I could, as she didn't seem to have any family around. I jammed the gearshift lever into park and yanked the keys from the ignition. Why hadn't I just called Sarah and gotten it over with on the phone? Answer: Because I thought she'd take the hint, that's why.

Alice's sweet face popped into my head. I'd fucked everything up this time. Majorly. Royally. Less than a month ago, my life had been boring. I think I preferred it that way. I know I did.

I slammed the car door harder than necessary and nearly came unglued when I saw that the Mazda sat empty on the graveled drive. Surely she wouldn't dare to let herself into my apartment? *Alice did*, a sly voice whispered in my mind. No. I hurried down the walk and rounded the corner, skidding on my heels when I saw Sarah looking down on me from the top of the stairs.

"Well, well, look what the cat dragged in. Hello, Henry." The smile on her face looked brittle, as though the skin on her cheeks might fracture if she held it more than a second or two.

"Sarah. What are you doing here?"

She stood with my jacket draped over her forearm. Her oversized boobs threatened escape from the hot pink spandex tank she wore. Spray-painted on jeans encased her lower body like a blue sausage skin. I thought she might've lost weight, but she was one of those girls that somehow always looked round, even when skinny—which she wasn't. Pink vinyl stiletto heels dug into the battered wood of the stairs. She'd done something hellish to her hair and it sprang forth in long tight spiraling coils like snakes from Medusa's head. To be fair, she didn't look much different than ninety-percent of the girls at U of I.

Alice made all of them look like whores.

"Hello Sarah. Good to see you, Sarah. What a nice surprise!" she mocked. "At least you could pretend you're glad to see me."

Guilt. It wasn't her fault that I regretted sleeping with her. I smiled and didn't mean that, either. "Sorry. You caught me by surprise. I wasn't expecting a visit. That's all." *Now get off my porch and quit staring at me like that.* Her pale blue eyes drilled into mine, waiting for my song and dance routine, no doubt.

"You brought my jacket. I didn't have time to call you back; it's been a busy couple of weeks. Thanks." I stood rooted to the walk and held out my hand for the coat. There was no way in hell I would climb those stairs and give her an opening to invite herself inside.

She hesitated, but then smiled as if she guessed the reason for my refusal to move. As awkward as the moment was, Sarah descended the stairs slowly, seductively, a modern day Mata Hari sizing up her next client, and handed me the coat at the bottom. Apparently, she still didn't get it, or else thought herself so irresistible, I might change my mind.

Her perfume surrounded me in a pungent cloud and I held my breath, then tried breathing through my mouth, where to my surprise, I could *taste* the shit. Awareness of just how much I didn't want to spend another minute with her nearly made me step back. Again, not her fault, but I couldn't help it. Beneath my polite demeanor, a battle of self-castigation raged.

Sarah tweaked my shirtsleeve and looked up at me from under heavily made-up lashes. "Would you come uptown with me for Happy Hour? We can have a couple of drinks and talk." She smiled again, a little sadly this time, and stroked my forearm. "I think we should. Don't you?"

Again I fought the urge to recoil, knowing it would be rude. She didn't deserve that kind of reaction from me. I didn't want to cross the street with her, let alone go back to the scene of the crime, but I suppose I owed her that much.

"Okay, but I can't stay long. My dad left a message at the school to call him and I've got a lot of papers to grade and a lesson plan to put together for tomorrow."

A bright smile lit her face and she was almost pretty beneath the makeup. Almost. Again, I thought of Alice's creamy skin and her shining, dark eyes.

We got into her car and she reversed out of the drive. I checked the right side for cars, and to my everlasting horror, looked right into Alice's shocked face. She stood twenty feet from the car, at the corner, no doubt on her way home. We shared a long look in the brief moment before Sarah shifted gears and tore down the street.

Shit. She wasn't kidding when she'd said we had a habit of bad timing.

***

"So what did your dad want? Did he say?" Sarah pitched her voice over the noise of the crowded bar and downed half a wine cooler in a couple of swallows.

"I think he wants me to go to some political function with him. He'd said something about it a couple of days ago. I didn't pay much attention to the message he left. Why?"

Sarah's questions seemed sly to me. Like she knew something I didn't and I didn't like that much at all. The last twenty minutes had been a coy inquisition with her asking the questions and mostly monosyllabic answers from me. Despite what she thought, there didn't seem to be much to talk about. After another beer for the sake of politeness, I'd let her down easy and walk home.

"Well, my dad is endorsing your dad's candidacy for Mayor. I'm guessing that's what he's trying to tell you—*if* you ever bothered to call him back." This, she delivered with downcast eyes, her hand moving the nearly empty wine-cooler bottle in small circles on the table. She'd ignored the coaster the bartender had put down.

That last dig was not lost on me. I hadn't called her back and wouldn't be here at all, but for the jacket. Dumbass. I dismissed it.

"What? Why would he do that?" This was Lincoln. Nobody endorsed anything. It was ridiculous in a town this size where everybody knew everything about everyone. In this place, you were lucky to take a dump without the whole neighborhood knowing about it.

She propped her chin on her hand, leaning on her elbow and pouted in what must have been her idea of sexy. "Don't act so surprised. They've been friends since we moved here."

I frowned into my beer. Friends was too strong a word—colleagues of a sort, maybe. "I guess. But why? Everybody knows Dad. He's into everything and in the newspaper at least once a month. It seems kind of silly."

Sarah's lips twisted into a secretive smile and she gave me a calculating sidelong look. "I told him we were seeing each other and thought he might help your father. He's hosting the soiree, a campaign fundraiser."

"You did *what?*"

She ran her tongue over her lips and beneath the table, her hand found my crotch and gave me a friendly squeeze. "Well, I didn't tell him *everything* or show him the video."

I recoiled in my chair, taking myself out of her reach. "What video?" My voice sounded flat, but I felt like my brain might just be melting as the horror of what she said dripped down into my gut and shriveled my balls.

She giggled and I wanted to bash her skull against the wall. "Oh Henry! You can't seriously sit there and act so innocent. As if you didn't know."

"As if I didn't know... what?" I'd gone numb from head to toe with dread.

"I got this super cool video camera for my birthday, remember? It has high-powered audio, too." She chuckled low and tapped her fingernail on her bottle, drawing out the suspense. "You wanted to do it; you positioned the camera and hit the record button. It was your idea. The result was, um, well, let's just say it's not PG rated. You are *quite* the man," she purred, and her hand crept up my leg again. "Creative, too."

Stunned, I sat there unable to speak or think, except this was worse than I could have ever imagined. This was a fucking nightmare. Literally.

Sarah giggled again and waved to the bartender, holding up her empty bottle. "So, I told Daddy we'd make an appearance at the fundraiser ball. I knew you'd want to go. He's happy about the two of us, but my mom is almost embarrassing. She's taking me shopping tomorrow to get a totally hot dress for it."

Her voice grated on my ears and I couldn't stand the sound of it. "I'm leaving." I shoved the chair back from the table.

"No, Henry, I don't think you are." She smiled again and it was utterly feral.

"Yes. I am." I rose to my feet and just wanted to go get impossibly drunk. Dimly, I realized that was what had gotten me into this mess in the first place. I couldn't seem to care.

"I don't want to be, um, blunt or anything, but I don't think you'd like the consequences of that, if you know what I mean."

Anger quickly took the place of shock. I shook with it. "No, I don't know. Why don't you tell me?"

"Well, first there's your dad. If he knew what... well, let's just say I don't think that video would be good for his career, especially since you tied me to the bed and the word 'rape' just might be whispered in the wrong ear. And then there's the coke we snorted. Oops. Camera rolling. The school board... Don't suppose they'd want a drug-addicted rapist on their payroll."

My mind frantically pawed over the blank space in my memory that held the events of that night. Nothing. The last thing I remembered was leaving the bar, and even that was a foggy, uncertain recollection. Waking up naked in her bed was the only clear piece I could retrieve. "I don't believe it."

"You'd better believe it. I played along with your little S&M fantasy to the hilt. I screamed and cried... very convincing, if you didn't know the script."

"But your parents..."

"Were gone for the weekend."

My knees buckled and I sat down abruptly on the chair as the bartender brought her drink. He must've been psychic because he plunked down a whiskey at my elbow, though I had a Bud on the table in front of me—but then, after all summer, he knew my drinking habits and probably figured it was time for Jack. He stood waiting for me to pay; another slap in the face. I paid him and tipped him, figuring it was only a tiny down payment on that one careless night. I slammed the whiskey without pausing for breath. Maybe the bartender knew Sarah, too, and this was a sympathy offering?

"Wayne! Hit me again, man."

The bartender grinned and snagged the bottle of JD from the end of the shelf, trotted back to the table, and poured me another generous shot. I doubled his tip that time and chased the whiskey with the beer.

Sarah scooted closer and cooed into my ear. "Henry, we were fantastic together. Give it a chance. You'll see." She rhythmically stroked my cock through my pants beneath the table and I swore beneath my breath when it began to get hard. Despite how I felt, it had a mind of its own. Always had.

"Shut up." I knocked her hand away.

She shrugged and raised the bottle to her lips.

"I've gotta pee." She stood. "Make sure you're still here when I come back, 'kay?"

My dick shriveled the second I'd pushed her hand away, and at the moment I could've happily cut it off for the trouble it had caused. But still, nothing added up in the right columns for me. Complete shock deadened my brain. What in the name of fuck had I done to deserve this?

And then there was Alice. I'd only gone out with Sarah because I couldn't deal with my feelings for her. That was wrong, but this was far worse. I went to the bar and ordered a double. This was going to be a very long night.

Sarah returned, strutting and flipping her hair over shoulder. She caught me standing with the drink in my hand almost at the table. Her lipstick glowed pink in the dim wash of the colored bar lights and I just wanted to…

"Kiss me, Henry."

"No."

"Yes." She leaned into me, put her hands on the back of my head and forced it towards her face, mashing her mouth onto mine, sliding her tongue between my lips. The scent and taste of the cherry flavored lipstick mingled with the smell of her face powder inhaled through a fog of cloying perfume. I stood with my eyes wide open, motionless as her fingers worked through my hair, while her hands kept the pressure on my head steady and firm.

The extreme close-up view of her did nothing to improve my mood, nor did the tongue probing the inner recesses of my mouth. I glanced around realizing that no one paid us the slightest bit of attention. But why should they? The typical shabby mob surrounded, caught up in their dramas and games. Public foreplay was not unusual here; I'd done it myself, plenty of times.

Sarah drew back after a time, frowning. I continued to stare at her for a long moment, then wiped her lipstick off my mouth, tipped my glass, and finished that one in three quick swallows. The whiskey burned my lips and traced a fiery track down my throat.

"I find it hard to believe you could kiss me like that after what you've said to me. The threats. It's…" I searched my rapidly fogging brain for a word. "It's despicable."

Her eyes popped open in surprise and then she brayed with laughter in that screaming shriek, wiping tears and grasping the table edge for support. "Oh, Henry. You're so funny. Henry does Daffy Duck: 'You're desthpicable!' he says." She whooped some more, then patted my arm. "This will work out fine; you'll be all right."

"As long as I play your game?"

Her washed-out blue eyes hardened in her face, all traces of laughter gone. "I'm glad we understand each other. You realize this wouldn't have happened if you'd acted right. I've waited weeks for you to call. Not once, but twice. *No one* does that to *me*."

"I don't know what you're talking about."

She crossed her arms under her heavy breasts and angry red blotches appeared on her chest, neck, and jaw. "Saturday, August 23rd. You spent the whole night in this very bar trying to get in my pants. I gave you my number. We made out against the wall in the alley and you promised to call me the next day. You didn't."

"I..."

"No." She held up her hand. "No more lame excuses. You took me to bed and I gave you what you wanted; now it's your turn. It's time for Henry to grow up and be a man—or else." She swiped her drink from the table and saluted me, the brittle smile back in place, only the hectic color splashing her skin above the pink spandex giving a clue to her real feelings. "Here's to the beginning of something beautiful."

I stared as she drank, angry, but maybe understanding her a bit better—though that changed nothing. "Sarah. This is crazy. Why are you doing this? It was a one-night stand, nothing more. We were drunk. I came here with you tonight because I was sorry it happened and I didn't want to mistreat you. What the hell?"

"Mistreat me? What a lovely choice of words! You've fucked over the wrong girl this time. I don't do one night stands."

"But you did and I don't want to see you anymore. Any sane person would realize that after what you've done and said, it's crazy to think I would."

"Too bad. I'm crazy, then and you're going to do right by me."

"You can't make me like you or want you. It's ridiculous."

"Watch me." She finished her drink and slammed the bottle down on the table. "Or I can mail the tape to the school board, the police chief, the newspaper," she tapped her long, pink fingernail on her lip, "and anyone else I can think of who will finish both yours and your dad's careers. I can blur my face right out of it. I think I'll do that when I get home. No sense letting the shit splash on my family. The act alone and the drugs will be more than enough to put you away. Then I'll decide whether or not I want to press charges anonymously—they protect the identity of victims of sex crimes, don't they? So maybe I should wait to doctor it, but that's no problem."

I still couldn't wrap my mind around what she'd done...what she was doing. Why? There were plenty of guys to sleep with. Plenty of fools to manipulate, and surely I'd not been the only one she'd ever brought home drunk. Why me?

"Finish your drink," she said. "I wanna get out of this pisshole. The bathroom stinks." She went to the bar and returned with a paper bag. I didn't care what was in it, but finished the dregs of my drink in one swallow, then wished for more.

Defeated and more than half-drunk, I swayed along behind her, out the back door, relieved to be going. We'd parked in the alley lot because there hadn't been room on the street. This town took Happy Hour seriously, and it had already morphed into a post-weekend bash, jammed to the rafters with the hardcore partiers and people who'd surely regret it in the morning. Waiting for morning was not necessary in my case. I already regretted it.

Full darkness lit only by a sputtering streetlight surrounded us and I sucked in a huge lungful of the crisp air. I wanted another drink. And another. Until I could forget this mess. I grabbed the bag out of her hands and shoved down the crumpled brown paper. Jack Daniels. Perfect. I uncapped it and took a slug and then another. It didn't burn this time.

My hand didn't seem to want to work on the passenger door handle, it was one of those funky little built-in deals, and not simple like my good old reliable Buick. She knocked my fumbling hand away, pinning me against the side of the car with her hips. Nearly as tall as I was in the high heels, she again kissed me and this time, I didn't resist. What was the use? There was nothing I could do. The time for that seemed to have passed.

She unbuckled my belt and unzipped my pants, her hand sliding beneath the elastic band of my underwear. I lifted the bottle again and drank deeply. Both of her hands wrapped around my cock and it felt all right.

"God, Henry. You're huge." She smiled up at me as I looked down on her rubbing my dick till I thought the skin would come off. She spit on her hand and I groaned when she started up again. I started to tip over when the world suddenly tilted to the left, and nearly lost my footing.

"You need to sit down, big guy." She opened the door and vaguely, I felt her tug my pants down until they puddled around my ankles. She pushed me into the seat, went to her knees and in a no-nonsense, mechanical way, began sucking my tool. I floated somewhere off in the distance, watching the streetlight blink on and off, its sick buzzing, frying sound vibrating my skull, as I occasionally raised the bottle. On and off. Light and dark.

A drunk stumbled out of the bar's back door and happened to glance in our direction. He stopped and took in the scene, probably not believing his eyes, because his mouth hung open. I watched his face as the streetlight stayed on a bit between the blinks. A huge grin lifted his cheeks and he shouted bawdy encouragement across the graveled lot, giving me the thumbs up as he reeled on by, shaking his head and laughing. I raised the whiskey bottle in a salute and drank as Sarah bobbed for apples in my lap.

Hours seem to pass. The streetlight went out. The last thing I remembered was her climbing over to straddle me in the front seat; no easy task in a Mazda, but it had a sunroof, so I guessed that's how she managed. I don't know where we were when that happened, but it was dark. Very dark.

I woke up in my bed around eleven a.m., my head pounding like the drum line in a marching band and sat up with a jerk, my hands clutching my skull, then fell back again when I realized I was alone. Painfully, I turned my head to the other pillow, half expecting a note to be there. I felt around on the one beneath my head. Nothing. I was glad.

I'd missed work. I'd missed a lot. I wanted to die.

What the hell was I going to do?

And then there was Alice. I began to sob in huge gasps, crying harder than I had since I was eight and racked myself on a bicycle too big for me. Daddy couldn't make this better. Oh no. He could only make it worse. I'd really done it this time.

Twenty-Four:
Alice 1980

To say I was angry would be an understatement. To say I wanted to kill Sarah was like saying maybe I wanted to breathe. That I didn't hunt her down and beat her to death was a credit to my self control. Though admittedly, she would tower over me and outweighed me by at least fifty pounds, I could certainly equalize the deficit with a Louisville Slugger in my hands. Sounded good to me.

Quietly I paced my bedroom floor, trying to calm myself and not wanting to wake my mom. The look on Henry's face as he spied me from Sarah's car nearly made me crazy with anger and yes, outright fear. Mom was still zonked out, had probably logged some overtime at the factory, and didn't know I'd been late coming home from school—so that part was okay, I guessed.

I paused at the window overlooking the wide porch roof, grabbed my old sweater and raised the screen. I stepped onto the shingles, hoping the peace of an autumn evening might clear my head. Kids rode bikes up and down the uneven bricks of my old street and lights came on in houses here and there as dusk settled murky shadows over my neighborhood. Jack-o-lanterns were making appearances on porches and the faint scent of the first burning leaves perfumed the air. The happy sound of laughter and shouts from a rowdy game of Red-Light, Green-Light a few yards down made me smile and I knew their moms would be calling them in for supper soon. It soothed and saddened me, too. I'd never been so carefree. Outwardly yes, but I'd always known too much. That took some of the fun out of it, I think.

My hands had almost quit shaking and the tears of anger and frustration had pretty much dried up. I settled into my customary place, using the outside wall of my bedroom for a backrest. The shingles still radiated warmth upon my bottom and the soles of my bare feet.

Once upon a time, Sarah had plotted against me and sent me to my death to insure Henry would marry her. Of course, he hadn't gone along with it, but had run away and hurt himself instead. I worried that some variant of that scenario was already in motion. Patterns tended to repeat themselves. Though times certainly changed, people in general only managed it in slow, painful degrees. All of the old sins were still playing themselves out in grand human drama. Only the stage scenery had altered.

Thankfully, they didn't hang anyone nowadays, and no one believed in or feared witches—I could probably rest easy on that issue, but that didn't mean something awful couldn't happen. I knew well that there were many things in this world that could make a person wish they were dead, and mean it, too. Henry Sayre's self-willed death in 1663 illustrated that point very well. I could think of more than a few instances in my own long history that supported that theory—priestess or witch, wise or foolish. Life in this world was complicated. Always had been.

I nearly reached for the Old Magic just to make myself feel better, but the spells and charms I still remembered, the most effective ones, would only come back on me three-fold—a quaint way of expressing the law of karma, real and binding. I'd learned that lesson the hard way a long, long time ago and it had kept me in line and off the Paths. There'd been times when my temper had gotten me in serious, serious trouble when I knew so much about that unseen world. I'd been a much younger soul then.

Death itself is not all that painful. It's kind of like peeling off jeans that are too tight and sighing in relief that you don't have to wear them anymore. It's the getting to that part that hurts like hell and can leave psychic scars on us when the ending is brutal and unwarranted. I'd left this life violently and way too soon a couple of times and I didn't know if I'd ever really get over it. I'd given up all but the Goddess part of my world, and still I'd burned and swung. Might not matter, really, but I'd kept that part of myself under tight control. I didn't want to die because of it—or of any cause that didn't fall under the "natural" category. I'd had enough of that.

So murdering her, harming her, or even disabling her in any meaningful way, was definitely out. That she'd come back for more of Henry after his shabby treatment clarified a lot. Sarah didn't know I existed, so this was not about me at all—maybe it never was and Alys Kerr had only been a minor obstacle eliminated from Sarah Holbert's path.

That meant she'd come after Henry alone. I knew what had happened to him after I swung from the oak tree in the town square. I didn't have the first idea of what had happened to her. Something told me it wasn't good and that she blamed him for it.

As for Henry going with her after dropping me off, I wasn't all that surprised. Despite what he'd done, Henry is basically a good soul with a conscience, even if it was a bit faulty at times. He would've gone because, inside that testosterone driven man-flesh and despite the contrary evidence, he's a gentleman. He'd misbehaved and felt guilty. No doubt he would break it off with her and be kind about it.

He could handle Sarah. He'd be all right. Wouldn't he?

Unfortunately, her move on him happened on the first of my mom's nights off and I couldn't get out, wouldn't get out, until she went back to work. On third shift all of her adult life, she was a night owl and haunted the house 'til the wee hours. I walked the borders of the roof to look for possible escape routes and found none. I'd likely break my neck if I jumped, and if I survived that, getting back in would be nearly impossible.

Sleep came fitfully to me that night, though I was worn out from worry. On my way out the door the next morning, I looked my mother in the eye and though I'd never shown the slightest interest in theatre, told her I'd be staying for auditions for the fall play, Arsenic and Old Lace, and probably wouldn't be home until ten. No, no, I don't need a ride home, I'll catch one with Sherry Phillips down the street and don't worry about supper, Mrs. Carey was ordering pizzas...

I raced to his classroom on a bathroom pass first hour. I had to see him and know that he was all right. When I glimpsed the Dean, Mr. Shaw, where Henry should be, I nearly lost it. The day dragged on and several times I looked in the History classroom. By third hour a substitute teacher had taken over—and stayed.

The dismissal bell finally rang and I bolted out the exit, took off my boots, and ran towards town. I'd finished my homework in study hall, so there were no books to lug.

His car still sat at the curb and I pelted up the stairs and hammered on the door. Footsteps sounded on the old floorboards and I breathed a sigh of relief. He was home. One wary black eye peered through a crack in the blinds at the door. He shot the bolt and yanked it open, then dragged me inside. "Alice! What the hell are you doing here? It's broad daylight!"

"Where have you been? What happened?"

He looked away and I noticed the pallor of his skin and that his hands shook so badly, he tucked them in his armpits. He looked like shit. Dark circles shadowed his puffy, bloodshot eyes. Black whiskers darkened chin and cheeks, and his hair stuck up in elf-locks all over his head. Pathetic.

"Are you sick?"

"You have no idea." He swallowed several times and I thought he might puke right there in the kitchen.

I caught a faint whiff of recycled whiskey and stale cigarette smoke, along with something else I didn't want to think about. "*What* have you done?"

He raised tortured eyes to me. "You have to leave."

"No. I'm not leaving until you tell me what has happened."

"I can't."

"You will." I latched onto his elbow and began dragging him towards his bedroom. "You're going to close that door behind us and tell me everything."

At first he let me drag him, but he stopped halfway across the living room. "Alice, my god, you have to go, sweetheart," he begged. "You have no idea of what's going on and I won't have you involved." Tears leaked from the corners of his eyes and I stared at him, my heart falling somewhere down around my ankles, I think.

The phone rang and he cringed at the sound. Four rings and a cheerful male voice played over the machine. "This is a courtesy call from AT&T. Now for a limited time, for the low, low price of just $9.99 you can…"

Henry nearly disintegrated with visible relief. He pinched the bridge of his nose between his forefinger and thumb. "I'm going to be sick." He ran to the bathroom and I heard him heaving behind the closed door.

A cloud of mint-flavored mouthwash surrounded him as he staggered from the bathroom, and if possible, looking worse than he had before. Sweat beaded on his forehead and dampened the hair at his temples.

"Listen, Henry. This is important. You have to tell me. I know things about Sarah that you need to hear. You didn't read the other Henry's journal, did you?"

He shot me an incredulous look. "What?"

"Never mind. We're going into your bedroom and you are going to tell me everything, or I swear, Henry, I'm going to stab Sarah in her sleep. Put a bomb in her car. Kill her a thousand times and then do it again."

"Jesus, Alice. What's wrong with you?"

He hadn't corrected me on her name. She'd chosen the same one as last time. Big surprise there. Not really.

"This isn't about what's wrong with me. It's about her. And you!" I yanked at his arm and he followed, reluctantly, I thought. I let him pass through the doorway and then shut the door firmly behind me. He collapsed face down on the bed and groaned. I crawled over him, curling around him, rubbing his neck and shoulders. He'd drank himself to death before, died in the gutter because of a situation she'd set up. It wouldn't happen again; not on my watch.

He abruptly shoved himself upright. "I forgot to lock the door!" He leapt from the bed and his running footsteps pounded on the floorboards. Soon he returned and fell down on his back beside me. He stared at the ceiling and I stared at him.

"You've really fucked up, haven't you, Henry?"

He looked almost shocked at my rude assessment of the situation, the details of which I didn't know, though I could probably guess. He opened his mouth, but then turned away. "Yes, I'm afraid I have. Big time." He hid his face behind his arm.

"Tell me."

"Alice, I can't. I'm…too ashamed."

This required drastic measures, I could see that now. In one quick movement, I rose up and straddled him, resting my bottom on his crotch. He yelped and yanked his arm from his face, his eyes wide and startled. "What are you doing?"

A sudden intuition hit me. "You haven't bathed yet and I can still smell her stink on you. I want you to go to the tub and wash. You need to. Her stuff is killing you."

He stared at me for a long moment. "You are the strangest person I have ever known."

"No, I'm not." I bent down and kissed his forehead, resisting the urge to settle in more tightly on the crotch I straddled. An electric wire somewhere down there built up a charge and sent it straight to my gut and brain, twanging invisible strings, sending freakin' Morse code up and down my body. Gooseflesh rose up on my arms from the contact.

I focused on the black eyes searching mine. "Washing yourself clean of her is mostly symbolic, but necessary for your well-being—me too, but mostly you." I sniffed him and wrinkled my nose. "Come on."

He appeared shell-shocked and boyish, younger than me by far, as I held out my hand and he took it. In the bathroom, I put the plug in the tub and turned on the taps, while he stood with his arms clasped around himself. Looking around, I couldn't find any salts or healing herbs to put in his bath. Men! They didn't know what was good for them.

When the tub was half full, I turned off the water and looked over my shoulder. "Customarily, one removes one's clothes before bathing."

"Nuh-uh, can't do that. Not in front of you." He shook his head. "It's not right."

I gave him the sweetest smile in my arsenal. "Aren't you a little tired of that high moral ground you like to stand on? I know I am and we both know it's bullshit. So yes, you can, dear. You did much worse in front of her, and I'm the only person in this world who can help you right now. I mean to do that."

He hesitated another full minute, but I put my fists on my hips and gave him the evil eye until he peeled off the holey t-shirt and then the crummy sweats. His physical beauty nearly took my breath away. Long, lean limbs, a well-defined musculature, and the fine, swirling hair on his chest and stomach caused my insides to clench.

He sank into the tub as I picked up a stiffly dried washcloth hung over the side and the mushy piece of soap on the dish and began to wash him. Henry jumped at my touch and I shook my head. "It's all right. Let me do this for you. You're a mess."

With a sigh, he leaned back and closed his eyes, as I worked the soapy cloth over his shoulders and chest, arms and hands, picking each up and spending time on them, using my fingers to massage and glide over his sudsy skin. He leaned forward to let me do his back and I saw the angry, blood-crusted claw marks running horizontal from the middle to his flanks. That fucking bitch. There I said it, at least in my head. She hurt him and I wanted to hurt her. I went easy over the scratches, hoping he wasn't brewing an infection from her venom.

I didn't hesitate over his man-parts and tried to ignore his response as I rubbed him gently beneath the water, then worked my way down his long legs and big feet. When I finished, I said, "Duck your head. I'm going to do your hair."

He took a breath and sank beneath the soapy surface. I rubbed shampoo into his hair, scrubbing his scalp and kneading his temples. He moaned with pleasure. "That feels so damned good. No one's ever done that for me. Not like that."

"I believe it." Foam ran in lazy streams down the sides of his face. He looked adorable. "Okay. Done. Now rinse."

He turned on the taps and held his head beneath the faucet, working the shampoo from his hair. While he did that, I stripped off my clothes. When he shoved his wet hair from his face and looked over at me, his mouth dropped open. "You. *Alice!* You…can't."

"Yes, Henry, I can and I will. You are the only man who will ever do this for me, and I won't let her leave her mark on you. You need healing and I need you. Now." I slid into the tub, straddling him. There was more than enough room for my knees and shins on either side of him. Big tubs. I've always loved them. "Consider it a ritual deflowering if you have to, Mr. Morality."

He gasped as we came together, not really there, but close enough. "You're a virgin." A statement, not a question.

"Of course I am. I'm only…"

"Jesus, don't say it!" he squeaked.

"Okay. I won't." I lowered my chest to his and my heart thudded in my ears. I wanted him. Despite anything he'd done. I put my lips to his and he kissed me deeply and surely. He shuddered and quivered beneath me as I ran my hands over him. All the old memories came flooding back and I nearly climaxed just squirming upon his hardness. Had to have him. Had to remove Sarah's filth from him. This was the only way. I reached my hand down between us and stroked him in a slow, tight fist.

"Alice." He murmured raggedly between kisses.

I drew back a little and looked into his eyes.

"You are the most beautiful…woman I have ever seen. You're…" He pushed me back a little, his eyes and hands roaming over my body. "Incredible."

I let my head fall back and enjoyed his touch, moaning a little when his fingers found the cleft between my open legs. I rose up and let them slide inside me. He paused, I knew, because my maiden state was obvious.

"Are you sure, Alice?" His voice cracked on my name and I smiled.

"I'm sure." Before he could say another word, I called upon the Goddess and my memories and ended the debate.

Twenty-Five:
Henry 1980

I'd expected a number of things at the sound of that knock upon my door, but I hadn't expected *her*. Alice being Alice—of course she flattened me with shock and a reaction to her that rocked the foundations of my soul. She'd drawn the battle lines between good and evil and stood as ready to fight for me as any knight with sword in hand ever had.

There was something gallant and fearless in her that I greatly admired. It took a lot of courage to be as different as she was in all things, from the way she dressed and her attitudes, to her unashamed, unrepentant desire for me. She rose up above me like a Goddess herself, white and shining, her goodness and purity surrounding her like a cloak.

Dichotomy. Enigma. Contradiction. Mystery. She forced me to question all things, not the least of which, myself. I will remember that moment for the rest of my life—and all the moments with her before and after.

Though I knew the difference between right and wrong, I honestly couldn't have told you where I stood in that black and white arena. My mind screamed No! And my heart and body roared Yes! Yes! Yes! Alice followed a moral code of her own making, a strange one, which left me breathless and disarmed. I was nearly twenty-five years old, and she held me at her mercy as though I were years her junior and under her command. I couldn't say no. I couldn't fight her or my response to her. I tried.

I failed and felt completely whole, maybe for the first time in my life. It didn't last, but that golden afternoon, I knew, would be the stuff of many dreams and future fantasies.

Before I could do much more than ask if she was sure, she took the matter into her own hands. A muffled cry came from her, and she closed her eyes. I started to ask her if she was okay, but she smiled, put a finger to my lips and said, "I am as I'm supposed to be. Love me, Henry."

We splashed half of the bathwater onto the floor and then continued in the bedroom, her glistening, damp body spread upon my sheets, the towel she'd wrapped around herself fallen away. A complete and utter awe descended as I looked upon her. Everything about her called to me—her smell, her skin, her dark eyes and I gave myself over to her without restraint.

From her there was passion, tenderness, two undeniable and unapologetic orgasms, a request for more when I'd rested up a bit, and a blessing from a Goddess whose name I did not know. Whoever she was, I thanked her, too. I'd never met or been with anyone like Alice. I doubted I ever would again. She was matter-of-fact about the loss of her virginity, as though she'd just changed her clothes, rather than changed her life. With a sleepy, sated look in her eyes, she thanked me for honoring her. Incredible.

The sun set and she asked for candles. All I had was a dusty, faded taper stuck in the junk drawer in case the power went out. She said that would work just fine. We jammed it in an empty beer bottle and took it to the bedroom. Instant romance.

She sat cross-legged on my bed with a towel wrapped around her, the dying rays of sunset glowed around the lopsided slats of the blinds, picking out the gold in her hair. The candle illuminated a face I'd only imagined in dreams. Angel. I'd been right the first time. Sappy, but true.

"Henry, I am ready to hear your story. I have to be home by ten and I can't get out tonight. It's my mom's weekend off."

The euphoric feeling vaporized. "Oh."

She patted the bed next to her. "I meant it Henry; you have to tell me everything. Nothing you say can change how I feel about you. It's all right. I can help. Forewarned is definitely forearmed."

I sat on the edge of the bed and wished that were possible. Brave girl. She had no idea. "No, it's not all right. I don't think it ever will be again."

She scooted around and climbed onto my lap. "Now, I'm going to hold your hands and you're going to talk. You need my help."

"It's too ugly," I choked out. My eyes stung with unshed tears and shame. "Especially after all this…with you." Inappropriate boners, virginity losses, and the tears I'd expected from her, not me, all came crashing down. I'm human, I guess, when you get right down to it. What I'd allowed Sarah to do to me was more than stupid. That, after thinking all day and having not found a way out of it, only made it worse. To admit it to Alice would surely kill me.

"Henry, that's more the reason. I've given you my trust and my self. Now you must give it back."

I swallowed hard and risked a look at her. Her brown eyes shone with compassion and suddenly I knew she truly was the only person on this earth I could tell this to and keep a shred of dignity. I spilled the whole sleazy story and left nothing out.

When I'd finished, for a long moment she did nothing but rest her face against mine, and I thought maybe she might wish she'd never come here at all. But then the words came, tumbling one over the other in a rush. "I should've told you everything, from the beginning. I gave you the journals because I wanted you to remember *me*...from then. I didn't count on Sarah turning up. I should've done something, anything, to stop you from going in that bar with her. I never dreamed things would go so far, so fast."

"The journals? What do those have to do with this?"

She muttered something and looked to the ceiling. "Henry, have you heard a word I've said? Remember yesterday? At the creek? Don't you get it?"

"Uh, not really." A smile twitched at my mouth as I remembered that fine ass cased in faded denim, climbing the brushy slope in front of me.

"It's no joke, but I messed up. I should've shown you *that* life, not one of the happy ones in Wales. It's just that I wanted you to see how it can be with us—not how it's been when it all goes wrong."

"Alice, time out! Stop. You lost me way back there with the journals. What are you trying to say?"

Alice fixed me with a look of impatience. "I'm telling you that Sarah, the one that is blackmailing you, is the same Sarah that sent Alys Kerr to the gallows. I am or was, Alys and you are that Henry, the one who refused to marry her and drank himself to death to avoid it—a pattern you are already showing signs of repeating. I hoped you would remember. She's come after you and unless we figure out what to do about it, she's going to get you."

Stunned, I tried to absorb her words, but they just kept bouncing off my brain.

"Listen," she said, "you are in deeper shit than you realize. People just don't do things like that. I mean, really. That you slept with her then blew her off is tacky, but not equal to what she's doing to you. Think about it!"

I shook my head, still groping for a logical, rational explanation for Sarah's behavior. Sick, twisted, and spoiled beyond hope of decency, all came to mind. But reincarnation? Even if it were true, I couldn't see how the events of three centuries ago between people long dead could affect the present.

Then doubt flickered in my mind. The things I'd seen in my own head at the creek yesterday, and the smell of burning and the terrible images that came when she'd spoken of witch fires in the classroom. The awful sadness that gripped me when I'd read about Alys Kerr's hanging.

"You really think we live more than one life? That we come back here over and over?"

Alice jumped from my lap, barely catching the towel before it hit the floor. With an annoyed jerk, she pulled it tighter around herself and tucked the end beneath her armpit. "That's what I've been trying to tell you since I handed in that paper! Think of how you've felt whenever I've talked of it. You've said you feel strange; there's a reason for that! You were there. Think about today. The things that lay unspoken between us! You don't do this with other girls my age, do you?"

"God no!" I looked at her and hoped she believed me. Prayed she did. "Settle down, okay? I'm listening. I am." I reached for her hand and she brushed me off. I tried again in a more even tone. "If what you've said is fact, how does that change anything now?"

With a frown, she said, "I admit it might not, but you need to understand what's going on. After what she's said about her parents, I think they are just as, if not more dangerous than she is. In 1662, they didn't hesitate to force William Sayre, your father, to bring an innocent girl to trial, even if he didn't want to. They stirred the townsfolk into a frenzy and left him no choice. Sarah has already brought them into it and threatened your father. They backed her before when she didn't get her way. They might do it again."

Staggered, I could do nothing but stare at her while she paced the floor.

Alice stopped. "Oh!" Her mouth popped open in surprise. "I'll bet she's been stalking you since you came back from college. Have you been in town long?"

Random pieces fell together in my head in a series of flashbacks. The education fundraiser I attended with my dad. His call to tell me about the summer teaching position that had suddenly materialized at the college a day later. Had he pulled some strings? Or had Thurmond called him?

Worst of all, the abrupt memory of meeting Thurmond's wife *and* daughter that night crashed through my tired brain like a charging rhino. Her hair had been pulled up in a tight bun and she'd been a lot fatter, with none of Sarah's dramatic makeup or bright colors. My eyes had slid right past her.

Months later, when she hit on me at the Watering Hole, I'd neither recognized her, nor remembered meeting her before. I wondered how many times she'd been there when I was wasted and I hadn't remembered until she called me sober. How many times had she come on to me last summer and I'd blown her off or left with someone else? She'd said twice, but honesty didn't seem to be her strong suit and that place was always packed with girls on the weekend. Oh… no. She'd asked me to dance at the fundraiser and I'd turned her down. I groaned and fell back on the bed.

"What? What is it?" Alice grabbed my arm. "Henry!"

I told her and the color drained from her face. She sat down hard on the bed next to me. "Now do you understand?"

I scrubbed my hands through my hair and sat up. She'd been way too close to the mark to not take it seriously. "All too well, I think. I'm screwed. There's no way out of this."

Alice patted my arm distractedly. "Unless..." Her brows knit together and then she smiled. "She's bluffing."

My heart leapt at the idea and then sank right back to the pit of doom.

"Can't you remember anything about that night?"

I shook my head. "No. I've tried."

"Have you ever done anything like tie someone to a bed and play out a rape scene?"

"That's not *my* thing." I took a deep breath; she might as well know it all. "But that doesn't mean I wouldn't have gone along with it, if it had been her idea. It's not the first time I've had to take someone's word for it when I'm on the Jack. I shouldn't drink the stuff."

She didn't comment, but the look on her face said she agreed with me. "But you remember what happened last night."

"Unfortunately, I do." I breathed the hopeless sigh of the damned.

"There's a good chance she's lying. If you were as drunk as you say, then she could've stripped you after you passed out."

"True," I said, but couldn't hide the skepticism in my voice.

Alice stroked a finger along her upper lip, seemingly deep in thought. "And then there's the cocaine. I saw her car go by at ten past two. If you'd snorted coke after that, you probably would've still been awake at eight playing her stupid games, don't you think? I watched you come home from my front porch."

Again, she'd surprised me. What in the hell could she possibly know about blow? A lot it would seem, but I doubted she'd ever touched the stuff. I hoped she hadn't. "You waited all that time? Watched for me? Why would you do that?"

Her pretty mouth twisted down at the corner a little and she shrugged. "I was worried about you. I had good cause and I'm not apologizing. So you can just forget it."

I nearly smiled. Feisty. I liked that. "Forgotten. Thanks for giving a shit. I wish I had, now."

"But anyway, I don't think there was enough time for all that and a blackout, too. You wouldn't have been up that early."

"I had to take a leak. I couldn't remember where the bathroom was."

With a skeptical look, Alice said, "It seems to me that if you'd spent all that time awake in the house, despite being drunk and high, you'd have remembered that."

"You'd think. But I don't *know* for sure."

Alice reached for her clothes. "You're going to have to play along with her for now. Try to catch her lying or get her to show you the tape—if there is one, which I doubt. It's the only way." Fully dressed, she combed her tousled hair with her fingers in the mirror on my dresser. Her eyes met mine in the reflection and I reached for my jeans, suddenly aware of my nakedness. "Even if you did all those things, she still might not expose you. She wants you. You'd be worthless to her disgraced and behind bars."

Somehow that worried me more than anything else. It was the *point*. "What if, since the threat of the tape is the only thing holding me to her, I can't get her to admit there isn't one? Or prove there is?"

An enigmatic smile lifted her mouth. "I think you can. Sarah, for all her tough talk is a plain little Puritan girl who is probably hiding some pretty deep insecurity. Look at how she paints her face and flaunts herself. Normal people don't react that violently to rejection, now do they? Charm her, make her fall in love with you and trust you. I know you know how to do that."

Her intense gaze pinned me to the wall and I thought she knew a lot more about me and the way I operated than I'd told her. Shit. I hope she never let herself think for a second that she was just another notch on my gun belt. Nothing could've been further from the truth and I didn't quite understand it. I'd probably spend the rest of my life trying to figure that one out. I think I was in love—not that I had the first clue of what that felt like.

I followed her to the kitchen and watched as she pulled a chair from my ancient kitchen table, sat, and yanked her balled-up socks from her boots. She'd been barefoot when she came in and had dropped them by the door. Everything she did seemed to hypnotize me. Watching her almost took my mind off the sick feeling of dread and the doubts that I could do what she seemed so sure I could.

I leaned against the door, rubbing my temples, the hangover headache returning with a vengeance. "I don't want to do this. I don't ever want to see her again."

She stomped her foot into her boot. "But you will and I'm going to help you. You need to call your dad and find out how deep he is in to Thurmond. I don't think that job at the college just came out of nowhere."

"Me, neither," I said, and shot her a desperate look as she stood

"Well, I'll see you tomorrow." She hesitated as though uncertain, but then threw herself into my arms. "This isn't going to be easy, Henry. What we've started here will be hard on us both—even without the other mess. Promise me you'll tell me what's going on with you, okay?"

I hugged her tighter and didn't want her to leave. I didn't want to be alone with this thing. "I will."

She leaned back and looked up at me. "Not that I don't enjoy riding with you after school, but I think we shouldn't do that again." She dropped her gaze. "Somebody might get the wrong idea and I don't want you to get into trouble because of me. This was my decision and I'm happy with it."

I smiled. "I'm glad. You're something special, Alice." I kissed her, softly this time.

Alice smiled as she pulled open the door. "I know."

Twenty-Six:
Henry 1980

"Dad?"

"Well, it's about time, Henry! I wanted to talk to you about two weeks from last Friday."

His jovial voice boomed in my ear and I held the receiver a good two inches from it. "I know. Sorry. What's up?" Ice water trickled through my veins as I waited for his answer.

"Well, a little bird told me you've got a girlfriend and I'd like you to bring her to my fundraiser."

Instantly I pictured dragging Alice through a crowded room full of stuffed shirts and introducing her to Charles and Abby Thurmond. The missus'd faint and Thurmond would suffer a convenient embolism, while I held Sarah's head in the punch bowl and drowned her. Dad would... die of shame. No good.

"Although, I've got the feeling you were coming anyway!" He crowed as though he'd just launched the Queen Mary or just won an all expenses paid vacation in Hawaii on Let's Make a Deal. The sound nearly split my skull.

"I don't know if I'd call it that," I said flatly and with the utmost sincerity.

"That's *not* what I heard," he sing-songed.

"Dad! It's not what you think."

"Okay, Henry. Say what you will, but pull the tux out of the closet for your old man, okay? This has to be the first big-wig gig of its kind for a mayoral candidate in this town. Can you believe it? In Lincoln? I could hardly believe my good luck. I'm going to spend every penny on advertising. I'm thinking about a billboard and ..."

He rambled on excitedly for the next ten minutes and if Sarah had been anywhere near, I would have gladly throttled her. He didn't need all this. People would vote for him because he was as wholesome as white bread and earnest as the day is long. My dad was not a politician as we know them; he was a good guy, though I will admit he was fond of the attention. Hell, he liked people, all people, any kind of people. He'd managed very well after

Mom died, filling his world with anyone he could help, any good cause he could throw himself behind. That he'd been so easily manipulated was no surprise. I think I'd inherited a version of that flawed gene.

"Dad!"

"What?"

"I need to ask you something."

"Shoot, son. I'm all ears."

I sucked in a nervous breath, dreading the answer. "I was just wondering… You know that job at the college last summer? Did… well, did something happen to cause it?" I screwed my eyes closed and pinched the bridge of my nose.

He laughed; his tone conspiratorial and chummy. *Well shit, I'm screwed*, I thought, as he waffled for a second, but then continued, protesting. "Well, is it my fault that Charlie was impressed with you? He said you had the firmest handshake since Ronald Reagan shook his hand on the campaign trail. That's high praise, son. He called me the day after meeting you the first time."

When I didn't answer, he continued, "I told him you were just finishing up your teaching degree and might leave us for greener fields. He agreed that we couldn't let that happen. A temporary position was all he could offer and I think he might've fired somebody to give it to you, but he's a good guy. He hinted there might be a better position coming open next year. You could go a long way with a man like him behind you, son. He knows quality when he sees it."

I forced cheerfulness into my voice. "Well, what's not to like? I'll see ya Friday after this one and we'll win for the Gipper, okay, Dad?"

More enthusiastic blather and it took me another fifteen minutes to get off the phone. Good lord. Alice had been right again. Sarah had stalked me. Funny how the word "stalk" could take on such vastly different meanings— Alice had done it and I'd only been glad her watchful eyes had seen it all, despite the ugliness. When Sarah had done it, bad things happened.

***

I stared at the phone for a long time before making the next call. It was the one I dreaded more than anything. In all my life I couldn't think of one chore, one single unpleasant thing I'd wanted to do less. Cleaning up my roommate's puke when he'd yakked on my bed last year had nothing on this—and worse, I'd have to find a way to be pleasant and play the game. Impossible, I decided, and unlikely, too. She wouldn't believe it—not yet. Or would she? Images of the drunken sex she'd initiated in the parking lot boiled through my brain and I wondered if she thought that would be enough to bring me around. I couldn't make up my mind and finally gave up trying to guess which way she'd play it. I stabbed her number into the phone.

She answered on the second ring. "Thurmond residence."

"Sarah."

"Yes, Henry?" Coyness laced her voice and turned it into a triumphant purr.

"I just talked to my dad and I'll pick you up Friday night at quarter to eight. Be ready." I dropped the receiver on the hook and called it good. She might have the upper hand and I would have to play mine eventually, but for this moment I could be exactly what I was: angry. The rest would just have to wait.

***

Alice gave me Henry's journal and I pored over it as though studying for a final exam on which my life depended. Every time I pictured Sarah, I saw the spoiled, pasty-faced brat of Henry Sayre's time until the two were melded in my mind. Fact or fiction, it didn't matter to me anymore. I copied the journal, translating Henry Sayre's archaic phrasing into my own words, surprised at times when I wrote for him without looking at the page.

From the little I knew of Sarah Thurmond, I could tell there were more than just physical similarities between her and Sarah Holbert. Both seemed to enjoy hurting people, playing head games, and causing emotional turmoil. A mask of wealth and respectability concealed the wickedness in both girls.

Henry Sayre had been nearly sixteen when he began his journal. That seemed to be the place where he'd succumbed to the pressure and had signed the marriage contract with Sarah, a document that confirmed the initial betrothal agreement between their parents and would not become official until a civil ceremony had been performed and signed by the authorities—probably his father and Reverend Holbert. He seemed concerned for the state of Sarah's soul, often detailing her many transgressions, and praying for strength to help her see the error of her ways.

Sarah did things to people she didn't like (and it seemed as though anyone at all could fall out of favor with her with little provocation) playing malicious tricks that were misunderstood and blamed on the person she targeted. He'd tried to talk to her about it, told her to pray harder for help from the Lord, but she only smiled and said she already did His work.

Sarah took credit for her misdeeds after the fact, confiding in him and laughing behind her hand as the chaos ensued. Reverend Charles Holbert's daughter disguised her true nature well—and his position in the community cloaked the rest. After a successful prank, she often did some small, outwardly considerate act for whichever of the wronged parties came out the winner, and that only increased her esteem in the eyes of the community.

By the time he signed the contract, Henry knew well that had he pointed a finger at her, no one would have believed him, and as bad as Sarah was, she would have surely found a way to turn the blame back on him. Perhaps, as her husband, he could take her in hand and shape her into a good woman. He knew not how he could accomplish this, but knew only that he felt he had no choice. Always he had been a good and obedient son, honoring his father and mother, and they seemed proud of him for signing the contract that would wed him to Sarah.

It boggled my mind that he had allowed this to happen, but then I supposed I understood it, too. Look what I'd allowed, through my own carelessness, to happen in my own life.

Henry Sayre worried a great deal about his father's position in the community, what a broken alliance with Charles Holbert—who seemed to be a faction leader as well as a minister—would cause. The man was rich beyond reckoning. Though a man of the cloth, he seemed unconcerned with the godly trait of poverty that most men of his stripe held in such high regard. Power seemed more a god to him than the one above, and he held the reins of it over the bustling village as a founding member, had the Governor in his pocket, and too many complicated ties with England to ever unravel.

Henry Sayre obsessed page after page, visualizing his family shunned and cast out of Camden—so much seemed to depend on being in Holbert's good graces. In the end, he'd become resigned to the path laid out for him, notwithstanding the fact that girls of marriageable age were scarce in Camden. There was no one else for him, and he thought perhaps, that was as God had ordained; his lot in life. Perhaps. This belief in possible predestination did not prevent him from praying for a fever to take her or a runaway farm wagon to run her down in the street (it had happened to Goodwife Finche not a year gone) and thus spare him from his fate. He prayed forgiveness for that as well.

When Alys arrived on the scene, I was engrossed in Henry Sayre's predicament and praying myself that Sarah might take one for the team. Alys was beautiful and smart, and in Henry's own words he'd been, "transported on a magical cloude, borne Aloft on a tyde of Ecstasie and Sweete, cherished Love." I knew exactly how he felt in every way that mattered. I didn't care who he was. He'd been in my boots and damned if I wasn't going to try to win a round, if not for me, then for him. I closed the book when Alys's trial began, knowing how that turned out and unwilling to put myself through it again.

I gazed out my kitchen window at the unimpressive view of the next building across the alley and wondered for at least the hundredth time how any of this would help. Even if I truly had been Henry Sayre and knew what I faced, what difference would it make in the end? The concept that Alice had explained so painstakingly had eluded me. The circumstances were so similar and the players so familiar that I could hardly dismiss it as impossible. But the problem lay in that my values and Henry Sayre's were still identical. I worried about the same things he did and all I held important in this world would be lost if Sarah prevailed again. Then what choice would I have but to either die or go along with it?

I didn't know.

***

Two weeks passed all too quickly and despite my growing fear of discovery, Alice slipped through my door just after sunset on the night of the soiree. Large dark eyes shone from her pale face, surrounded by the hood of a long, midnight blue cloak. Half dressed in my tuxedo and heading to the bathroom, I nearly yelled with surprise when I saw her standing in the archway to the pitch dark kitchen. She'd brought with her the smell of the night air, clean and crisp, now that autumn had settled in.

In that breathless, frozen moment that we stared at each other, I could've sworn I saw standing stones, hulking monoliths glowing white beneath a starry night sky behind her. I blinked and the image was gone.

"Alice! You scared the shit out of me. I thought we agreed..."

She took a step toward me. "I agreed to nothing. I couldn't let you go without seeing you and giving you what protection I could." She crossed the room in rushing steps, her cloak swishing against her legs, and hurled herself into my arms. Only she could wear such a garment in this day and age and not look ridiculous. She looked like the priestess she claimed she once was.

I pushed back the hood of the cloak and kissed her forehead. "Protection?"

She looked up at me with an expression so sweet it melted my heart. "I brought you something. It's... been in my line, the matriarchal line, well sort of, since..." Those magnificent dark eyes looked upwards as though searching then came to rest upon mine. She shook her head. "...a very long time."

Alice opened her hand and within it was a beaten iron pendant in the shape of a half moon. It hung upon a blue satin cord. "This symbolizes the Goddess." She caressed the dull metal with a fingertip. "I want you to wear it."

The look on her face made me hold my tongue and I could tell this was important to her, so important that it hurt her to give it to me—that was crystal clear. I bent down and let her put it over my head. It hung on my chest, still warm from her hand. "Thank you, Alice." I smiled, though it was probably more of sick grimace. My stomach had twisted itself into tight knots of dread. "I need all the help I can get tonight."

She rose on tiptoes and kissed me, then murmured against my cheek. "I hope you won't need it, but it's all I had, all I could think of." She pushed away and traced the half-moon with her forefinger. "This was with the diaries. Branwen left it for me. I had no need of it the last time…"

I frowned. "You knew it was there? You remembered that?"

"Oh yes. Remember the inside joke I mentioned in my paper? Branwen and I always leave things for each other and she hasn't arrived yet—I'm pretty sure I told Henry Sayre, and that's why his journal ended up in the cellar with hers. No other reason that I can think of… This charm we have passed back and forth since the beginning of time. When she comes, I will give it to her and she will leave it for me again to find next time. I never forget."

Amazement caused me to shake my head. "But…what if the building had been torn down or somebody had stolen it?"

"It's never happened yet." Her delicate mouth turned firm and resolute, the rounded lower lip tightening into a thinner line that denied all doubts. Meanwhile, my mind crawled all over the things she'd said. "Even so, I don't doubt that I could've found it, wherever it may have landed. I am very strongly attuned to it."

My thoughts still followed the impossible lines she'd drawn. "So, Branwen, your mother in that life will be here again with you in this one? She's not your mother now and you know for sure that's she's not reincarnated? How?"

"It's a long story, but the short version is that we were sisters in the beginning and we were priestesses. I have a little carven stone earth mother figure that belongs to her. Our father made it for her in what we now know was the Late Stone Age. These two possessions we keep as a covenant to each other. This time, Branwen is not my mother. I have no siblings or best friends…" Alice shrugged. "There is only one option left. I will bring her forth."

I grabbed her shoulders, the absolute terror of what she'd just said nearly caved me in, body and soul. "Alice, you're not… I mean we haven't…"

She laughed, a delightful sound, like small bells ringing. "No, no. I took care of that after the first day of school, the first time I laid eyes on you. Planned Parenthood is a wonderful and much-welcomed thing. They opened a clinic over on Walnut Street this summer."

"What?" Shock seemed to be my primary expression these days.

"One of us had to be responsible, and quite honestly Henry, that has never been your strong suit. I know you. We've been lovers almost as long as Branwen and I have been connected as sisters or mother and daughter. But anyway, I can wait for her. I want to be able to take care of her and I'm not exactly in that position right now."

Shocked again, this time to speechlessness, I stared at her like the huge dolt I undoubtedly am. I didn't deserve her. That thought clobbered me where I stood.

Alice glanced at the clock. "You've got to finish getting dressed. We'll save those stories for another time."

"Can you stay until I have to leave?"

She shook her head. "No, I'm sorry. I can't. My folks think I'm in my room studying right now. I slipped out the back door while they were watching TV. I had to come."

As much as I wished she hadn't risked it, now that she was here, I didn't want her to go. I didn't want to go where I was going. "Well then, give me a kiss…for luck."

Her eyes turned serious and she took my hands. "For luck, and then some."

The kiss she planted on me was warm and sweet, then she picked up the iron pendant and kissed it, murmuring something I didn't quite catch. The tip of her nose had turned pink and tears sparkled on her lashes as she turned away and then was gone.

My strange, sweet, bewitching girl. If only she could turn Sarah into a toad. I would toss her into a lake and never have to think about her again.

Twenty-Seven:
Henry 1980

I rang the bell, corsage box in hand, unsurprised when a tuxedo-clad Charles Thurmond answered the door. I'd expected the prom night/first official date tripe and here it was. A smile creased the lines at the corners of his pale blue eyes as he looked me over. Sarah's arctic gaze in his weathered, but amiable face still held all the warmth of a raptor sizing up its prey. His hair, dark and closely cut, had begun to go gray in all the right places. He looked like what he was: a successful, middle-aged man.

"Mr. Thurmond, I'm here to pick up Sarah."

With an air of a man with only slightly less than the entire world at his command, he chuckled and held the door open for me. "Come in, Henry, and please, call me Charlie."

"Thanks," I said, as I followed him through the foyer and into the great room. I searched my memory for some recollection of the night I'd been there, but was again, disappointed, knowing that the kitchen and the interior basement stairs were all I was likely to recognize up here.

"Would you like a drink? Sarah and her mother are putting on the finishing touches." His grin and eye roll were predictable and though it was meant to put me at ease, it actually worked. This was familiar ground; a place to stand and rest for a moment, even if it didn't mean a thing.

I chuckled, returning his smile, painfully aware of myself and wondering if I came off as only a nervous date, or something else. "Sure, Charlie. A drink would be great." I momentarily wondered if he were privy to any of the details of this sham. "Whatever you're having will be fine with me."

"I'm in the mood for Glenfiddich," he said as he turned to a sideboard. "I often find myself in that mood around this time of the night." He flashed another smile and the measuring glance back over his shoulder. I didn't think I was the only actor here, though he had far more practice. I reminded myself to be careful.

He handed me the glass. "So, Sarah tells me you've been dating since this summer."

"Yes." I smiled and sipped at the thirty-year old single malt, and noticed that he did not invite me to sit down.

"I was glad to hear it. There's not much here in Lincoln that meets my standards."

As a nearly lifelong resident, except for my detour to college, that pissed me off, but I smiled anyway, my face already beginning to ache from the forced grins. "There's more here, sir, than meets the eye."

He laughed. "You haven't been around much, have you kid?"

To my relief, Sarah, followed by her mother, entered the room. I placed the glass on a coaster on the end table, turned to them with the corsage box in my hand with yet another stupid smile on my face. "Mrs. Thurmond, it's nice to see you again."

I shifted my eyes to the barracuda on her left. "Sarah. This is for you." I held out the box and realized that the pink and yellow tinted flowers looked too innocent for the sophisticated, skin tight, plunging black-beaded gown she wore. She must've thought so too, because she didn't put it on, but handed the box to her mother and then told me flatly that she was allergic to orchids. With her hand clutching my arm, she hustled me out the door.

I glanced over at her as I held the car door open and caught a smug smile upon her face. The gown's side seams looked tortured to the point of splitting as she levered herself awkwardly into the front seat, the slit down the side revealing her plump leg to mid-thigh.

As I turned the key in the ignition, I cracked the window; her strong perfume immediately sucked every ounce of oxygen from the car.

With effort, I said, "You look very nice, Sarah."

She giggled her signature screech. "Thanks. You, too." She turned her face to the window, away from me and I wondered what she was thinking.

I took her arm as I escorted her through the decorated arch of the ballroom with a false smile on my face and an air of detachment, which wasn't hard, really, since the Sarah I knew seemed nowhere to be found. She moved through the crowd with me at her elbow, paying compliments and allowing herself to be drawn into superficial conversations.

Gone was the threatening, poisonous girl who'd blackmailed me and twisted my arm into playing this sick game, replaced by a socialite in control of both herself and her audience. She seemed content with my silence, and I assumed that contentment was mostly due to the fact that I'd caved in to her and given her what she wanted. The rest? Well, I figured she was mostly just showing off, showing me that, I had in fact made a mistake when I'd walked out on her.

As I'd planned, I gradually allowed myself become warmer as the evening progressed in a slow-motion, frame-by-frame act of vigilance. I tipped glasses of champagne in my father's honor, kept my head, and gave a speech worthy of the man Thurmond had compared me to.

I didn't kid myself that this was a one-time deal or that I had one ounce of freedom. Whenever we'd become separated by the crowd, I would look over to find those glacial eyes upon me, whether they were hers or the old man's.

Around ten o'clock, my dad addressed the crowd from the stage; the quartet had taken a short break. I hadn't expected it and neither had anyone else, because people milled about, socializing, turning at the sound of his voice over the sound system. I glanced over to find Sarah at the edge of a group of women staring at me. I let my gaze turn hungry as it passed over her, the simmering resentment turning my gut to writhing snakes put aside, as I attempted to turn the tables on her. Message received. She bit her lip then ran her tongue over it, seemingly unaware of herself.

By the last waltz, I held her not at arms length, but closely, her body a warm, yielding pillow against mine.

At a quarter to twelve, I said I needed to go work on the upcoming midterm final exam for my freshman class, and it would likely take the rest of the weekend. She smiled at that and I could tell she approved.

I walked her to the front door of her house, pulled her to me and kissed her like I meant it. I did it again, just to make sure I got my point across. I'd slept with uglier woman than Sarah, but none with her evil proclivities. I made sure I had my hands on her broad ass and my cock in the upright position. Not that difficult. I pretended she was Alice, Deborah Harry, Farrah Fawcett, or just about anybody else. This was survival.

Sarah giggled and the ridiculous stiff curls cascading from the pouf at the top of her head bounced. Diamonds glinted from the shellacked, loopy mess and twinkled at earlobes and neck. I had no doubt they were real. The size of the house and the cars the Thurmond's owned—her father drove a Mercedes, let me know that rhinestones were out. How they'd come to be in this one-horse town was beyond me.

"Henry, I'd almost think you enjoyed yourself tonight."

I pulled back and said, "I did."

"Would you like to come inside? My folks would love that."

"They're not here yet, are they? Wasn't a senator or something supposed to make a late night appearance?" Ridiculous, all of it, but the event had attracted stellar turnout—no doubt more of Thurmond's machinations

"They won't be home for hours, but they wouldn't mind if you stayed late…they totally approve. Besides, those rooms downstairs are mine. I come and go as I please. There's an outside entrance on the drive, further back. I thought you'd remember that."

I automatically stiffened, but caught myself. The Chamber of Doom had an escape hatch I'd missed the first time. "Um, well that's often a side effect of whiskey, I'm afraid." This was dangerous ground and a hot spot for me. She knew that and I got the feeling she tested it, probing it like a barely scabbed-over wound. But then, I guessed it might be the same for her, considering I'd snuck out on her. Maybe she wanted to know which way I'd gone?

Then it hit me. She'd been trying to get me inside and either misunderstood the reason for me wanting to leave early, or just wanted me to hose her again. She thought I wanted to be alone with her! This had worked far better than I thought it would. I'd guarded my drinks, keeping them in hand and taking them to the john. After talking with Alice, I almost wondered if she'd drugged me that first night. I wasn't chancing it.

"Sarah, I've been thinking…" I gazed long at her and thought of the fifth of whiskey in my sock drawer. It called to me.

"Yes?" She shoved her pelvis against my groin. I fought the urge to jump away but stood fast as she pushed against me, my arms a loose circle around her.

"Well, I realized after what you said that last time, that it *was* pretty crappy, me leaving you and all after we'd, uh, you know. You deserve better than that and the longer I thought about it, the more I understood that you were right." I ducked my head in what I hoped was credible portrayal of shame. "I think we should start over. After tonight, I've realized that I like you, Sarah, and…you're beautiful." I traced her cheek with a reverent fingertip. "Can you forgive me?"

In streetlight's blue glow, she surprised me with a look of satisfied triumph. Did she think it would be so easy to make me fall into line? I couldn't believe my luck. Alice had been right about her from start to finish.

"Maybe." She ran her tongue over her painted lips. They looked almost black in the blue-tinted street light. "Why don't you come inside and prove it, big guy?"

I stared at her for a second longer than I should have. Revulsion washed over me and I hastily looked away, afraid the truth would show on my face and felt myself unequal to this sort of game. "Sarah. We need to do this the right way. I'd like to date you. Be romantic and get to know you. Is that allowed?"

That did it. Or at least I hoped it did. She giggled again, and a sneaky hand found the deflating bulge in my pants. "Henry, what's gotten into you?"

It sure the hell isn't you, I thought. "That's easy. You're a beautiful woman from a good family. I'm from a good family, too." Charles Thurmond's quality control statement came to mind. "There's not much on my level here in Lincoln, really, and I mistook you for the usual type of girl that hangs out at the Hole. It was wrong. I'm sorry."

Her eyes glittered. "Do you mean it? I mean, really?" A barely restrained eagerness had crept into her voice. I heard it and knew that I'd finally hit the right note in this fool's overture.

"Yes. My dad would be ashamed of me. I should try harder to be like him. My mom would turn over in her grave if she knew what I'd done." Now *that* was the bald truth. I almost felt relieved to tell it after all the lies.

She blinked rapidly and looked to be both flattered and slightly undone by my words. Bingo. A radiant smile brought that fleeting prettiness I'd glimpsed before to her face. "I told you it would be fine. We were fantastic together. Both times." Her glance slid towards the door. "We *could* go inside, Henry. It's definitely allowed."

Immediately, I kissed her again, knowing my chance of escape could slip away in a heartbeat. I hugged her tight. "No Sarah. We need a fresh start. I want a chance to make it up to you," I said against her stiff, brittle, touch-me-and-I'll-break curls—such a contrast to Alice's wild, untamed honeyed tresses. Henry Sayre's eloquence had crept into my head.

I planted a gentle kiss on her temple and backed away. "I'll call you tomorrow. Maybe we could see a movie Sunday?" Alice's mom went back to work Sunday. I could satisfy the protocol and dump this bitch before Mom ever hit the driveway.

"Sure, Henry, I'd like that."

"Goodbye then, until Sunday."

Again she giggled, nails on a chalkboard, a banshee scream. "Until then!" Her fingers fluttered in a silly, girly-wave, and I stifled the urge to run as I walked to the car. I collapsed into the driver's seat, my legs suddenly rubbery and my face hurting fit to crack from smiling so much. I kept my pace sedate as I pulled out of the drive, though I wanted to floor it and lay a six-foot patch of rubber on the pavement. Maybe, if I kept this up, I'd sweet talk her into showing me the tape or get her to admit it hadn't happened. Until then, the oblivion of Master JD awaited and I looked forward to unconsciousness.

I wished Alice would come and wipe the stain from my lips and my soul. She couldn't. Her mom worked a revolving schedule and sometimes her days off meant real weekends.

I called Alice the next morning and asked for her under the pseudonym of Joe Williams from her history class who needed help on the paper that geek Spears' had assigned. I figured they wouldn't trace the call. She'd die if she couldn't know how I'd done and I wouldn't risk her getting caught trying to see me. I had the feeling that Joe was going to need a lot of help with his homework for a while. I suggested I park my car in the public library's lot downtown and she could climb in the back seat and hide while I checked out a couple of books. We'd go on a road trip. She loved the idea.

Twenty-Eight:
Alice 1980

The Saturday morning before Halloween found me crouched down in the back of the Buick in the Public Library's parking lot. I jumped when he yanked the door handle and slid into the driver's seat. He pulled out of the lot without a word and finally I said, "You'd feel pretty silly if there were only an empty seat back here."

"I looked before I got in."

"Cheater."

"Yup, that's me, all right."

That peculiar vibration one can only feel when sitting on a car's floorboard worked its way through my body, making it feel as though every crack and bump on the road were being conveyed directly through my nervous system. The old, uneven bricks of McLean Street were rough beneath the wheels. Cramped and tired of it, I crawled onto the backseat and lay down. Better.

"So how did it go? Really?"

He adjusted the rearview mirror and smiled at me. "Good, I guess—if anything about that could be called *good*. It's really hard to tell with her." He shuddered theatrically and his face turned serious as he flipped on his signal for the turn that would take us out of town.

"I don't know if I'm going to be able to pull this off, Alice. It's not easy pretending you're in love with somebody you can't stand. I kept thinking she'd catch something in my voice or a look on my face…"

He glanced back in the mirror. "But she seemed to buy it and I guess it's okay for now."

"Yeah, that's what you said on the phone this morning."

"Have you had any more insights on Sarah? Motives? Possible next moves?"

I sighed. "The only motive I can think of has to do with the fact that you were supposed to marry her and didn't. She seemed to have a vested interest in that marriage, all I suspect having to do with status—her family's expectations and both families' position in the community. Not to mention that she was ugly, had the personality of a warthog, and likely had no other prospects after you left her."

Henry laughed. "That's putting it bluntly."

"No, not at all. I'm being kind."

That set him to laughing harder. He turned the car again. "Come on up here. It's safe now."

I'd come camouflaged today in jeans and a t-shirt, my hair French-braided and trailing down my back. He smiled when my sneaker hit the front seat. "What's this? No witchy-wear, today?"

"Nah, didn't want to stand out." He often teased me about my clothing choices, but I also knew he thought them wildly erotic, so I let him.

He cast a sweeping glance over my faded Levi's and Led Zeppelin t-shirt. I'd tied a plain, black hooded sweatshirt around my waist by the arms in case it turned chilly.

"Didn't work. You look great, outstanding, even. Black is a good color for you, even in Zep t-shirts."

Heat bloomed in my cheeks as my last lifetime jumped into my mind's eye. Yeah, I looked good in black all right. Damned near irresistible. "Thanks." I turned my face to look out the window. Combines and farm wagons and trucks lined the sides of the fields. Arcing waves of gold filled empty beds and then were trundled off to an elevator. Only wispy clouds showed here and there in the crisp, blue sky and sunlight warmed my face through the glass. I rolled down the window and let the rich fragrance of Indian summer flow through the car. "It's a gorgeous day."

"Yes, it is. Better now that you're here." He patted the seat next to him and raised his arm and I snuggled in under it, then planted a kiss on his smoothly shaven, good-man-smelling cheek. I absolutely loved his scent. Shaving cream and wholesomeness, like the forest or…

He said, "You don't know how much I count on you taking away the Sarah Sickness."

"Yes, I do."

"You would at that, I suppose. You were the one who gave me the initial cure."

I smiled and admired his profile against the wide open vistas of the fields and occasional farmhouse whizzing by behind him. His straight nose and the flare of his jaw. The sweetly curved lips and those ridiculously long eyelashes. All his colors blended together into an enticingly masculine package. I ran a hand under the hair at his neck and played with his curls. "I'm glad you give me credit for that. This is not… easy, any way you want to look at it."

Truthfully, the sneaking around part was not all that hard on me. I got a regular old buzz out of it. The hard part was hiding what we were and letting Sarah have the place I should occupy. When I thought about it, things really weren't all that different from that medieval life when I burned, the Colonial life, or the one following it. I'd snuck around to see him in all of those existences and never had the recognition of being a fiancée or wife. It had been a very long time since we'd been legit and I couldn't seem to remember just exactly where we'd gone wrong on that issue—a rarity for me. Maybe I'd never really known what had happened. Or...maybe it was just one of those things we'd had to learn and we'd practiced it upon each other. Who knew?

But those last few times were a *lot* like now—different of course, but the framework still existed. We'd missed something important, I think.

An angle to consider: what if I'd gone about this the wrong way again? Adhering to a pattern myself? But no, there simply hadn't been a choice this time. Sarah moved on him like a school of piranha on an unsuspecting wildebeest at a watering hole. I smiled. Watering Hole—funny how that name just kept coming back to haunt me. I tucked a lock of hair behind my ear that kept blowing into my eyes, became annoyed when it immediately blew free again, and reached over to roll up the window some.

These thoughts darkened some of the day's golden quality. Henry hadn't used Aleysia Robson, Alys Kerr, or Carrie Robinson, nor was he using me in the current vernacular, now. But circumstances had once more forced a covert relationship. Neither of us could change it, nor would we until I turned eighteen and graduated from high school almost four years from now. It seemed an eternity.

Henry found another hidden lane in a miniature forest, ignoring all the No Trespassing, Private Property signs, and carefully lined up the Buick's tires alongside the deep ruts that might've damaged the underside of the car. This time, we crossed a small bridge over another creek before he stopped.

"How do you know about all these places?" I asked and shut the car door.

"My dad and I used to fish a lot when I was younger. He knew all the good spots. We also know the guy who owns this land. He doesn't live around here, so no worries there."

He retrieved a blanket from the trunk and took my hand, leading me to the grassy bank of a small stream. "It's deeper over by the bridge and better for fishing, but I like it here. I used to come to this place just to think sometimes."

I smiled. "It's very peaceful."

Henry spread the blanket and we sat upon it, staring at the water. A comfortable silence ensued and he held my hand, stroking the knuckles with his thumb. Without warning, his other hand shot out, parted the long meadow grass, and I jumped from the swiftness of the motion. He came up with a cluster of Queen Anne's Lace, which he tucked behind my ear. "For you, my lady." He smiled wanly. "Alice, I really wish things were different."

With a sigh, I lay back on the blanket and stared at the not quite noonday sun shining through the crimson, saffron, and rust-colored leaves above our heads. The sight of that little weed flower brought an immediate wash of tears I struggled to hold back. He didn't remember, but still he did the same silly, lovely things he always had. "I know. I'm just glad you're not so hung up on the age difference anymore. You did that, you know."

"Oh I'm still hung up on it all right, but was smart enough to know when I'm outgunned." His eyes narrowed. "What do you mean *I* did this?"

"I mean you were pissed at me when you died last time and you did this to us on purpose. That's all."

"Huh." He looked away, back toward the water. "What happened?"

I pulled my hand from his and closed my eyes. "I don't want to talk about it."

The light dappling my eyelids turned dark. I opened them to find Henry looming above me, his dark wavy hair surrounding his face. His hair had grown since school had started and I wondered when he would cut it. I liked it long. His brows drew together in a frown. "Why not? You talk about the rest of them, why not that one?"

I smiled, suddenly nervous. "Why dredge up things that make no difference now? We're here. We've found each other and have overcome several obstacles. There's no need to go back there."

A frown creased his smooth brow and his mouth turned stubborn. I'd seen that mulish twist of the lip in so many of its forms, I wasn't likely to forget it any time soon.

"I don't think so, Alice. You sound like you blame me for this situation and if you do, then you should tell me what you did to make me do…" A smile twitched his mouth. "Man oh man, this is convoluted. How do you keep it all straight? You say you remember them *all?*"

"I do. But it's not like they're there in my head playing nonstop like a movie, but like all memories, they're buried in the background unless—I'm reminded of something or choose to remember."

Henry stretched out beside me. "Very clever. Now what happened? To us?"

I turned on my side and faced him, looking into his black eyes. With an outstretched hand, I traced the curve of his cheek and the angle of his jaw. "I'm not perfect, you know. I made a mistake."

He reached around my neck and pulled the band from my pigtail, then worked his fingers through it until the braid loosened. "I love your hair. You should always wear it down. What kind of mistake could my sweet girl have made?"

The heat flooded my face and emotion nearly choked off my words. I was so content to be here with him, why did I have to ruin it? "Well, you see, Henry, after the Colonial lifetime, I determined that we were not good for each other. It wasn't the first time I'd lost my life because of my involvement with you."

Maybe it wasn't fair to blame him for the witch burning in the 15th century, after all, I didn't know for sure about that one, but I had my suspicions. Priests should not take lovers and make them pregnant. Story of our lives. A grim story. And one I was determined to prevent this time around until I said it was time for it. I'd be safe then.

Henry played with a lock of my hair, twisting it around his finger, his eyes heavy-lidded and his long dark lashes casting shadow crescents upon the cleanly cut planes of his cheekbones. "And?"

"You followed me to that life. I should've known you would; your heart had been broken when Sarah hung me… but I…" Tears seemed determined to spill from my eyes; holding them back grew harder by the second. "Eventually, I left you for someone else, Henry. You wouldn't marry me and I left you. When I came to flesh as Carrie Robinson in 1905, I came determined to change the course of that life and vowed I would have nothing more to do with you. But the attraction between us was more than either of us could withstand. That lifetime, in its own way was more miserable than the one before it. I begged your forgiveness, but I don't think you really did."

Henry leaned in and kissed my brow and temple. "I forgive you, Alice, for whatever you think you did. You're very romantic, you know that? And why wouldn't I marry you?"

"It was the '20s and you were a wealthy white Chicago businessman and I…was a black jazz singer. You found me at a speakeasy, wailing the blues." I nearly smiled at the shock on his face. "I guess you can see the problem?"

He flushed. "Uh, maybe. It sounds pretty complicated." His brows rose skeptically. "How did you know I wouldn't choose the same race, considering the times, just to be with you?"

"Lucky guess. There was no purpose in your choosing it—and no karmic reasoning for it being chosen for you."

"But you did."

"I had thought to set myself out of your reach; that even if you followed me, you wouldn't…"

"But I did."

"Yes, you did and well…we made a mess of that one, too, with no help from anyone else."

"And you say I refused to marry you? Did I tell you that?"

I shook my head. "Oh no. You just *didn't*. You couldn't. The times were so different then. Years went by and…well, it was the 1920s and I couldn't have expected that you would, though I did hope. Instead, our worlds were separate. You could enter mine whenever you pleased or could take the time, but yours was closed to me."

"Did I marry anyone else?"

"No. I did."

He lazily stroked my hair, nuzzling his face into my neck. "I'll bet you were beautiful. I'll bet you had me standing on my head before you finished your first set."

I giggled because his breath against my neck tickled. "That's pretty accurate. Are you sure you don't remember?"

He pulled me close, hugging me to him and somewhere in my mind, I smelled cigar smoke and tasted gin. A piano played the blues, tearing at my heart.

"I'm sure. But I wish I could."

"You might hate me now, if you did."

"Well, according to what you've told me, I wouldn't have to remember, but would hate you regardless, just going on instinct. I think we've proven that hating each other is just damned near impossible."

I felt him smiling against my cheek, but knew that this life had only just begun. Forgiveness is not an easy thing to give. We'd both proven that, as well.

He rose up on his elbow. "We could've both still been alive when we were born this time. How did we die?"

I sighed. "I don't think this is a good idea."

"I do. You said I need to remember, that I always forget and that's part of the problem. I would also like to show you that maybe it's not so important after all. I'd still feel the same way about you. Nothing you've said yet has made me angry. I want to know."

My eyes slid away and I turned over to my stomach, resting my chin on my crossed forearms. After a time, I said, "There came a day, after long years of waiting, that I made a decision. It took me a long time to tell you, because despite it all, I loved you…"

"And I loved you too, I'm sure, even if I was uptight and white, right?"

An involuntary giggle slipped out. Henry could always make me laugh when he chose; that was also part of his charm. "Yes. I think…no, I know you did. But the memories of Alys Kerr's abrupt departure from life at seventeen still stung. I'd grown tired of waiting and wanted to settle down. Jim Swan, the man who own the speak, well, he wanted me. Always had. And he'd chased me whenever you weren't around.

"He cared for me, I guess, the best he could, and one day, when he asked me for the ten thousandth time to give up on your white ass and marry him before it was too late, I turned around and said I would.

"We were drunk when we did it. And when you came to me… I…"

Henry shifted on the blanket next to me. "What did you do?"

"I flung it in your face. All of it. You bolted out the door and…were killed in the street by a car. I saw it from my window. I ran to you as you lay dying, begging you to forgive me…" Tears welled up and spilled over and down my cheeks. "Too late. I'm always too damned late."

"And you? What happened to you?"

"I drank a lot. I sang a lot. I discovered drugs and passed that existence in a sick, brief fog. After you'd passed and after I'd done what I did, there wasn't much left for me. I thought I knew better, but sometimes, we have to go back and find out. We forget." I dropped my head into the shelter of my arms. "It's harder to forget when you remember it all. Drugs can bring oblivion, at least some of the time. I died young. An accidental overdose. Thirty years old. I wasn't far behind you."

His big, warm hand rubbed my back. "This shit isn't easy, is it?"

"No."

"Well, I'm sorry for both of us. Where was Branwen that time?"

My head came up, surprised he'd thought of her. "Oh, she wasn't there. I, well, I broke a few rules that time. She wasn't ready to come—they got her in the second wave of witch hunts. She was an old woman by then and still keeping the Old Ways and … well, that's neither here nor there. But I wasn't ready to reincarnate and neither was she, but I did anyway. I didn't give myself time to heal in Spirit. Free will and all that jazz."

He turned me over and lifted my chin. I gazed into his eyes, so dark and so bright. "And this time?"

"I don't know, Henry." I swallowed hard. "I get the feeling we still have a lot to learn."

His strong arms enfolded me and he stroked my hair as I rested my head on his shoulder. "Me too, Alice."

Twenty-Nine:
Henry 1981

I reached for one of the baggies Alice had given me and dug out a handful of aromatic herbs to throw in my bathwater. She said they would help. I poured two fingers of whiskey into my glass and knew it would help more.

Lies. My life had become an unending stream of them over the last six months and I didn't like myself a whole lot most of the time. I'd been known to bend the truth a little when it came to girls, but this added up to a double life—a triple life, if you counted Alice. Round and round I went. I fabricated feelings for Sarah I didn't feel, putting on a front that had no basis in reality whatsoever. I told Alice everything, but had to hide her from the world. I played my high school teacher role during the day and broke all the rules with her at night. Daily, I waited for my world to explode into a thousand pieces of deadly shrapnel.

Alice was a sacred island of truth for me, and only with her could I be all that I should be—and it was so much less than I wanted! That just couldn't be helped and I comforted myself with repeated promises that our time would come. Whenever I came home from the nightmare with Sarah, I prayed for the end of it and the beginning of an above-board relationship with Alice.

If only I could find a way out of this mess with Sarah. If only I could push a fast forward button and make Alice eighteen. I tried not to think about what would happen if we were exposed. She was about the only thing holding me to sanity. I couldn't give her up. It was way too late for that. I loved Alice, body and soul.

I sank into the steaming water, wincing as it set the claw marks down my back on fire. Sarah had marked me up pretty good this time. Bite marks on my chest, scratches, and bruises on my shins where she'd kicked me. My cheeks still stung from the two roundhouse slaps she'd delivered before I could get her arms pinned to her sides and subdue her. High romance, there. She seemed driven to hurt me, marking her territory like a feral cat.

At Alice's prompting, I sent Sarah flowers for no reason and sappy greeting cards—which she'd purchased at Woolworth's on her way home with her allowance. I'd wined her. I'd dined her and did whatever Sarah wanted except have sex with her; that omission seemed to be her biggest problem. My time for excuses was running out. I knew that.

I lived alone, but needed a reason to keep her out of my bed, so I invented a roommate, a divinity student from the Christian college across town named Steve Bailey, with whom I'd made a pact not to bring girls to the apartment. A shocked look came to her face at this news and she immediately agreed to the line I'd drawn.

I puzzled over that one for quite a while, because she rarely agreed with me on anything. Maybe I'd pushed that button of outward respectability that seemed so important to her. Appearances, despite the hellish private reality, seemed to be all that really mattered to her—well, that and her goal of trapping me, a task she seemed well on her way to achieving.

Or maybe she didn't want to offend a future minister with premarital sex? She didn't seem all that religious, though I know she went to church every Sunday, without fail. Lutheran, I think. A weekly opportunity to show off her designer clothes was more likely the point to her attendance than a devotion to the faith.

Our Sarah is a shallow bitch, oh yes, she is, and every day that passed I found that personality puddle shrinking. Her current depth reading stood at about two inches.

I kept her out of my bed, but then the alternative was hers, in her rooms below the mansion. Ready for that line of attack, I somehow managed to tell her with a straight face that I would not be disrespecting her parents' home without the benefit of marriage.

She closed her mouth with a snap, biting off the cutting remark I knew was well on its way out her stupid mouth and a look of deep, inner absorption took over her face, transforming it, scaring the bejesus right out of me. After a long moment, when she solemnly agreed to that restriction as well, I realized she'd set her sights pretty high, and this was a sure sign that I was coming along nicely.

Sarah liked to drink. And when Sarah was drunk, she wanted sex. Putting her off, pissed her off, and that led to screaming, crying and kicking, and brutal near-sex, or worse, anger-driven, painful blowjobs in the car—thus, the reason for my current beat-to-shit state.

All that I'd done had failed to get the result I wanted. No matter how drunk I got her, she would not talk about the tape or the lack thereof. I'd begun to think I'd been right all along. She'd never admit that it hadn't happened or give me the tape, because then she'd lose her hold on me. This would go on indefinitely.

I sloshed more whiskey into my glass, its pungent, comforting reek filling my nose. I leaned back in the steaming tub, letting the warm green-tinted water do its work on my tired, sore body.

Alice never got mad at me for doing things most women would've bashed my skull in for and been justified in doing so. Sometimes, I felt so full of self-hatred, I almost wished she *would* hit me over the head, scream, and throw things. Anything. But she grimly accepted it as part of what both of us would suffer until Sarah could be neutralized—*if* she could be; that still remained to be seen.

Since the charade began in earnest, Alice had been strangely silent on the subject. I'd asked her point blank what I should do, though we both knew what was coming. She only frowned and said I'd know when the time came, and whatever that ended up being, she'd be there for me when it was over.

Oh. Right. Thanks, sweetheart. My navigator and co-pilot seemed to have put on her parachute and jumped right out the fucking hatch on me.

Well, now that wasn't accurate. She patched me up all the time, listened to my endless angry rants over Sarah, and never once let me down. For all her powers of insight and uncanny, near psychic abilities, Alice just didn't seem to be able to see the end of this. I almost bought her a crystal ball at Spencer's, just to see what she might do with it. When I'd joked about that, she'd gone rigid and fearful, and begged me not buy it. I laughed a little and suggested an Ouija board as an alternative, but she started to cry, so I stopped that pretty fast. She was scared shitless and I was sorry. Very sorry. I never, ever wanted to make her cry again.

I didn't suffer a shred of guilt over deceiving Sarah; I suffered for Alice and what this must be doing to her. Sometimes, that other life she seemed convinced we'd lived worried the shit out of me. Though the similarities of both existences were undeniable, a part of me still doubted, because I couldn't quite break myself away from the awful reality unfolding daily, in my face. It didn't seem to matter one bit that I knew these things about Sarah, she countered me at every move. Part of me hoped it wasn't true, because she seemed indestructible in both lifetimes, a cunning adversary with the devil's own luck.

Even so, I wanted at least a chance of winning. I didn't want to give Sarah supernatural powers along with her considerable natural ones. Disbelief seemed the only way to keep her in perspective. Alice kept telling me, "Remember!" All I could seem to want to do was forget. Whatever it was that she knew or remembered, the path seemed blocked for me. I'd tried. Even Alice couldn't bring those memories to me like she had at the creek that one day. I couldn't seem to go there at all, except for the way I felt when I read the journals or thought about them hanging her.

That seemed to be the worst of it, the very real fear that Alice's life might be on the line if Sarah ever discovered her presence here. Most days, I convinced myself that it couldn't be possible—but dread followed me, crouching like a gruesome jack-in-the-box, popping out in dreams and unguarded moments. Sarah was something I'd never come across in either woman or man. She scared me.

I didn't want her. I didn't like her. I lifted my glass, enjoying the slow, smoky burn and decided I would do it one more time. Just once. I'd have to bang her and that thought was enough to make me want to cut my wrists. I'd have to get her shit-faced (not the hard part) and search her basement rooms for the tape. That would be the last time. Whatever I found or didn't find, I couldn't take this anymore. I refused to take it. I'd half-convinced myself she'd lied, because she if she hadn't, after almost six months of a relationship that would make a romance novelist puke, surely she would trust me enough to talk about it or give it to me?

Not again. Never again.

Thirty:
Henry 1981

The night it happened was so nearly identical to the first one with Sarah that it felt downright creepy. We went to the Watering Hole to celebrate our six month 'anniversary.' A live band played. The only differences were that this time, I drove us in my car, nursed my drinks, and didn't go to the can without them. I also held her hand, let her hang on me, and endured it all until the band quit playing and the lights came on. She'd slammed wine coolers all night long. The bartender yelled "Last call!" and it was music to my ears.

Act I concluded. Act II, about to begin. I dreaded it more than anything. Sober for the most part, I'd remember it all this time. It wouldn't be pretty.

We'd barely closed the doors on the car before Sarah jumped me, had my pants unzipped, trying her damnedest to take the first layer of skin off my penis with both her teeth and hands. After about five minutes, I'd started the engine and pulled out of the parking lot. I don't think she noticed. This time, when I pulled in the drive, I reluctantly killed the motor. I never did that, because I never stayed.

I patted her back and pulled her head up gently by her hair. "Come on, baby. I gotta zip up."

"Hen-*ry*. You want me to stop *again*? Don't you wanna cum? I'll make you feel soooo gooood…" She glanced down at my less than enthusiastic weenie. I was so friggin' sore from her rough treatment, I didn't know if I *could* finish what she'd started. The woman couldn't give head to save her life—not like *someone* I knew. I shoved that thought away, because if I didn't, I was going to start the car and get the hell out of here. Like I should. Like I wanted to. In all my life I never thought I'd be used and abused this way. Shit happens, right?

I smiled at her, realizing I changed into two people when I was with her—the outwardly solicitous gentleman and the hidden resentful, angry man behind the smooth facade. Neither of them resembled the person I was with Alice. Not even close.

"Of course I do, you get me so hot I can hardly stand it." I'd become a master at double meanings in this last six months. "Aren't you going to ask me in?"

She pouted. "What's the point? You never want to. Always some limp-dick excuse."

"Not anymore."

She peered at me suspiciously, so drunk that she squinted through one eye—but I knew damned well it didn't mean a reprieve. She was near insatiable when she was sloshed, which these days, seemed a lot of the time. Getting her off was just about impossible and I'd often give up, tired and bored, with some flimsy promise for another night.

Sometimes, I'd get lucky and she'd let it go with an insult and slamming the car door hard enough to break the glass. Other times, she'd scream and cry and try to hurt me. Those times were the worst. It'd take another hour to get her settled down enough to dump her off at her house. The next time, from the way she acted, you'd have thought nothing had gone wrong with her. She'd either not remembered or didn't care.

Her mascara had smeared into raccoon rings around her eyes and I thought Alice Cooper might've looked a shade better to me than she did at the moment. I seemed to be obsessed with Alice's of any kind tonight.

"You mean it? You wanna come…" A hiccupping belch rocked her body and I jerked, thinking she might hurl in my lap. "…in?"

That struck her as hysterically funny. I opened the car door, slid out from under her and slammed it, happy to just have the volume turned down for a second. I tucked myself back into my shorts and zipped up, taking in the neighborhood's wee hour stillness. Sarah's shrieking laughter, muffled by the car, seemed swallowed by the night.

No lights burned in any of the big houses' windows along the street and the cold, crisp early spring air felt good after the overheated, smoky bar and then the close confines of the Buick. I breathed deeply, steeling myself for what had to come next, fighting the unending stream of excuses that had been on parade in my head since before I left the apartment to pick her up. I walked around the back of the car, opened the door, and pulled her out of the passenger side. This had to be finished. Tonight.

"Whoopsy-daisy, up you go." I hauled her to her feet and we staggered around the house to the rear entrance. She babbled non-stop every step of the way about how much she loved me, how long she'd waited for me…blah, blah, blah.

I watched from a distance, somewhere outside of myself. I had to, because inside I was crying for Alice. This disgusted me in a way that casual sex never had before and it kinda shocked me. When Sarah dropped her clothes and walked naked in front of me, I felt nothing at all. Zombie-like, I stood while she fumbled with my belt. I shook myself, peeled her hands from it, and said, "Lay down, Sarah, I'll do it."

She giggled, fell on the bed, and never took her eyes from me. As I came to her side, I was sure I couldn't get it up. I knew it like I knew my own name. My dick was raw already and the salty, sweaty skin of her palms set it on fire. I panicked a little, because if I couldn't manage it, she'd be at that all night or want me to go down on her. She'd hinted at it before, but I'd wiggled out of it. She had a bush the size and depth of the Australian Outback; the very idea of putting my face in it made me nauseous. I couldn't help comparing her to Alice—but other than sharing the same gender, there was no comparison. None.

I closed my eyes and imagined the rough mouth working my cock belonged to my gentle, sweet witch. I often called her witch, teasing, and it made her smile. One of our little things, an inside joke. I tried to forget the pain Sarah inflicted, and before long, Alice's magic worked on me and I knew I could do this. I only had to keep my eyes closed and her sweet face in my mind, regardless of what was going on.

The vacuum with teeth released me and heavy breasts settled on my chest.

"Henry, sweetheart. Tie me up."

My eyes flew open, startled from my whimsical dream of Alice. What the *fuck*? "No."

"You know how that turns me on. I can't really get off any other way most of the time. You get tired and give up so fast." She pulled scarves out of her nightstand drawer. "Please?" She threw a leg over and straddled me. "Or maybe I could tie *you* up. That'd be different." An unholy light glowed in her eyes and I recoiled only to find that she had me momentarily pinned.

"Sarah. I don't want to be tied up." I heaved her off me and kneeled, staring down at her. With a deep, unwilling breath and my voice flat and dead in my ears, I said, "Let me make love to you."

She rolled her eyes. "Oh all right. Whatever."

That pissed me off. Like she was doing me some *favor* all sprawled out there and… I jumped on her and slammed into her, taking her breath away. If she liked it rough, I'd give it to her rough. "You're a whore, aren't you, sweetheart?" I pulled her hair and she moaned and opened her legs wider.

I stopped, suddenly inspired. "Turn your fat ass over, bitch."

Her eyes flew open with surprise, but they were glazed with desire. "Okay, Henry, if you want." She bit her lip and turned over, showing me her dimpled rump. If she'd shown one sign of reluctance, I would've stopped, regardless of what she'd done to me.

I landed a good smack on it and then did it again. Red handprints immediately showed up on her skin. Sarah's breath came fast and ragged, and it was clear that she liked this approach. A lot. Well, good. It would be over quicker. "Get it up here."

She propped herself up on all fours. "Like this?" she asked in a little girl voice.

"Good enough." I rammed my cock in to the hilt and she screamed and bucked against me. This wasn't sex, it was anger. Fuck it. I *was* angry—maybe more than I'd ever been in my life. I dug my fingers into the squishy flesh of her hips hard enough to bruise and she moaned again but didn't try to move my hands.

I rode her hard, banging her forehead against the headboard, pulling her hair and slapping her backside like I was the lead jockey on the final furlong at the Kentucky Derby. She got off at least three times and when I was ready to shoot my load, I flipped her on her back and spewed on her face. A lazy smile came to her lips as she licked off what she could reach with her tongue, the rest she wiped off with her fingers and guided them to her mouth.

My stomach did a tidy back flip and the judges all held up 10s on their scorecards. Bile rose in my throat. Easy, Henry. Easy, boy. Hang in there, almost done, almost over.

I fell back on the bed, spent, but realizing as I did, that I felt almost vindicated for what she'd put me through this last six months—*that* would come when I gave her the kiss-off of the century she deserved. I'd wrestle with the rights and wrongs of it later. Within minutes, she turned over, farted, and began to snore. Minutes after that, I started opening drawers and looking for the tape.

In her underwear drawer, I hit pay dirt. There lay a video cassette labeled in a lazy, round schoolgirl scrawl, "Henry & Sarah, 9/21/80." I'd thought my anger spent, but I was wrong about that. I grabbed my clothes, dressed, and ran out the back door. No more. No more.

***

My mind raced along with my heart as I parked the Buick on Pekin Street and then bolted up my back stairs. My hands shook as I slammed the plastic cassette into the VCR. I punched play and then froze in front of the television, my eyes riveted to the screen. Tinkerbell whizzed around an animated castle while Jiminy Cricket sang *When You Wish Upon a Star*. What the hell was this? I pushed fast forward through the opening scenes, of all things, *Sleeping Beauty*. The screen turned snowy for a few seconds.

Sarah sat naked on the bed I'd recently vacated, a martini glass in one hand and a cigarette in the other. She took a long, dramatic drink and a drag from the cigarette, then turned to the camera.

"Henry, Henry, Henry." She shook her head. "What am I going to do with you? If you've got this tape, then that means you've left me high and dry again. Damn. When are you going to learn? That is *not* allowed. I got your number, babe. Oh yes I do!"

She cackled. "And worse? You must think I'm stupid if you thought I would leave that other tape where you could find it. I think we've just discovered who the stupid one is in this relationship, haven't we, Henry?"

Sarah shifted and raised her glass in a toast. "You've been a very bad boy, and now...," she sipped from it, "you will pay." She rolled up onto her knees; pendulous breasts rolled and swung. "But it's not all bad, not really, because..." She set down her glass and cigarette on the nightstand, picked up a small gray box from the bed, opened it and held it up to the camera. "These are our wedding rings. I've already picked the date." She began to laugh in gasping shrieks. She closed the velvet ring box close with a crisp snap.

Horrified, I thought of the night last fall, early on in this disgusting sham when I'd said I'd not disrespect her parents' home without the benefit of marriage. The look on her face had scared the shit out of me and I knew, without question, that this idea had sprung from that one sentence, like a single windblown spore will soon throw up a weed even in the most carefully tended garden.

"I know what you're thinking," Sarah addressed me from the television screen. "You're thinking, like hell you have, but that's okay, think it all you want, because this is the last time you will.

"You made a huge mistake, Henry, thinking that I was so desperate and naïve as to buy your lovesick act. Nope, it didn't happen. You think I don't *see* those looks you give me when you think I'm not looking? You think I don't *know* why you won't sleep with me? Ha. I'm not the naïve one in this relationship—and you're not that good an actor.

"So a while back, quite a while back actually, I got this idea that you might be hiding something, something that might be keeping you from me in all the ways that count. I'm pretty sure you're not queer, and normal guys just don't turn down sex the way you do all the time. You're too young to be so damned limp. So I figured..."

Her baleful eyes stared at me from the screen, contempt written on her face. "God, you are such a dumbass."

Dread and denial fought for supremacy as she prepared for her revelation. Demon. That's what she was, had to be.

She looked at the camera and winked. "Hang on a sec, the slide show will follow my presentation." She laughed again, spread her legs and began to idly stroke herself, talking to me, talking to herself. She reached off camera and brought back an enormous dildo and I turned my head.

"Watch, Henry! Here it comes!" My eyes flew to the screen where she obviously faked, or maybe not—a bucking, screaming orgasm.

The picture faded and to my abject horror, photographs of Alice and me appeared one after the other. They were set to music: *Someday, My Prince Will Come*. Some of them had been taken through the windows of this very apartment, and I thought of the two-story vacant building across the street. Others had clearly been taken from inside—the long, dark walk-through closet adjoining the bathroom, the door of which faced my bedroom across the empty space of what had once been a sitting room. Someone had been in my house.

My beautiful Alice naked. Alice in my arms naked. Alice beneath me, on top of me, while we made love. Alice leaving the apartment, taken with a night-vision lens. Alice and me on a blanket by the creek in a compromising position, then in a field full of dry autumn grass and wildflowers. Alice getting out of her mom's car and going through the front doors of the high school with books in her arms, wading through deep snow. Alice and me in my car, and then beneath budding trees on bright green grass and my old blanket in early spring. There were more, but...

Sarah's voice narrated the slides, dripping with sarcasm. When at last they were done, she appeared on screen, wearing a red silk kimono. "You have a problem, Henry. Your little Alice is just a few years shy of what a high school history teacher's respectable reputation will allow. You notice that there are dates and times clearly stamped on each photo? Fourteen years old, fifteen now, but shame on you! And you think I'm fucked up? Oh, Henry! You are perverted beyond even what I can imagine!

"I shudder to think what will happen when this hits the paper." She picked up the gray ring box and turned it over and over in her hands. "But there's a way out. Always a way, where there's a will." Her screams of laughter vibrated the TV's ancient speaker and I stabbed at the volume button and abruptly sat on the floor; my knees buckled.

"But wait! There's more!" Sarah screeched.

"Christ."

"This is how it is, Henry, how it's gonna be, so listen carefully, okay? My father is an important man with connections you can't imagine. He is going to make your father almost as important—at least here in this little shithole town and maybe a bit further down the road, bigger places. That is, if Billy can manage to not be too big a fool.

"I want you, and what Sarah wants, Sarah gets. My future husband, namely you, is going to be a good boy from now on. He's going to take a more prestigious job at the college, Dean, I think is what Daddy said, and that's just the beginning. You are going to be respectable and worthy of me. No more little underage whores. No more pretend. I think we're straight on that, right?

"And you will do these things because if dragging your dad's name through the mud, a prison sentence, and a life-long label as a child molester isn't enough to decide it for you, then think about your little sweetheart, Henry. I'll hang her high, darling, *real* high."

Those words broke a cold sweat on me and I shivered from it. Fear. I admit it. She'd done it before; I couldn't help but believe she'd make good on the threat if I didn't... I couldn't even frame the words in my head. Did she remember? Or was she just being an asshole? I didn't want to know and I didn't think it really mattered. Nothing mattered anymore. Nothing at all.

As I rolled to my knees, already reaching for the whiskey I'd left on the end table, the cartoon prince on horseback appeared where Sarah had just been and slashed his way through a forest of thorns, intent on a gloomy castle in the distance. A green fireball exploded and the Evil Queen appeared on the long bridge spanning the moat.

"Now shall you deal with *me*, oh prince...and all the powers of *Hell*!" She shrieked, laughing madly and turned into a menacing dragon.

I didn't bother with a glass, but cracked open the seal, glad that I hadn't tucked it in a drawer or put it away in the cabinet. On my knees and swigging right from the bottle, I was suddenly mesmerized by the message being communicated through the television screen. A momentary cloud of superstition passed over my head. I couldn't help it. Bad omens and all that—they'd never made much impression on me, but this... the absolute correctness of the scene compared to the wreck my life had just become, well, that was just too much. Way too much.

The Evil Queen-turned-dragon towered a hundred feet or more above the stalwart prince, all sharp teeth, scales, and claws. The longsword in his hand looked puny and unequal to the task in front of him—a deficit I could definitely relate to. She laughed again and snorted green fire and smoke, taking out the bridge in front of his horse's hooves.

Disney princes always triumph over evil. Always. But in real life, dragons and evil queens just didn't leave any gaps for tiny long swords. They killed and maimed and destroyed people, along with the bridges their flames burned to cinders. My bridges seemed to all be just piles of ashes. Of the one I needed the most, the bridge to my sanity—the one that led to Alice, nothing remained but empty space. Sarah had blasted it into a gorge that couldn't be crossed.

I reached forward and hit the off button. Coincidence? I didn't think so. But this prince, the one kneeling here like a limp doll on my living room floor, wouldn't defeat this Evil Queen. He could only put his heels to his horse's flanks and run it headlong off the damned chasm and die—or he could bow down to her demands and become enslaved.

I just couldn't make up my mind which it would be.

Thirty-One:
Alice 1981

I'd fallen asleep with my hand on the bright yellow trim-line phone, not just an extension, but my own line, a Christmas present from my parents, (my mom, of course; Dad would never have thought of it), waiting for his call. He'd thought that tonight would be the night, though nothing Rod Stewart ever imagined could've covered this.

Faerie circles, standing stones, and dreamscapes revealing memories. In a picturesque 17th century village, a young woman swung by a rope from a tree limb. I turned from the body, unsurprised to find myself outside of it. From above, I watched as a young man sobbed, his dark, curly-haired head in his hands on the other side of a barn with clear view of the oak tree.

He ran through a quiet house, his boots thumping on the floorboards. With shaking hands, he emptied a tin full of coins into a handkerchief and knotted the ends together.

Up a narrow flight of stairs he flew, skidding to a stop in front of a desk. He yanked a leather bound book from a drawer, opened it, and using the quill and inkpot hastily filled a page. He set the ink with a pinch of sand, then shoved it into the inside pocket of his coat. I'd read his words, three hundred years after he'd written them, but I'd not lived this scene with him.

On his way out the door, he grabbed his hat from a peg on the wall and didn't look back. Down a long, dusty path he ran, tears streaming and sobs racking his body. He stopped as he came to a small clearing and fell to the ground, screaming his pain to the almost bare trees and dry November grasses. In the place where he'd known unparalleled rapture, he now knew a sorrow equal in its painful depths. A cold wind reddened his cheeks and nose as he removed the book from the inside of his coat.

I would've cried for him, had I been able.

Gently, he parted the long grasses, searching for something I think I already suspected. I remembered him tucking those wildflowers in my hair, giving them to me; a love offering. The tale of that poor queen, an innocent who'd lost her head for the sake of love had always made me cry and he'd always found those flowers whether it be spring, winter, summer, or fall with the unerring grace of a magician. I'd never known how he did it. But he did. A heavy, rasping breath which sounded desperate as though his life had depended on his success, escaped him as he found a tiny flat-topped cluster of Queen Anne's lace. He pinched the flowers off at the stem and placed them in the book, then wiped his nose with the back of his hand. When I'd found the journals at age eleven, there was nothing but crumbled dust between the pages… his last love offering to me in that lifetime. I should've guessed.

Arthur Kerr, my father in that life, opened the door at the urgent pounding, his long narrow face worn with grief and as tear-stained as Henry's own. Henry thrust the book into the large, herb and potion-stained hands.

"Give this to Mistress Branwen. She will know what to do with it."

He shared a long, tormented look with the older man and then turned.

Sarah Holbert smiled from the open garden gate, her plain face turned radiant beneath her white lace-trimmed cap. Lashless, pale eyes glowed with the confidence of an assassin whose dagger had just found its mark; the handle of an empty marketing basket lay across her arm. He strode toward her, a deadly look upon his face. The smile fled from her pouty lips and her round eyes widened as she took in his expression. He didn't slow as he approached, but knocked her out of his way, into the mud next to the horse trough.

"Henry, my beloved! You are at last delivered from Satan's evil, why do you not rejoice?" she shouted at his back as she scrambled to her feet, seemingly unmindful of both the insult and the mud that sullied her skirts and hands, and ran in his wake. The basket lay forgotten in the muck.

Henry halted at the sound of her running feet.

"Where are you going? It is nearly time for services." Breathless, she caught up and faced him, high color staining her plump cheeks. "My father has planned a grand sermon to celebrate Camden's liberation from wickedness. Our Lord in his righteousness has prevailed!"

He stared at her, his face a frozen mask of disbelief.

She pawed at his arm, leaving wet, dirty streaks on his white, bleached linen shirt. "He shall also announce our wedding feast. My mother makes ready for the celebration. It is but two days hence." Her chest heaved and she spoke in a blowy, puffing voice.

Still he stared, his eyes red-rimmed and furious. "Marry thee? I shall not. Never."

A frown puckered her smooth forehead and her pale blue eyes filled with false concern. "Then I must tell my father that our trials have not ceased. The witch has corrupted thee and the Devil still dances in thy soul. The oak in the square has not yet seen its last ornament."

His eyes turned to onyx shards in his rigid face and his mouth, already twisted into a bitter grimace, spat his words in a clipped New England accent.

"*My* father was mistaken in his verdict, Mistress Holbert. An innocent has been murdered and the true evil stands before me now, spewing lies and filth. Thou hast sickened me to my very soul. The Devil's arse awaits your kiss, you wretched, foul creature."

She smiled sweetly and opened her mouth to speak, her hand outstretched and resting on his arm.

"Touch me not! Demon," he hissed, and made the sign of the evil eye. "Be gone, fiend!" He batted her hand away and when she did not move, he turned briskly on his heel and left her standing in the street.

As he rounded the curve which led north to the open road, she shouted. "I shall see thee Fourth Day, Henry. The contract is signed. It is thy blood which sealed the pact."

"I shall see thee in Hell before that day arriveth," he shouted back.

***

Henry Sayre's body lay curled in a gutter choked with garbage and human waste. He clutched an empty bottle in his rigid, frozen hand. Frost clung to his eyelashes and brows. His skin was blue and his eyes were closed.

Unemotionally, I watched Azriel lead him away, knowing it was for the best.

Seeing me now might unhinge him. Seeing me now…

I woke with a cry that came out as a whimper. A sending, surely? Things had gone terribly wrong, I knew. My heart pounded and adrenaline flooded my chest. With shaking hands I snatched the phone and dialed his number.

One ring. Two. Three. I held my breath for the fourth, knowing if the answering machine decided the time was right, I would hear his cheerful voice asking me to leave a message I couldn't leave. The phone rang on and on… and on. Maybe the machine had finally quit altogether.

Damn.

Blood is a powerful fluid. Forever it has been the key to many binding oaths, rituals, and yes, sacrifices. He'd signed the marriage contract with his own blood. A quaint, old-fashioned practice, that people often joked about in this time. No joke. He'd not been given sanction to break his oath, though in Puritan times, it was possible, if all parties, the parents, and the Magistrate agreed to it.

He'd skipped that part when he'd skipped out on Sarah.

Thirty-Two:
Alice 1981

I found him on the living room floor, still in his date clothes from the previous night and curled into a position so close to the dream, it nearly stopped my heart. His normally healthy olive complexion was a nasty, greenish-tinged white. Next to his hand lay an empty whiskey bottle, another lay on its side on the coffee table. A puddle of vomit had soaked into the carpet not far from his head and he'd wet himself. The reek nearly knocked me over. Paralyzed with fear that I'd come too late to save him, I could do nothing but watch his chest for some sign of life. After what seemed like an eternity, he twitched in his sleep, sucked in a gasping breath and blew it out in a snort.

"Henry." I shook his shoulder and he cracked an eyelid.

"Alish." He muttered something unintelligible, and as I turned to go make him some coffee, the TV screen caught my eye, glowing blank and blue, Channel 03 showed in block letters at the top right. The VCR. For quite a while I stared at that innocuous blue screen and knew I didn't want to see what had put him in this state.

In the living room he groaned and sat up, then crawled towards the bathroom. I felt badly for him, knowing that he'd never have wanted me to see him this way. The coffee brewed and the sound of running water and the toilet flushing drifted into the small kitchen. As the long minutes passed, my pulse hammered a Funeral March drumbeat in my temples and anxiety gripped my heart.

I poured two cups of coffee and opened the windows. It didn't help.

He stumbled across the threshold and fell into the chair, immediately covering his face with his hands. His hair lay in damp curls and his sweats were rumpled, but dry and mostly clean. Minty fresh Scope and stale whiskey filled the air around him. I reached for the bottle of aspirin he kept over the sink, shook out three tablets and filled a glass with water.

"Here," I said, and peeled one of his hands away, tucking the pills inside.

He dry-swallowed them and blew on his coffee, sipping as though it hurt his mouth.

"Henry…"

With a weakly upraised hand, he rasped, "Not yet. Please."

I sank into my chair and drank the coffee, eyeing him beneath my lashes as he drained his. Finally, he raised dull, bloodshot eyes to me. "Go into the living room and watch it. I don't want you to…" His face crumpled and his voice cracked. "But we don't have any choice." He put his head on his arms and sobbed.

My eyes immediately filled in response to his tears. Like a sleepwalker I did as he'd asked, side-stepping the wet spots and punching the start button, then perched on the edge of a sofa cushion. In a trance, I watched Sarah deliver her coup de grace.

When the prince faced the dragon, I turned away and stared out the window for a long moment, rose, then switched it off.

I paused at the archway and took in the broken man sobbing with his head down on the table and knew that I couldn't heal this kind of hurt. It was a mortal wounding. I recalled Alys's words as she begged her Henry to run away with her and his practical reasons for not doing so. A thick veil of helpless surrender descended over my soul; I think I'd been here before. I might not die this time, but I'd certainly want to.

Too late, said the voice in my head. *Way too late. Always too late.* "Henry? Will you run away with me?"

His shoulders stopped in their shaking and he lifted a tear-streaked face that held my answer.

At least he spared me the reasons. I knew them well. I stepped to the door and opened it.

In a strangled voice, he said, "Alice, I love you. I always will."

I didn't turn around, but said, "I know, Henry. I love you, too."

The screen door banged shut on its frame behind me. I walked home.

Thirty-Three:
Henry 1981

I stayed drunk the entire weekend.

Monday morning, bleary-eyed and wanting to die, but doing the best I could to go on, I checked my pigeon-hole in the office and pulled out a lavender envelope with a gold seal on the flap.

***

Dearest Henry,

I realize I shouldn't leave this here, but felt it was safer than any other place from prying eyes.

I've started and thrown away a dozen copies of this letter, finding that nothing I can say, nothing I can write, describes how I feel. There are no words to make this better or way to make this right.

My heart is broken and so is yours…

If there's one thing I would tell you, though it's small comfort and hard to believe, this is not the end of our story, Henry, but only one chapter in a very long book. Eternity is a long time, my love. We shall meet again, in better days of our own making. We must bend ourselves to our destinies and accept our fate the best we can.

It is important to tell you that regardless of how you hurt, how desperately unhappy you might become in the months and years ahead, you **must not** give in to despair and end your life again. That act, coupled with a blood oath given and a failure to honor it, or break it honorably, are what led us to this place. Whatever you do, however you can survive this disaster, draw a line over which you refuse to cross, and live out your days, Henry. I think it is one way to free your self of her.

She has made a future divorce all but impossible… for even when our love is no longer illegal, she will have evidence of a transgression which she will hold over your head for the rest of your life—or until she tires of you and leaves you. It must be her decision, but until that day comes, the destructive magnitude of the evidence she holds will never lessen. I am only sorry that she used me to get the job done.

You might already understand this, but I need to be sure you do. I will spend the rest of my life trying to forgive her, or risk finding myself pitted against her next time. For you, I have already forgiven as I always have, and likely always will. I love you! But you know that already, don't you?

Hold me near in your heart and memories, Henry. I don't hold you blameless in this, but I do hold you human, and will love you all my life and beyond.

I wish we could… be brave, throw Sarah's filth back in her face and withstand the consequences. You know well that I would stand by you through it all. I wish…we could fight this somehow. But for four lousy years on this planet, we might've had a chance. The gap between 14 and 18 is a bottomless pit.

There are many ways, I suppose, to look at this. If you'd forgiven me last time and waited for me, we might not be suffering now. But then, if you had, you would've only postponed the inevitable confrontation with Sarah. We never escape ourselves, Henry, only return to the lessons we refuse until we get them right. It is The Way It Works.

I would go anywhere with you. Do anything for you, except make you withstand a price too high to pay. I can't help myself, either. I can't help wondering if an honorable opposition to her, say a lawsuit or permission from my parents to see you would make a difference?

Still, my mind searches for a solution. I find it hard to give you up.

I love you and somehow, those words seem inadequate to the way I really feel.

Alice

***

I folded the letter, returned it to the envelope, and tucked it inside my jacket. Woodenly, or maybe hollowly, like the Tin Man I'd once told her I was, I walked into the Principal's office and gave him my resignation.

I stayed drunk for a week, but I lived.

Thirty-Four:
Alice 1981

Two weeks after the video, I sat in the living room on the couch with my mom as Samantha bewitched Darrin for the ten thousandth time on the late afternoon re-run schedule. Despair claimed me and I didn't have the energy to fight it. Henry had quit his teaching job and I couldn't go to him anymore. I was dead inside. Hollowed out and empty, holding onto life by the fingertips.

I didn't expect him to call me after the letter. I didn't expect anything at all from him. I just hoped he'd be okay. Somehow, I didn't think he would be. Every day I looked for his obituary. Every day that I didn't see it made me think that maybe he'd really listened to what I'd said. Maybe.

I glanced over at my mother, who seemed distracted and distant. She sat with her legs curled under her, leaning on the armrest, in faded jeans and flannel shirt, her hair still a little damp from the shower. She'd not been up long; she held a coffee mug in her hand, but seemed to have forgotten it was there.

"Mom?"

Her blue-green eyes turned to me. The look on her face said she hadn't been watching the sitcom any more than I had. "Yes?"

I faltered. This quiet version of my mother, so lacking in her usual Pollyanna zest, kind of threw me. "Do you remember that day I told you I found Henry, and then said I was joking?" I waited, dreading the cheerfulness or silly remedy she would suggest or worse, an immediate subject change, but I needed to say something, talk to somebody about this. I couldn't seem to stand it by myself.

"There's something wrong, isn't there?" For once her lip didn't quiver and her eyes stayed dry. She set the coffee mug down with a thump on the end table. "Come here and let me hold you."

I scooted down the length of the couch and tucked myself into her warmth. She smelled good—like coffee and Irish Spring soap and Gee Your Hair Smells Terrific shampoo, combined with her own unique fragrance that had always spelled security for me.

"I love him, Mom, but I've lost him and there's no… way to fix it." I began to cry then, the tears that had been frozen inside me since I watched the video, were unleashed in a furious flood. To my surprise, she didn't try to make me feel better or dismiss anything. She only stroked my hair until I quieted.

Finally, she said, "Is this something I need to tell your father? Has he… forced himself on you?"

I sat up and looked at her through the blurry shimmer of tears, begging her with my eyes to understand. "No, Mom. Never."

"I didn't think so, but I had to ask." She looked away for a second, as if embarrassed.

I wiped my nose on the back of my hand. ""I… I went after him. I know you don't understand…"

Mom reached back and yanked tissues from the box on the end table, then gently wiped my face, the skin around her eyes creasing in a watery smile. Her tears this time seemed different to me, not weak or girlish, but belying strength I hadn't known she possessed. She handed me the wad of tissues and kept one for herself.

"I think I do, now, but I didn't for a long time." She blew her nose, then tossed the crumpled Kleenex in the can in the front of the table, snatched the box and placed it between us on the cushion. I squashed it when I grabbed back onto her, clinging like a two-year old afraid of the dark. Truly, I *was* afraid of the dark, but it wasn't on the outside, it was all inside, a black pestilence that might take me over and kill me. I needed my mommy, badly. She popped the box from between us and pulled me onto her lap. I was just about as big as she was now, but that didn't matter a bit to either one of us.

She stroked my hair as she cuddled me, sighing. "I remember how when you were ten, you begged for an entire year to go to Camden, and once we gave in and took you, your fascination with the Apothecary's house and how you cried at those two graves. I remember the names on the stones, Alys and Henry." Mom shook her tousled blonde head above me; I know she did because I felt it and knew her gestures very well. I didn't need to see it.

"I nearly fainted when I saw that, but couldn't believe it. I really thought you might need psychiatric help. That you'd over identified with people you'd read about…or something. You were only eleven that summer and we didn't quite know what to do with you or what was going on.

"You had a vivid imagination, and then there was your obsession with the witch trials—all those trips to the library. I think you read every book they had on it. We were surprised when you bypassed Salem for Camden. We took our vacation there because you wanted to go so badly, we thought it might unzip you altogether if we didn't."

I leaned back against the arm of the couch and stared at her, floored by these revelations, and hoped she'd go on.

Mom twisted another Kleenex between her hands, distractedly, her forearms resting on my thighs, which were covering hers, my bottom now sunk down in between the cushion and the arm of the couch. I'd not been this close to her in quite some time and found myself surprised at how comfortable it was.

She continued. "And then there was Henry. Did you think I never listened when you talked about him when you were little?"

"I didn't think you believed me."

"At first, when you told me you'd found him, I thought you'd lost your mind, but then I was almost relieved. At least I didn't have to worry that you might be delusional. He became real to me, then."

"But you talked about medication again. You didn't…"

"Move over a minute, baby." She shifted out from under me and levered herself from the corner of the over-stuffed sofa cushions. "I want to show you something."

Mom returned with a battered magazine. The covers were missing and the pages dog-eared. "A few days after you'd said that you found him, I took Grandma to the doctor, remember? I found this in the waiting room." She handed me the magazine. "There are people like you all over the world. You remember your past lives, don't you, Alice?"

I looked at the article header. *Reincarnation: Three Strange Cases.* "Yes, that's right."

"The children in those articles took their parents to the place they'd lived before, too. They knew things they shouldn't have known, couldn't have known, and I realized then what this had been about. I even gave you your proper name: Alice. Alys. Amazing. You must be a very strong soul. No, you *are*. I know that already." She smiled, and pride stamped itself upon her face. She not only understood me, I realized in a sudden bolt of awareness, but she liked me, too. I'd wondered endlessly about that. Love was something you expected from a parent. Liking was another thing altogether. I hadn't been easy to like through all this. I felt bad about that. Mom didn't seem to care.

She perched on the edge of the sofa while I scanned the article. "I think you're different, though, even from them. You remember more than just the last one; you remember all of them, don't you?"

I raised my eyes from the article and searched her face, realizing that she was, in her own right, still a beautiful woman and most of my looks, except for my dark eyes had come from her, including my small, compact and curvy frame, which would probably stand the test of time. Hers had, most definitely. My eyes were open now and I almost wondered if she'd wasted herself here, working herself to death in a factory, married to a truck driver. Everything seemed to change in a single moment and I could barely comprehend it.

I said as much. "I can't believe you're saying these things, Mom. Why didn't you tell me about it? Surely you suspected that I'd be relieved, even happy to know that at least one person in this fucked up world understood me."

She drew back a bit at my use of the ef-word, her mom-stuff triggered momentarily, but then rallied. "I'm sorry, baby. You know I am. But it was just too weird, off the freakin' wall, really, and so…," she shrugged. "But it in my mind, it was so much better than psychosis. You just can't imagine what happened to me when I read that article. I've been to the library myself these last few months.

"Your father and I," she paused and looked at her hands, worn from years on the assembly line, the nails cut short, the palms and pads of her fingers callused. When she raised her eyes, a faint sadness seemed to touch them. "We're just everyday, common people—and that's all right. But you, I think, despite being our daughter, are not like us at all. And as wild as the reincarnation angle is, at least I had an explanation I could live with—all the pieces fit. I didn't have to worry that I'd be visiting you in an institution anymore."

"Does Dad know?"

She shook her head, her wide eyes suddenly panicked. "Hell no! I didn't tell him or show him the article or the books I've been reading. He'd shit a sparkly purple *brick* if he knew about this. Our last conversation about your mental health was after Camden and when he was offered the over-the-road gig with Behrend's Trucking, I pushed him to take it, figuring he wouldn't be around so much if you started talking about Henry again. He loves his trucks and driving. It was a win-win situation for all of us. Though I do miss him. You're father is a good man, if *only a man*, Alice.

I nodded. It was the simple truth.

"But, then you'd stopped talking about Henry and seemed satisfied by the trip, so I left it alone."

In the spirit of honesty, I said, "I overheard the two of you talking therapy and I shut up. I wasn't going *anywhere*. Honestly, Mom, that totally pissed me off. I'm not crazy."

She nodded and a little smile turned up the corner of her mouth. "I know that *now*, Alice. After you quit talking about Henry, Stan finally stopped obsessing about you and talking about sending you away for help—and that made *my* life easier."

Holy shit. He'd tried to give me to the fucking faeries again! I loved my dad, but for the love of all that was sacred, he was a damned slow learner.

I looked on my silly little mom with a brand new respect. She'd been the only thing standing between me and a mental ward. I should've known that. I should've known. And Dad would've thought he was doing the right thing, the best thing. He'd always been that way. Always. I hoped with the utmost sincerity he got his boy next time around. She'd broken the spell and I thought they'd have five or six kids to lavish themselves upon. I shook away the image. Sometimes, I *could* see things very clearly, except it seemed, when it came to my own business.

"I kept it to myself when you started sneaking around to see Henry, too."

The magazine slid from my hands. "What? You knew about it the whole time? About him?"

"Yes. He lives down the street, on the corner. His dad is our new mayor. I…voted for him. He's a good man. I thought there was a good chance his son might be, too."

I started to say something in agreement, but she cut me off.

"You're too *much,* Alice, so beautiful you break my heart. I couldn't blame him for loving you, regardless of the rest. You seemed… well, absorbed, with him. Happy. I thought it might work."

Abruptly she stood and hurried to the sideboard, where she began rummaging in a drawer. "It's why I got you your own telephone line. Joe Williams doesn't exist and I figured there'd come a time, if he kept calling, that your dad would start asking questions."

A thousand questions of my own whirled through my stunned brain. I thought my mom an open book, a shallow pool where everything was visible right down to the shiny shells and colorful stones decorating the sandy, reliable bottom. Fifteen minutes ago I would've agreed to her claim to ordinariness; not anymore. It was like someone had stolen my mom and replaced her with someone more like…me.

"But Mom, weren't you worried about my age and all?"

She smiled grimly over her shoulder. "If you'd been a typical fourteen year-old, I would've thrown his ass in the pokey and never thought twice about it. But to be fair, Alice, you've never been a child, even when you were little. You've always known what you wanted and you've always been sure of yourself."

"Part of the problem, I think," I muttered and she heard me. The slight snort she made gave me to know that she agreed with me on that score.

She returned with newspapers in her hands. "I've seen teenage crushes and grown men know how to handle those. This wasn't that at all, but something that had followed you from then. I knew you'd go after him. You said as much that day in the car. After years and years of hearing about him before it all happened…"

I spoke up. "Even before then and before that, for as long as I remember."

Mom nodded, a slightly glazed look in her eye. This had been a lot to take in, I could see that, but as usual, she'd done her best to educate herself and help me—though she'd been wrong in her previous theories. I was nearly overcome by the affection I felt for her.

She spread the papers out on the coffee table in front of us. "This was the part I didn't understand."

On the front page of both papers, Henry posed with his father, once at the soiree back in October and again on election night just a week ago. Bill Spears had won both the primary and the election by a landslide. Sarah hung on Henry's arm in both photographs, a plastic smile in place, her father and mother squarely behind them. Henry just looked dazed.

"She's the reason he left you, isn't she?" Mom sniffed and flicked Sarah's face in the photo with her blunt fingernail. "She doesn't look like much to me. He must've been an idiot to pick her over you."

I smiled a little at that, touched and surprised again by her mother-bias and the aplomb with which she seemed to accept the situation. "He didn't pick her, Mom. She blackmailed him, took photos of us together, and said she will ruin him if he continues to see me. She wants him. He left her at the altar for me in Camden. She and her family hung me for a witch and he drank himself to death a couple of months later. It all has to do with that. It's called karma, and it's serious shit."

She shook her head, sadness creasing weary lines onto her pretty face. For quite a while she sat immobile, seeming to think it over while I waited, hoping she might have some solution. Finally, she said, "I'm so sorry, baby." She sighed and folded the papers. "We just don't have the power to fight something like that. We're nobodies and they're somebodies—and you know who always loses those showdowns.

"The laws…even if we didn't press charges against him, and we wouldn't, the state could and your dad and I might be arrested for letting it happen. They could put you in a foster home; take you away from us…" The thought of that brought a fresh wash of tears spilling down her face. "I would *die* if that happened. I could never let that happen!"

Faerie mounds and abandoned babies flitted through my mind and I knew she meant it, knew she was right in her grasp of the whole sickening mess. I'd come to that conclusion myself. I whimpered as a wave of utter hopelessness ripped through my heart. This had been my last chance, my final hope; though I think I knew it would never work.

"It's over, then. There really is nothing we can do." Twin fangs of loss and grief sank into my battered soul, driving the reality deeper. I'd lost my Henry again. Lost him! Impossible, but oh so true.

Mom put her arms around me. "No, baby, I don't think there is." She drew back a bit and looked me in the eye, the tears turning her eyes a glowing shade of turquoise.

"I'm not going to tell you that you'll get over it or that you'll feel better in a few weeks or months, though you probably will. You'll just have to take it one day at a time, and I'll be there for you when you need me—every step of the way. I'm not losing you… again, Alice. You're my baby and I'm keeping you safe." She'd heard me. Really heard me, and that made *me* lose it, but good.

I wailed in her arms and she wailed with me until we were both spent. That night, she called off work for the first time ever and I slept with her in her bed for the first time since I was three.

***

Dressed from head to toe in black, I stood hidden among a row of dwarf maples and shrubbery outside the Lutheran church. A mob crowded around the front entrance and soon, the newlyweds emerged. A shower of birdseed. Applause. A thousand or so mauve and pink balloons went up, and my Henry squinted in the August sunshine on the steps as he held Sarah's hand. A camera flashed and he rudely dropped the hand he held, his haggard face hardly that of a happy bridegroom.

Stuffed in a white gown with at least ten yards of tulle and lace, Sarah waddled at his side, obviously pregnant. As though the rest of the nightmare she'd constructed hadn't been enough to effect this end.

A limo idled at the curb and I lost sight of him as the crowd closed around them. I wiped tears and sweat in the late summer heat. At least I'd spared myself the torture of watching the ceremony. It was done.

Thirty-Five:
Henry 2033

Azriel floated on a cloud of light in Alice's bedroom, his head propped on his hand. "Henry, had you forgotten the letter Alice wrote?"

I didn't answer for a long time. "I don't want to look at this anymore, Azriel."

He sighed. "You must."

I stroked Alice's hair while she slept. She'd taken another pill. This time, she didn't venture forth but stayed inside her body and mind. "Of course I didn't forget the letter. I memorized every word." I picked up a lock of her hair and rubbed it between my fingers, then held it to my lips. She smelled so *good*.

"There were times it was the only thing that kept me from loading that revolver I kept in the closet and eating the barrel. She told me I mustn't, because I'd never be free of Sarah, if I did. I believed her." I glanced over at him, suddenly nervous. "She was right about that wasn't she? Sarah still blames me for everything. She told me so right after I died. Will I have to do this again?"

"Let us save that for later, hmm? Did you see anything in that letter differently this time?"

I thought back and couldn't say that I did. It still hurt. I knew that much. "What am I supposed to see? That it hurt so much I drank whiskey almost every day of my life just to bear it?" I shook my head. "If that's your point, Az, I think I got that one down cold."

He chuckled. "No, I knew that already. I am referring to Alice's invitation to oppose Sarah honorably and acquit yourself."

My eyes flew to him. "You're kidding, right?"

I found myself standing in my old apartment on Logan Street with the letter in my hand. I'd read it several times, sometimes having to stop because I was crying too hard to see it. Effortlessly, I'd melded with 1981 Henry. His tears were mine and my heart shredded all over again from the pain. Azriel stood at my shoulder and I jumped at the realization that this had not just happened, but that a younger version of myself stood there with the letter in his hand, weeping and wanting to die. I was already dead, but you sure couldn't have told it from the way I felt.

"There, Henry." His glowing finger pointed to the final paragraphs. "She gave you the opportunity to fight it."

I looked to him incredulously. "Azriel, did you read the first part? She knew it was hopeless. What kind of life could I have given her, branded as a sex offender? I couldn't have worked in education or earned a decent living, but would've had to hide in the shadows all my life. My father…"

Azriel shook his head and held up a hand, silencing me. "And yet, the life you settled for with Sarah amounted to the same thing, except loveless, miserable, and alcoholic. This is not the first time this lesson has been before you. Think!

"You never gave your father or either girl's parents an opportunity to make a decision. Remember, Henry, the contract could be dissolved by committee."

"Azriel, I keep telling you I didn't know about the contract. I didn't know what this was." I almost believed it myself.

He fixed me with a disappointed look and handed me Henry Sayre's journal, which I looked upon with dismay. "You did. He wrote about it in great detail."

The pages turned by themselves to the passage which described Henry's signing of the contract with his blood and the conditions under which it could be broken. I shook my head. "How could I have known those rules applied here? Besides, Henry knew he didn't stand a chance in hell of getting out of it."

"You are untruthful and that is not allowed in this place. Henry Sayre let himself be led, the easier course than standing up for himself and what he knew to be right and just. Telling the court at her trial that he loved Alys was not enough—and he knew it. He had known for almost a year that he wanted to break the betrothal with Sarah to marry Alys, but he lacked the courage to face his father and Reverend Holbert. He'd watched Sarah destroy lives and yet he couldn't find it in himself to oppose her—and exposing her was the only thing that would've changed the course for all involved. That is the crux of this particular instruction.

"You knew your identity, knew that all of you walked the earth in new forms. How many times did Alice tell you? Show you? What would it have taken for you to believe her?" Azriel asked gently. "I invested a great deal of energy instructing you between your ventures into flesh and you did not heed me."

A bright, hot flare of anger lit me up. "You are a Heavenly Being; you are supposed to be nice. What the hell is this? You scold me like I'm a five year-old who just shit himself in front of God and everybody."

Azriel laughed. "I only tell you the truth. If you view yourself as a child with bowel control issues, then you must be." He raised a golden eyebrow in comic speculation and I laughed, unable to help myself. Compared to him, I knew I certainly was an infant.

He continued, "Now back to the lesson at hand. Sarah's parents in this life never knew the extent of what she'd done to you."

"But Thurmond…"

"Took your measure accurately and gambled on your cooperation. He did not care how Sarah had accomplished it, but he had eyes, he saw your misery. She was his child and learned much from him. He only insured her success." Azriel shrugged.

"I don't understand!" I shouted, but the words lacked power and force of conviction. I lied to myself and watched as my younger self re-read the letter and broke the seal on a fresh bottle of whiskey. The old apartment walls, paneled and warped, seemed so real to me and for a moment, I found myself lost in just looking at the sun coming through the big beveled front window, shining on the scarred hardwood floor. I'd lived most of the happiest moments of my life here in this place. The sheers blew with a spring breeze, renewing and sweet. But not for him. Not for Henry. Never again for him.

"You do. Charles Thurmond had more to lose than did your father or you, not to mention the human laws against blackmail and coercion—of which he played a part. I will repeat myself: the contract could've been dissolved by the parties involved. It was an equal balance of power. Sarah herself gave you the way out."

I cringed. Azriel knew about that, too. I should've known better than to think he wouldn't. But it wasn't Azriel I'd wanted to deceive. It had only been myself.

For a moment, I witnessed an alternate reality, on the outside looking in for a change, and saw the eight of us, all five parents, Alice, Sarah, and myself standing in my father's living room. I confronted Sarah, confessed my love for Alice and she for me. I held up the tape and put it in the VCR and watched the horror and revulsion passed over every face but Sarah's, which turned sulky and bored, as though the whole thing was beneath her notice. She tried to leave and her father stopped her.

In the stunned silence following the tape, Alice stepped forward and told them all that if they sent me to jail, she'd go right along with me, because she'd seduced me, not the other way around and that we were going to be married—even if it meant a prison wedding and conjugal visits. The expression on my face at this announcement was priceless, and I almost smiled and forgot for a moment that this did not happen. Alice always did know how to drop a jaw—this was no exception. She made me proud to know her and sad that I had not risked it.

In minute detail, I saw how it might've played if I'd only had the courage to call them together, confess it all, and let the factions work it out. Viewed this way, it seemed an even trade—my reputation and my father's, in exchange for Charles' and Sarah's.

Alice's parents, of them all, seemed the least upset, and I believe that after questioning her and making sure of me, they might've stood behind us. They stared at me, not with accusation in their eyes, but amazement, and kept exchanging looks as though my presence there had hidden significance. Lila Keyes nearly smiled when introduced to me.

None of the rest might have happened.

"Jesus Christ."

"He might have been a good one to call upon about then." Azriel turned a benevolent smile upon me. "He knew a thing or two about courage in the face of impossible odds. Your own odds of success were much greater than His ever were."

Azriel towered over me, suddenly huge, his presence overwhelming and I felt very small in front of him, though his kindness and patience with me were seemingly inexhaustible. Even as he spoke the words that humbled me to the core, he smiled and touched me with a loving hand. I trusted him. I couldn't deny that.

He turned a look on me loaded with significance, like a teacher coaching a slow-witted student. "You did not completely trust Alice, but she never took another lover."

I recalled the night Alice told me of Branwen's arrival at some point in the future. I turned to Azriel. "But what about Branwen? Her mother. I mean, baby? Was Alice alone the rest of her life, then?" Guilt and abject misery weighed upon me heavily. I remembered her empty house on both occasions I'd been there.

Azriel smiled an almost cocky grin, for him—which always, no matter the subject, seemed suffused with understanding and kindness. "She outsmarted you, Henry. You gave a child to her the night she called to you."

You coulda dropped me with a feather, or maybe a soft breath, so great was my shock. I approved with every fiber of my being. "Well, hot damn. Good for her," I said and meant it with all my heart. I'd had a daughter— and she'd been no accident. Alice would not have allowed that. A daughter! Branwen. Someone important to Alice. Vital to her. I thanked God sincerely for that—and then thanked Him again that I'd been the one. After all the heartbreak we'd suffered, that one little thing stood as a solid black checkmark in the Good Column.

Again I let my imagination wander over what might've been—saw myself with Alice and Branwen at Scully Park. Alice sat in a swing smiling, as I pushed the little one in the one next to hers. This Might Have Been image brought its sorrowing partner, Regret, to ride shotgun with me through the park. I expected that feeling now.

I never wanted Alice to be alone, even if I couldn't be with her, even if I'd never known the only child I'd created in that life—and yet, I did know her. I loved and respected Mistress Branwen as Henry Sayre. She'd been a kind, loving woman—open in ways that simply weren't allowed during those uptight, Puritan times. Alice was meant to give love and receive it. Branwen was the one person I knew would do that very thing for her.

"Not Branwen this time. Elyse." Azriel paused, taking in the confusion that probably showed on my face. "Different name, same soul."

"Oh." The night she called to me? Darkness fell around us in a swishing curtain over the brilliant spring afternoon in my old apartment, circa 1981 and I found myself in 1985.

Thirty-Six:
Alice 1985

The summer of my sixteenth year, 1983, I finished high school. They mailed my diploma and that was all right with me. I never liked it much there anyway, and why should I drop out when I could pass the finals? No probs.

My parents then signed the papers which emancipated me as an adult. I did that for them as much as for myself, because Mom worried night and day that I might end up in foster care if this thing went south. If I were an adult, then they couldn't remand me to the custody of the state. Dad, as usual, went along with my mom—and never had the first idea of why we both wanted this so badly. She'd run quite an emancipation campaign for me. He caved.

At seventeen, I began selling my past life stories as fiction to magazines and sold Alys and Henry's journals to a private collector. After all, I didn't really need the journals; those lives were stamped on the very cells and crenellations of my gray matter. They'd served their first purpose and now would stand for the second.

At eighteen, I wrote a novel, which was really only a memoir sold as fiction. The women's magazine editor, who devoured my short stories like peanut M&Ms and never wanted the bag to come up empty, nearly shouted in the phone when I told her about the novel I'd written about Henry Sayre & Alys Kerr. She knew somebody who knew somebody else further up the chain and so it happened. Just like that.

The paper I'd turned in for Henry's assignment in 1980 held the seeds of my future. The irony was not lost on me that he'd called it historical fiction himself. It seemed only right that out of the ashes of that lifetime, I might find the security of this one. I wrote my stories and books under the penname of Carrie Robinson. I didn't want celebrity; I wanted solitude.

With the proceeds from the sale of the journals and an advance from the novel, I bought my small Queen Anne Victorian house on Lincoln Avenue, its steeply pitched roofs, scrollwork and gables a strong echo of the stately 19th century. I settled in, making a life for myself. At the back of my mind, Henry waited, as all unfinished business will, like an ax above my head.

Perhaps I thought these things I'd done were solely for my own satisfaction. That's what I told myself. But still, I held onto hope that my independence, my sanctioned adulthood, (the notice was published in the newspaper in the legal section and I knew Henry read that paper, cover to cover, every day) would lessen the guilty burden of our illicit relationship somehow and he might find his way back to me again.

As the days passed into months and then years with no word from him, I realized my longing for him had not lessened, nor had I grown out of it. No. It had grown with me. Spending so much time in our past, reliving it and committing it to paper had what should've been a predictable effect, but one I hadn't foreseen until it crushed me flat.

An early spring midnight found me in the backyard of my new home, weeping and naked with a ceremonial dagger in my hand, calling desperately on the Mother, my beloved Goddess, to remove this pain from me. I held the blade, waiting for a sign that my time was done here in this world. Branwen was not here to cut the bonds holding me to the flesh. I called to her, but she did not come. She'd never failed me. Never. But then, this body was very much still alive.

For all that I understood, and the wisdom I'd gained through memory and experience, this despair and desolation of heart was more than I could stand. I could not release myself from it. It did not lessen with the passage of time. I could take no action to alleviate it. Caught in a trap of my own making, I could see no clear path out of it but the one.

Azriel stood before me, his golden light brilliant against the deep shadows. Dark of the moon; dark of the soul. One and the same to me.

"Alice."

I lifted my head and smiled, wiping tears with the back of my hand. I laid the dagger on the damp, springy grass. "I had not thought to see you again until... Has this life ended then?"

"No." His wholesome light drew me to him, like a candle in a lonely inn's window will lure a small and very tired traveler. He held open his arms and I climbed into them. "You cannot escape this, little one, but only prolong the inevitable. You know this well. Need you reminding, then?"

"I don't..." I paused, looking up into that implacable, yet impossibly gentle face. "Azriel, I can do nothing to resolve this. There is no point. It is useless."

"There is a purpose to all suffering. You need only to seek the cause."

I nodded, but felt my heart squeeze painfully in my chest. "I am willing."

Azriel took my hand and in the span of a heartbeat, I stood once more in the street where Henry Sayre died. I watched Azriel lead him away and the thing I had missed before came clear.

I turned to the angel at my side. "You guide us both."

"Yes."

This simple thing, the thing I'd known but doubted, leapt up before me, plain and undeniable. Soul mates and choices. Lessons and failure. The pattern I detected within myself and denied had led me to this place. My depression deepened, becoming even more a death shroud than it already was. "It doesn't matter, then. Does it?"

"It matters a great deal." Azriel shook his head, in what for him passed as mournful, which wasn't quite. "And then, it does not. One way or another you will arrive at the answer. Whether it be this lifetime, or the next dozen is your decision. It is all the same to me. Suicide will mean a setback. You know that. But it is in your hands, Alice."

I walked at his side down a twisting dirt road back into town. Long skirts now belled at my ankles as I paced down the street, raising small dusty puffs with every step. I paused at the great oak on the village green, the new spring grass brilliant beneath its spreading limbs, glistening with dew. Tender leaves sprung forth madly. I could almost hear them unfurling, as the life force rushed beneath the rough bark on the ancient branches. Azriel tugged my hand and I let him lead me on down the main street where I faced a two-story, whitewashed clapboard home I knew belonged to the Holbert's—the best, most imposing one in the tiny village. Revulsion caused me to turn away, but Azriel blocked my path.

"You must look, Alice. You asked for the Mother to remove your pain, but you have not considered the pain of the one who was also wronged."

Sarah's weeping could be heard where I stood and I knew her wedding day had come and gone. Perhaps she'd heard the news of Henry's death? Could she have really cared? No. This was more likely self pity. "She accused me of witchcraft and had me hung, Azriel. She is evil and deserves what she has wrought upon herself."

"Really? Do you believe it, then?" Azriel pointed at the window. "Shall I remind you that there is nothing in this world without purpose? Without adversity or opposition, there would be no growth in your kind. She is fulfilling a purpose just as necessary and strong as yours. Sarah is as imprisoned by this as are you, and yea, Henry, too."

I stared at him, feeling the rebellion churning my insides.

"Your hatred burns like a dark flame, visible through the heavens, little one. It will consume you and tie you to her as surely as is Henry in your present time."

This had *not* been all about Henry, then. I looked to the window and tried to put myself in her place. Somewhere along a forgotten corner of my heart, perhaps the one behind which I'd hidden my pain when as Carrie Robinson I'd waited for him to marry me... No. It was not the same.

"Look upon her."

I stepped to the window and observed Sarah, who lay on the floorboards in her shift. A candle burned next to her. Her right hand gripped a straight razor and I could see that she'd cut herself superficially in a hundred places—places the modest black uniform of the Puritan maiden would conceal. Bloody rags lay on the floor next to her where she'd wiped away the evidence. I glanced to the fireplace and realized she'd burn the proof of her self-mutilation.

She'd rucked the long skirt of the thin undergarment up around her waist and along the tender white flesh of her inner thighs I could see burns. The presence of the candle close at hand took on greater significance. The acrid reek of burnt hair assaulted my nose and horrified me. I wondered how far she'd gone with this self-abuse.

I glanced at Azriel who looked upon the scene with compassionate eyes, and said, "She harms herself. This is not my doing. I am not responsible for her actions."

"No, but she too, has made sacrifices, Alice. Have you forgotten that all souls be equal in the realm of Spirit? That all will do their turn in every role, be it evil as you say, or good. She is no worse than you, nor is she the better. Sarah is playing her part and suffering for it, because for all that she has done, there has been a purpose—yes, she has wrought much grief upon herself and others, too, but any human is capable of that and must do it to learn the importance of consequence.

"This you know and this you have chosen to forget. The path away from this can only be walked with forgiveness in your heart."

The crackle of flames and the smell of burning cloth assaulted my nose and I was transported to another time and place. I stood tied to a stake in an earlier era, waiting for the flames to consume me. My eyes fell upon the priest who had condemned me to death for the practice of witchcraft. Henry was on the ground, held fast and made to watch. He wept and struggled against the men who held him.

Cold, pale blue eyes held mine above his head.

The child in my womb, the one Henry had put there, though he wore the Dominican robes and had sworn himself to celibacy, had stilled its restless turning, as though it had already departed for Spirit. I resisted the urge to curse the priest, knowing full well that it would only cause harm to my soul in the end. He didn't understand. For all of his spiritual teachings, he did not know, lest he would not be doing this terrible thing. The Christ's words came back to me, echoing through my head. The wisdom of the Masculine Element balanced in perfect harmony with the Feminine, embodied in one great, loving teacher: *Forgive them, for they know not what they do.* Over and over I said those words as the flames burned me, took me, and consumed me until I was dead.

Unable to bear this melding with the burning young woman, whose skirts smoldered around her ankles, I parted myself from her and returned to Azriel. He took my hand and I leaned against him. His arms came around me and held me securely. I drew strength from that heavenly embrace.

The priest chanted in Latin, his eyes never leaving Aleysia Robson's face. While Aleysia's tortured screams split the air, I watched from the safe blanket of Azriel's protection as the soul that shaped the priest revealed... Sarah. I should have known.

I'd paid him no heed, having no knowledge of him at all and no understanding of his relationship to Henry. That he'd tried, tortured, and convicted me meant very little to Aleysia Robson in the end. I'd stood accused with three-score others and had not known the cause to be personal—though I hadn't missed the link between my involvement with Henry and death. I just hadn't known the details.

Agonized and twisting with the throes of the flame's white-hot cruelty, I had not understood the significance of Henry's enforced presence at my burning. I could not think beyond the moment, and that they held him so to bear witness to my destruction had no meaning. After my death, I had fled to the safety of Azriel's keeping, soul-sickened and hurting. I left Henry behind and thought of him no more for a very long time.

Then, I stood at Azriel's side in a majestic cathedral as Henry received his holy orders in a still earlier time, though it was clearly the same lifetime. The blue-eyed priest, a bishop, I now understood, looked upon him with something close to adoration as he placed his hands upon Henry's bowed head and invoked the power of the Holy Spirit upon him.

Vows given and broken without dissolution. Illicit congress and retribution.

Love offered and love thwarted—on all sides.

Moving forward through time, minutes after Aleysia's death at the stake, I watched as the black-clad brothers pulled irons from the conflagration of my pyre and held them to Henry's eyes. His screams tore through my very soul. They stripped him of his priestly robes and dressed him in peasant rags, then dragged him beyond the city gates, where they left him to die or to beg for his sustenance. He chose death.

Unsurprised, I watched him take Azriel's hand. That the angel could be in two or more places at once didn't surprise me in the least. The afterlife was a strange, interesting place. Angels were angels; they were not restricted by the rules of the earth plane. That is an exceedingly good thing. We need them so badly.

After my body had been reduced to bone fragment and ash, and Henry maimed and left to die, the bishop retreated to his rooms and turned an ancient key in the lock of a stout, iron-studded door. He wept as he slowly removed his robes of office, and then fell upon his knees, naked, before an altar. From beneath a gold embroidered cloth he pulled a metal-tipped scourge. He held it to his lips, mouth moving in prayer, and then began to flog himself, scoring his flesh until the blood ran on the flagstones. He lost consciousness, and upon regaining it, he staggered to his feet, swaying and bloodied, and reached for a woven garment of rough goat hair. He fell again, moaning from the contact of the brutal shirt against his open wounds. One final time he mortified himself with the scourge, this last stroke he wielded with brute force between his own legs. He cried out in agony, curled upon the floor, weeping and vomiting.

Then I saw no more.

I turned to Azriel and we stood once more outside Sarah's window. "I cannot."

"Be it so, then."

I found myself alone in my backyard.

Thirty-Seven:
Alice 1985

The time had come, I decided.

I had not scryed in centuries, nor attempted it in many lifetimes. Negative associations had prevailed in my mind and I'd left it alone for so long, I wondered if I would still know how to find the Paths, and once found, if I could still journey down them.

For months I revisited my former existences, becoming priestess again for a little while. The rituals came easy to me. The Old Paths still survived, though lay hidden beneath many layers of humanity's refusal to walk them. I reached within and could vaguely sense their glowing trails, winding through timeless skies, earth, water, and fire.

The outdoors always appealed to me far more than darkened rooms, so at midnight on the first night of a full moon in May, only a day or two past the traditional Beltane, I filled a large silver basin with water and took it to my backyard.

I invoked the Mother and dropped the cloak I wore. Naked, I sat upon the cloak and stared intently at the silver mirrored surface, recreating Henry in my heart, mind, and soul.

Nothing of him remained with me; I had no articles of clothing or keepsakes to draw myself to him. Nothing but the feelings lingered, still raw and unhealed after four years, as did crystal clear memories of the man himself. I remembered everything, right down to the way his chest hair swirled, the curve of his cheek, and the hard, masculine cut of his jaw. His dark, intelligent eyes with their bristly black lashes looked into mine. I chose a happy Henry to remember, though sadness, fear, and hopelessness had chased us through much of the time we'd spent together. Our golden moments, fleeting but beautiful, flickered through my thoughts of him.

The long, finely formed limbs came to mind, as did the arch of his feet and the tenderly soft skin of his neck in that sweet spot beneath his ear. His scent was the easiest of all to summon—the irresistibly potent masculine essence, spicy and clean, yet so warm. I loved crawling into a bed where he lay sleeping, his smell concentrated in the sheets and reaching out to envelop me when he raised them and drew me in.

Reflected in the shining mirror of the bowl, Henry appeared in a blue, flickering light. In my mind, the luminescent Paths glowed, beckoning, and I stepped onto one and willed myself to him. In his living room at the palatial home he shared with Sarah, I waited in a shadowed corner not far from the television. He sat in a recliner, staring at the screen, a drink in his hand, his clothes rumpled; his face tired and sad.

Henry lifted his glass and his eyes darted to the corner where I stood, then flew wide. The glass slid from his hand and bounced on the carpet, spilling whiskey and ice cubes. He tripped over the footrest as he leapt from the chair and fell, sprawling to the floor, his eyes wide and frightened. "Alice?" he squeaked.

I smiled, remembering a bathtub and a younger version of him. I showed him the way to my house. "Come to me, Henry. I need you." I blew him a kiss as he nodded and then returned to my self.

The scent of flowers blooming in my garden surrounded me and I fell back on the cloak, smiling into the lunar face of my Goddess.

He would come.

Thirty-Eight:
Henry 1985

Alice had picked a rare evening to visit me. I'd come home late from an out of town meeting and had only just poured my first drink when I glimpsed her standing in the corner. To find me sober at midnight on a Friday was nothing short of a miracle.

Was I shocked at the sight of her standing naked in my den? Certainly. Half-freaked when she disappeared? Check that. Surprised? Well, though I'd never seen her do it, I'd have to say I wasn't, not really. Mostly, I wondered why she'd waited so long.

To me, she'd always been a creature of dreams and magic, capable of things I'd never imagined. Despite the terrible reality we'd suffered, she'd remained in my mind as almost a myth, one that grew by the day as my memories became more refined, more real to me than my present life. I smiled. An angel come to earth. Alice.

In a state of high, anxious anticipation, I circled through town, wrestling with the idea of going to her. My heart did back flips in my chest from both excitement and terror. I must've driven thirty minutes, just trying to get myself under control.

Struck by the urgency and the utter foolishness of what was likely a dream, or maybe a hallucination, I tried to talk myself out of it and then couldn't stop the elation of knowing I might see her again. It had been so long. Just this one time couldn't hurt. Could it? Round and round I went, in both my head and on Lincoln's deserted late night streets.

I didn't completely waste those thirty minutes, but spent quite a lot of time checking my rearview mirror. The private investigators that had dogged me the first couple of years had found me a drag and given up—or so I hoped. For a moment, I visualized Sarah barging in on us in bed together, coming at Alice with a knife in her hand, stabbing her before I could move.

I shuddered and the ever-present, much worn mental video of my trial as I faced charges of child molestation played, the invisible finger in my head pushing the start button. I couldn't say after four years of marriage that I knew Sarah any better than the night I took the tape and my life truly ended.

I avoided her as best I could, played my part at the never-ending public functions, and fought daily to not be drawn into the conflict that always waited, just below the surface with her. I often failed. The release of anger was too much to resist most of the time, though there was no resolution for it. The rest I drowned in liquor—and even that was a faulty remedy, as any alcoholic could probably tell you. It was all I had.

Sarah's car had not been in the garage when I left, and I didn't care where she was, though I cared deeply that she not discover my whereabouts. Like Henry Sayre, I wished daily that she might die in an accident, that there might be an oak tree or a semi out there with her name on it. Only the vehicles had changed over the last three centuries. In my opinion, a terminal illness would take much too long.

In the last month, the ever more frequent dreams of Alice had nearly driven me out of my mind, but then, I was pretty close to that on a daily basis anyway. I thought back to all the things she'd said about her time as a priestess and wondered if she'd been practicing what she did tonight—I didn't have a name for it. Astral projection seemed close, but really didn't cover it. What she'd done was too deliberate, and she'd spoken to me, told me to come to her, showing her house, number and the street. Impressive.

I turned onto Lincoln Avenue. Azriel sat in the passenger seat.

Confused I glanced over to him. "What are you doing here?"

He smiled broadly. "I want to leave you with a parting thought, Henry, as you revisit this next phase of your life. Consider that perhaps this is not so much about whether or not you will have to go through this with Sarah again, but whether or not you will fail *yourself* again."

I stared at him so long, the car should've left the road or crashed into a telephone pole. It was then I realized that 1985 Henry drove it and I'd only come along for the ride. I'd merged with him so effortlessly, I hadn't noticed. The afterlife was tricky.

"I will, Azriel. I promise."

"Enjoy your trip." He disappeared.

Smartass.

Thirty-Nine:
Alice 1985

I waited in the dark on my front porch step and nearly scared the life out him when he stepped upon my walk. My heart raced and I almost came out of my skin for the sheer joy the sight of him evoked.

"Ah!" was all he got out before I launched myself into his arms and covered him in fierce kisses. Tears ran down my face and onto his, small joyful noises of reunion came from us both in those first seconds when our mouths, hands, and bodies found each other for the first time in four long years.

Hope filled my heart and mind with impetuous visions of waking up with him by my side, the two of us together the way were meant to be. I let it take me over in the first sweet moments, but knew that whatever came of this night, the decision must be his alone. I could only show him I held a place for him, give him a glimpse of what awaited if he could only break Sarah's hold. Knowing that I could help Henry and yes, myself too, take the next step in our soul's journey stiffened my spine.

My cloak parted when I put my arms around him; his clothing the only barrier between us. His breath caught when his hands fell on my bare flesh and I knew then that we would have to get this out of the way before any talk would be possible.

"Come, Henry," I said against his lips.

He laughed and nearly choked. "I think I almost did. I'll be hard as a rock on my deathbed if you're anywhere within a mile of me. It's automatic—you've always had that effect ...on me." He held me at arm's length for a long moment, keeping my arms spread and the cloak open, his hungry eyes raking my naked flesh, then finally returning to my face.

"Alice!" He laughed with delight. "I've missed you every day for the last four years. I can hardly believe you're real." He took my face between his two big hands and then wiped my tears with his thumbs. The sound of his voice filled my ears and his closeness and intensity made me shiver. "You are even more beautiful now than I remember ..."

I placed a trembling finger over his lips. "Shh… there'll be time for talk, later."

His eyes burned into mine and we understood each other. He lifted me into arms that shook with the passion that existed between us. "Where?"

When we stood next to my bed, he let me slide to my feet. Bathed in moonlight, we never took our eyes off each other as I dropped my cloak and he quickly shed his clothes. I lay back and admired him, loved him, and wished so badly that he could stay with me.

Our lovemaking, as it always had been, was effortless and forthright—as though hours and not years had passed since we'd last loved each other. I held my arms wide for him and he came to me, running his hands over every inch of my body, his lips hot against my skin. His hair had grown long again and it shone in the silvery, uncertain light on his shoulders as he rose above me. I looked into his eyes, and love glowed hot and fierce in their black depths. I began to cry again when he entered me, became one with me; the feelings so intense I could not contain them. I remembered lifetimes of this singular passion and pulled him down, holding him like he was the only thing rooting me to this very earth. Perhaps, he really was…the only thing.

Release was not far and the ripples, shudders, and cries rent the darkness of my once silent and empty room. Filled now, with all I had ever wanted or needed.

He had come to me.

I lay in his arms and reveled in his warmth, unwilling to break the spell for a moment. Our ragged breathing soon quieted and a cool breeze blew the white sheers at the floor-to-ceiling windows into billowing, benevolent ghosts. Gooseflesh rose on my skin and I pulled the quilt over us. "I love you still, Henry."

He sniffled and reached his free hand up to wipe his face. "Alice, I haven't been the same since… To say I love you is not enough. Every day you are with me in my mind. Tonight, I saw you in my living room. I can't…"

"I know." I turned toward him more, and traced his dear face with my fingers, wanting to memorize the small changes that had occurred since the last time we'd been together. "I called to you. The Old Ways still work."

Smiling, he said, "Still up to the enchantments? It suits you, Alice." He kissed my damp brow. "Promise me it won't be the last time?"

My heart sunk at that. "I don't want you to leave."

"I don't want to, either." He breathed a gusty sigh. "I don't want to ruin this night for either of us, but so much has changed and then, so much is still the same."

"Tell me about your life." I moved away from him a bit and propped my head on my hand, my elbow supported by the old-fashioned feather pillows I couldn't sleep without.

"I think it's about what you'd expect, under the circumstances." His face fell into bitter lines, the not-so-distant future Henry already showed himself, though he'd not seen his thirtieth birthday yet. "I'm miserable. I drink too much and think about what might have been. I endure. That's all."

"You listened to that part, then?"

The corner of his mouth twitched, but didn't quite turn into a smile. "I don't want to go through this again. I couldn't."

Progress? Maybe. "You would have little choice, I think."

"I remember you saying that. I only wish..." He shook his head, his voice resentful and harsh. "There's no way. She'd never let me go. Though I don't know why she wouldn't. She has to be as unhappy as I am. Strangely enough, I think she thrives on it."

"I see." I'd come to understand that things with Sarah were much more complex than I'd known five years ago. Understanding her purpose in our lives did not make it any easier. "Have you ever asked her for a divorce? Told her you wanted one? I know what I said in the letter, but if you talked to her..."

"Like she might be a human being with actual feelings? I've done everything but commit suicide in front of her and she won't budge. She says she is satisfied with..." He sat up and pulled at his hair, uttering a growl of frustration. "I haven't slept with her since the night I took the tape from her bedroom. I... she's sick, Alice. Really sick. And it's become worse over time. She tells me she wants a baby, and demands I give her one, because people in our position should have children or others might wonder about us..."

"I thought she was pregnant at your wedding."

He smiled and shook his head. "You were there, weren't you?"

"Outside. I watched you leave."

"She told me she was, but gave up the charade a month later, throwing it in my face as though it were somehow my fault she'd lied and it hadn't turned out to be true. Now, she harps at me every day about a baby."

"But you can't do it. Can you?"

He groaned and scrubbed his hands over his face. "No, I can't. I won't touch her again that way as long as I live. She bought and paid for this sham of a life. That's all she gets. From me."

I thought of the bishop and wondered if his physical abhorrence of Sarah was rooted there. "And if you don't comply with her wishes?"

Henry shrugged. "It's a complete stalemate. For every move there's a countermove." He shuddered. "I think that's what she wanted."

I believe I knew what she wanted, though the meaning had eluded me; it was her methods that made me want to kill her. "She could've made that tape with just the photos of us on there, and confronted you personally with her demands. Why did she implicate both herself and her father?"

Henry looked away. "I've thought about that many times, why she'd given me ammunition to use against her. She's too smart for that. But what I think she wanted, as twisted as it sounds, was to equalize our power so she could...I know it sounds crazy."

"She wants you, but she doesn't love you. She doesn't know the difference between domination and love. They're one and the same to her and always have been..."

Again the Bishop rose in my mind. Complete power over another person— those things equaled love to that soul. I felt a momentary twinge of pity, something I had not felt when witnessing both Sarah's and the Bishop's self-mutilation. The memory of Azriel's compassionate face as he looked upon her moved me now in a way that it had not before. She did not know, or had forgotten, the meaning of love and that, of all human conditions was the saddest. And still, it was not enough to forgive her—not when the other half of my soul still suffered every day of his life because of her. All the pity in the world could not change that simple truth.

I shook these thoughts away, realizing he waited for me to continue. "Sarah has always believed I was just a mistake and in time, you'd forgive her and come around. She thought the same thing when she was Sarah Holbert. She underestimated your feeling for me." Simply said, and so inadequately. The Bishop's cold eyes burned into my soul. Unknowingly, I'd put myself right in his path again, interfering with his plans, taking Henry away from him, not once, but three times now. So we come full circle, meeting ourselves and our enemies again and again. Until we get it right.

"Yes. I think that's it. She's never stopped trying to," he shook his head, "you know."

"I know." But I also knew that in Sarah, he and I had both found the reaping of what we'd sown. The only way to banish her was to give her an honorable dissolution of all bonds—and expose her for what she was. It didn't have to be a tabloid front page exposé, or anything so dramatic, just a reckoning with the people whom she'd hurt.

That was an important element of this situation. Otherwise, she could never be free of herself. Not that I gave a tiny turd for the state of Sarah's soul, one way or the other, but as Azriel had shown me, she was no different than the rest of us. We think we can do it all by ourselves, but we can't. Other people have to act as catalysts for change in us—it can't be done alone.

"Do you have anything to drink?" he asked, breaking into my thoughts.

I nodded and retrieved a bottle of wine and glasses from the kitchen. "And what of the other tape, the one she used to start this mess?" I asked as I poured.

His eyes were upon me; I could feel them tracing my curves as I'd traced his more angular lines earlier. He scooted back to sit against the headboard and accepted the glass I handed him. "It doesn't exist."

I sat on the edge of the bed. "Knowing I thought that from the beginning almost makes it worse." I shook my head. "I should've tried to see, attempted to walk the Paths like I did tonight when I came to you. I might've been able to see the truth of that night as it happened. You could've ended it then, when she first threatened you."

He shook his head. "No, Alice. The damage was already done when I went home with her and then bailed before she woke up." Henry shrugged. "I wouldn't have stopped seeing you, couldn't have, and she would've had those pictures taken, regardless."

"But…"

Henry sipped from his glass and sighed. "No. That's where the die was cast —not in the lie she'd told about that first night, but that there was a *first* night. She made one valid point in that whole twisted mess: I was drunk and played with her feelings. I treated her like a whore."

"What?"

"I'm. Well, I *was*, nothing more than a dog after a bitch in heat. No, I still am, but not by choice, only by circumstance." He pinched the bridge of his nose between his fingers and heaved a heavy sigh. Black eyes met mine and the naked truth shone in them. "Okay, I've always been that way and you, my sweetheart, have been the only exception in my whole pathetic life. You know that don't you?"

"Yes, Henry, I know you love me."

He nodded solemnly, satisfied, because some truths just *were* regardless of what was on the surface. We both knew that one.

"I led her on, and while I'm pretty sure I didn't tie her up that first night, I am reasonably certain that I did have sex with her. It's who I am and what I would've done, whether I remember it or not."

"But…"

He took my hand in his. "The only way to have prevented what happened was to either not have gone home with her, or told her from the start I just wanted to get laid, nothing more, and let her decide if she wanted to go ahead with it."

"Instead…," he shrugged, "Well, I knew better, but I did it anyway." A grim smile twisted his mouth. "Did I ever tell you she told me "You've fucked over the wrong girl this time,"? I couldn't have said it better myself."

I could only stare at him. "And you think you deserved this? That *I* deserved this?"

"No, not at all. But had I never crossed the line in the first place, or better still, told her I wasn't interested and left her alone, she would've had no reason to continue. She wouldn't have had a hold on me—then."

He patted the space next to him and I snuggled in under his arm, thinking that for all that Henry didn't remember, there was a great instinct in him to do the right thing. That he'd failed consistently left me awed.

What he said felt true. Had he taken either course, that old pattern might never have been triggered—or the requirements might've been satisfied. In many cases, simplicity often solved knotty problems. It could've happened just that way. I thought about the bishop, his long somber face rising up in my mind's eye. Could Henry have wanted to give him a taste of his own medicine? Even if he hadn't remembered it? Using Sarah the way the bishop had used him?

"After that point, nothing could've changed it. The tape she had of us together was all she really needed, and not even you could've guessed that." He sighed again. "I've gone over how it might've been different, played the "If Only Game" a million times. It always comes out the same."

We sat in silence for a time, each absorbed in our own thoughts. Henry shook himself a little and looked around as though suddenly noticing his surroundings. "This house... is it yours?"

I smiled. "Yes."

He looked at me, as though he expected me to elaborate. I didn't. "Is it rude to ask how you've done all this at, what are you now? Twenty?"

"Almost." I waved an airy hand. "I work. I save. I pay bills. You know how it is. I've been fortunate, in that regard."

"Very much so; you deserve it, Alice," he said, giving me a little squeeze with the arm beneath me, and seemed content to let the subject drop, though I didn't know too many nineteen year olds with houses like mine.

More subconscious resistance, something I didn't think he'd overcome in one sitting, though I'd try again before this night had ended. The smile I remembered transformed his face and for a moment, all those years fell away and I was fourteen, maybe fifteen, and the whole lovely future lay before me. I never believed Sarah would win. But she hadn't. Not really. He still belonged to me, even if his life belonged to her. She'd taken it from him and he let her.

I steeled myself and said, "Henry. I needed to see you, because I think that giving into Sarah was wrong. Surviving isn't enough... or at least it isn't for me."

A mask of pain descended over his face. His curving lips, the ones that so easily formed into that charming, careless grin, clamped together and grim lines framed them. He reached around me for the wine bottle on the nightstand and refilled his glass.

I began again. "I could sell this house and buy another somewhere far away. We could leave Lincoln and put this behind us. I am nearly twenty now and if I don't press charges against you, there is no case. If we left and they couldn't find us, what would be the point?"

He swallowed hard. "Alice, you are so sweet and still so young. And I would keep you that way, if only so you never had to know the dark side." He kissed me, his lips tender against mine. "I am... not bullet proof. And neither are you. Charlie Thurmond has some not-so-nice friends. I know, because I've met them upstate in Chicago. Sarah said she would hurt you and I believe her. She keeps her promises. That's for sure."

I flashed him a startled look, but then bowed my head as I felt this chance slipping away from us, the strong echo of the past settling around me. I'd just asked him to run away from it again, and that wasn't part of the deal. He still refused me. These patterns were so ingrained, I'd unwittingly tried once more to do what I'd always done—and with the same result.

"There is one thing left that we could do, Henry."

"What's that, my love?" He cupped my breast in his large, warm hand and deliberately misunderstood my meaning.

I placed my hand over his and held him with my gaze. "Since every last one of us is implicated, the Thurmond's, your dad, my folks, Sarah, and the two of us, we should call them together in one place and put it on the table. Let them decide."

His hand froze on my breast and his eyes widened. "I could never do that."

"I would tell them the truth about us. You could be free of this."

He set his glass on the table and turned to me, placing his hands on either side of my face, stroking my temples and cheeks. I loved it when he did that. "Alice, they'd tear us apart. The laws... if it became known, it wouldn't even need to be your parents pressing the charges, the state would... and then there's..." His hands dropped to my shoulders. The sudden awareness of just how large those hands were struck me and my very bones felt fragile and small by comparison.

His voice trailed off and I knew I'd said all I could or ever would on the subject. The rest he would have to come to on his own. I could do nothing more. I knew there was only one way I could forgive Sarah, and that lay with Henry's parting himself from her, taking full responsibility for his actions, and ending it honorably—a course I strongly felt that she would accept, because she'd been waiting for it for so long. While the suffering Azriel had shown me did not move me to forgive her, I understood the toll it had taken. She would not be finished with either of us until the terms were met. We were all hopelessly tied together and Henry held the key.

"If it were just me, I'd do it, but I can't risk hurting the people I love best in the world. And you don't know how many times I've thought of… Alys. I couldn't lose you like that again. It killed me the last time."

I melted against him, sad, but still thrilling to his touch. We took our time and when he left me, the moon was on the other side of the sky…the gulf between our desires and reality just as wide, if not wider than it had been before.

On the front porch, I heard his car start up down the block and saw his headlights cut the predawn shadows. I hugged the sheet I'd wrapped around myself to my body and already felt the new life beginning there.

Branwen. I would not be alone for much longer… though I would be again after she'd grown.

There are worse things, I supposed.

Forty:
Henry 1988

How do I hate thee, Sarah? Let me count the ways...

I lowered the newspaper in my hands, nearly knocking over my coffee cup, when Sarah appeared in the kitchen. For all the clubs, civic organizations, and do-gooder memberships she held, it was almost an unheard of event to see her awake before I left in the morning.

Her face, scrubbed clean of makeup looked chalky; the pale, almost colorless eyes round and rabbit-like without the paint. In the last seven years her weight had see-sawed. Today, her normally rounded cheeks looked hollowed out and I knew she'd been starving herself again. That was her business, but I wondered why she bothered. It wasn't going to change anything between us. But then, maybe she'd take a lover and lose interest in me. There was always that hope.

Using the paper as a shield, I raised it between us and tried to continue the article I'd been reading. She poured herself a cup of coffee and sat quietly at the table across from me.

"Henry, we need to talk."

I lowered the paper an inch and peered at her over the edge. "Unless you're ready to discuss the terms of our divorce, I have nothing to say to you." I flipped the paper up and pretended not to hear the sigh.

"I want children. You are my husband and it is your duty to give them to me."

I lowered the paper, feeling the barely tethered rage blistering through my chest, lighting me up, torching my brain cells. "So divorce me. Your rights as a wife are being violated. I've even given you ten other good reasons: Kate, Tanya, Melissa, Karen, Annie, Laney, Barbara, Sasha, Vanessa, and Kara. Infidelity at its finest and undeniable grounds for divorce." *And Alice three years ago*, my mind stubbornly added, though she didn't belong on that list of party girls. I pushed away the well-thumbed memories attached to that enchanted evening, and her name, for fear my thinking it would cause it to come out of my mouth.

Sarah didn't flinch at my conquest list, but only shrugged. She already knew about all of the girls I'd notched on my gun belt. "So what? You've not crossed the line with them. Nobody knows but me. I want a kid."

"I have no duty other than to keep up appearances, so that you can carry on this stupid, shitty vendetta of yours." I snapped the paper up. "Get a fucking dog."

"Okay Henry, if that's the way you want it. Don't say you weren't warned."

I slammed my fist on the table, bouncing the cups; the paper fluttered to the floor. "Don't threaten me, Sarah. I'm sure the Children's Foundation board would love to see their president jamming a foot-long dildo into her cooze."

Sarah fixed me with a glare. "Did you hear what you just said? I am the president of the Children's Foundation and I *have no children!*"

"You should've thought about that when you railroaded me. I don't want you and I'm not giving you another hold over me."

"You are not keeping your end of the bargain."

"My end? I never bargained anything more than my name on this. Children were not part of the deal. I'd never bring a child into this fucking nightmare. What kind of a sadist are you?"

"You're the expert on child abuse, not me."

"Nice one, Sarah. That'll help your case."

She smiled. "I've thought about adopting, but that's no good—you'd never make it through the interviews and screening sessions. Besides, I don't want to raise somebody else's kid, I want my own. I've gone to the doctor. Everything checks out and I'm ready."

With a snort of derision, I said, "The world couldn't take another Thurmond hell-spawn. Forget it. It's not happening."

Her lip curled downward in a sneer. "You poor miserable man. What a victim you've made of yourself. All you had to do was give this a chance, but instead, you have to ruin it. All for a teenage tramp."

"Leave her out of this."

"No, she must've been a great lay, 'Don't hurt me Daddy!'" Sarah's eyes burned cold fire in her white face. "You're a sick fuck. Why don't you just get over it? Most men would kill to be in your position. You're wealthy, you've got a job most people only dream about, and a wife who wants to sleep with you and have your children. Why can't you do the right thing for once in your damned life?"

I rose from the chair so fast it tipped over backward and crashed on the floor, treading the same battleground we'd been over so many times without resolution, and disgusted with myself for letting her bait me this way. "The right thing? The *right* thing! End this misery for us both. That is the only right thing. You have the power to do that."

The futile sense of hope that always came at this point in these empty exchanges fluttered in my chest. I knew where it led. She'd dangle freedom, then snatch it away just for the pleasure of crushing me. I couldn't seem to stop myself from thinking that one day she'd get tired of this and just give it up. I'd be moved in and living with Alice before another sun had set. If she'd still have me, that is. No word from her in over three years. She might've met someone else. Truly, I'd been surprised she hadn't been attached in '85. A beautiful girl like her could have her pick of men.

"I can't do that," Sarah said with a small shake of her head, then raised the cup to her lips. "Besides, you said the vows. This time I'm holding you to them."

This time? I didn't think she heard herself and I wasn't sure I heard her right either. Those two words lodged in my brain and refused to be banished. "You're still young enough to find someone else and have a family. I'm a dead end, Sarah, and after seven years of this hell, it should be clear that I'm not changing my mind. You'll not find whatever it is you're looking for with me."

She eyed me over the rim of her cup. "You have no idea of what I'm looking for, or what I'm…" She set the cup down and rose from the table. "Never mind. You'll see soon enough. You really just blew your last chance, darling."

My eyes followed her as she moved to the door. "Way to go, Sarah. Way to take the high road."

She threw her hair over her shoulder and chuckled as she moved toward the stairs. Somewhere in my gut, an iron band tightened and squeezed. Fear.

***

My nose itched, but I couldn't move my hands to my scratch it. I hated dreams like this where I was paralyzed and unable to wake. My eyes opened on bright morning sunlight as the alarm clock began to ring. I reached for it, but was stopped. I tried to rise, began to struggle, but quickly found that I'd been tied flat on my back, ankles and wrists, to my bed. Jesus, my head throbbed and my tongue seemed swollen in my dry mouth—not that unusual for me in the morning.

"Oh, there you are, Sleepy Head."

I turned to the sound of her cheerful voice, blinking because she'd moved in front of the east window and all I could see was her silhouette against the glare as she leaned over to shut off the alarm. "Sarah, untie me. I've got to work this morning." I struggled against the bonds, trying to sit up, but found that the harder I struggled, the tighter the bands around my wrists and ankles became. She'd tied me with plastic, locking restraints first, then with thin nylon cords leading to the bed frame. I'd stayed up late drinking the night before and hadn't felt a thing.

"I've called you off sick. It's okay," she giggled. "I know your boss. Nasty virus going around, you know."

Understanding dawned in my pounding skull and panic whipped through my chest. My hands felt sorta numb. I had to stop fighting or I'd cut off the circulation. "I said untie me, you bitch. This is will never work. Don't you understand the mechanics of it? You're wasting your time."

Her robe fell to the floor, revealing a body I'd not seen in seven years and still had no desire to see. She flipped her hair over her shoulder, baring her heavy breast. "I don't think so."

I steeled myself for contact, her hands icy and rough on my cock. She settled herself onto the bed, stroking herself as she stroked me. "It's been a long time, Henry. Haven't you missed me?"

"Sarah, you were the worst lay I ever had. I'd rather fuck a handful of raw liver." Henry Jr., I proudly noted, played dead; a fat pink, lifeless worm in her hand. There might be a God after all.

She laughed. "Aw now, you don't mean that. I know you don't." She bent down over my groin, her hair tickling my thighs and belly. Before she could take a good grip on my penis, I bucked and squirmed, trying to ram my hip into her face and hurt her.

"Damn it, Sarah." I panted from the effort of trying to block her. I wasn't in the best shape of my life and it showed. "I don't want you. How many ways do I have to say it?"

"That really makes no difference…in the long run." She heaved a sigh and looked up with an exaggerated expression of disappointment on her face. "Well, I guess you're right. This isn't going to work."

She swung herself off me and padded over to my dresser. I fell back on the bed, gasping and trying to catch my breath, my heart knocking around my chest like a loose, erratic hammer.

"What are you doing? Untie me. *Now.*" I craned my neck, trying to see, but all I saw was the two white moons of her ass, twin dimples demarcating the flesh above them. I could hear the sound of bottles clicking together, maybe, and it did nothing for my state of mind. She could just as easily walk away and leave me here until I gave in. That is, if I *could* give in. A stiff cock is not exactly encouraged with this sort of stupidity. I felt myself go cold at the idea of laying here for days until she got what she wanted. She was sick. Very sick.

Finally, she returned with two syringes, one in each hand.

Terror caused me to struggle against the bonds, my eyes felt near to popping from my skull and my balls tried to climb up inside me. "What the hell are you doing?"

She held up one hypodermic needle. "This one is to make your disposition sweeter. I can't get anything done with you all upset." Before I could move, she rammed the needle into my thigh and pushed the plunger. The drug burned like fire beneath my skin, but I soon felt a pleasant haze spreading over my body.

She gazed down on me with an almost friendly look on her face, reminding me in that instant of her father. "Quit your whining, Henry, it's just a mild sedative, nothing too much. I want you at least able to perform."

"Sarah… Don't. Itsh not gonna work." My tongue thickened in my mouth and time seemed to slow to a crawl, each moment passing in a sweetly hellish slow-motion frame. The other syringe in her hand waited and I did my best to ignore it.

She leaned over me, smiling. "Henry, you silly boy. You've underestimated me again!" She then settled herself between my splayed and useless legs. "Now be still. I don't want this injection to go astray. That could be bad news for you. Permanent damage and all." With the ice-cold fingers of her left hand, she pinched my limp penis and stretched it upwards on my belly. In her right hand she held up the syringe.

Through the pleasant fog surrounding my brain, I felt a distant kind of horror, as though watching a movie where this was happening to someone else, somewhere else, a long ways away.

"This is phentolamine, and in a minute or two, you'll understand why your protests are just plain silly. Don't move."

I felt the needle slide in at an angle at the base of my penis, and knew that somewhere in my head, sober Henry was cringing and screaming, having a complete fucking cow, but found myself unable to react. Honestly, it didn't hurt all that much, it was the horror of the thing which had me parting company with my sanity—or would've if I could've managed it. I couldn't seem to grasp onto that terror and run with it.

Soon the head of my cock tingled maddeningly and then it got hard, very hard. A raging erection rose up at the fork of my legs, the likes of which I hadn't experienced since I'd been a teenager, back when that thing between my legs had been a brand new toy. I looked down at myself with a jaded sort of detachment. Not so new anymore. Time…it passes and takes us with it…

Sarah giggled interrupting my drug-induced epiphany. "That's better. Much, *much* better. At last, something I can work with." She gazed happily at my crotch like a scientist who'd finally grown the right kind of bacteria in her specimen dish.

"Where'd you get it?" I panted, my hips involuntarily moving, straining for contact with something, anything. My head spun a little, but I just couldn't care.

"My dad. He's not quite as young as he used to be," she said as she straddled me. "I told him you're impotent, and he wasn't surprised, either. How do you like that, you arrogant, prissy bastard? You think you're too good for me, but we both know better, don't we?"

She wrapped both hands around my cock, skinning it slowly up and down. I thought I might come in her hands. I groaned and she let go. "Oh no you don't. After all this work and drama just to have sex with my husband, I'm not going to waste a drop. I'm ovulating."

"You are a fucking psychopath," I said, as she rammed herself downward on my dick.

"And you are a fucking…spineless…wimp. Ah," she moaned and ground her ass into my groin.

"I…hate…you." My head seemed to be clearing, but my cock wanted more. My hips pistoned upwards to meet her.

"Oh god. Jesus Christ. I'm gonna come," she screamed as though surprised by it.

That did it. My balls tightened and I came until I was sure the top of my head had blown clean off. Immediately after, Sarah flipped over onto her back and placed a pillow beneath her hips.

"Get off my arm, you stupid cow. I'm losing feeling in it."

"Henry, your pillow talk could use some work," she said, dripping acid, but scooted down and off my arm, taking the pillow with her.

"Untie me."

"Hmm. No. I can inject you without worrying about your future usefulness to me for the next three days. Perfect really, because that's how long I'll be fertile."

"What? You can't keep me tied up here for three days. It's crazy and…" I felt panic rising again, filling my chest, banding it with iron until I thought I might not be able to breathe and I wanted to babble and beg. This woman was insane—of that there was little doubt, and I had been naïve in my belief that she couldn't rape me, for that is certainly what she'd done and apparently planned to do again. I thought about telling her the truth of just what a waste this had been, but, tied up as I was, she just might kill me.

"This is your doing, Henry. It always has to be the hard way with you. Never easy. So now, the path is chosen."

"I have to piss. Am I just supposed to do it right here in the bed?"

"Hold it. I'll get a urinal for you in ten minutes. The books said I have to keep my hips elevated for fifteen minutes. So shut the fuck up." She yanked the hair on my testicles and I yelped. "You are such a baby. I can't believe I married such a big sissy-boy. Are you sure you're not queer?"

I bit off my vitriolic, almost automatic request for a divorce—knowing full well that she could hurt me, badly, until she finally decided she'd had enough. She meant it. She really meant to do this. I'd surely lose my mind before then. When she came at me with the hypodermic needle again, I was grateful for the stabbing pain in my hip. High as a kite, I could sleep through most of this and then it would be over.

***

Sarah kept her promise. Three times she injected me with phentolamine and three times she rode me until I came. The rest of the time passed in a narcotic dream. During one of the brief periods of near lucidity she allowed me, Sarah explained her system, as though proud of herself. She used Valium on me the first time and then morphine in between, timing the shots for her attacks on me. She did not elaborate on where she'd got the drugs—but I supposed it wouldn't have been that hard with the kind of money she had to throw around.

On the final day, after the hip-elevating and more taunting, she injected me with morphine one final time and cut the ties on my wrists. In the seconds before the drug took me over, I rubbed them while she snipped the ones at my ankles. Weak and woozy, I felt the overwhelming urge to just put my hands around her neck and squeeze until her stupid face turned purple and then blue and finally black…

The memory of Alice's face when she'd described Henry Sayre's feelings toward Sarah Holbert played through my drifting mind. I didn't seem to be capable, at the moment, of holding onto any emotion or thought for very long. Lucky for Sarah. I closed my eyes, replaying old memories as the morphine rocked my brain on its oblivious clouds.

Distantly, I heard the door click and opened my eyes some time later to find myself alone in the room. It was dark outside, though she'd left the lamp at my bedside burning. I struggled to my feet, still dizzy, but gaining strength by the minute. My limbs were stiff, but very wobbly, and but I needed to move. Slowly I began to weave my way around the room, sometimes grabbing at furniture to steady myself.

I staggered into the hallway, looking for her. A light shone beneath her door and I headed for the stairs and for the coffeemaker. I wanted to be halfway sober when I delivered my punch line to this hideous joke. I slid down the steps, bouncing one at a time on my ass, not trusting my balance.

Still naked, I gobbled leftovers like a madman, scooping out handfuls of mashed potatoes and gravy and gnawed a hunk of roast beef, cold and congealed, without using a plate. She'd fed me enough to keep me alive, but found the result of feeding me not so pleasant when a bedpan and baby wipes were the only option. She'd surely not thought of that part, or I'd have been hooked up to an IV upon awakening for sure. I slugged down three quick cups of coffee, took a shower, shaved, and put on the first clothes I'd worn in three long days, feeling my strength slowly returning. My wrists and ankles were raw, and she'd left other marks on me as well. Typical. Bruises from the needles darkened my arms and legs, adding more resentment to the load I already carried.

I paused at her door, then opened it. She lay on her bed, propped up on pillows, reading by the light on her nightstand; a peaceful scene at complete odds with both her nature and what she'd done to me. You'd never thought it possible seeing her like this, relaxed and so occupied with such an ordinary diversion. She looked up in surprise as I stood at the threshold.

With my hand still on the knob, I said, "I had a vasectomy three years ago."

The look on her face was almost worth the price of admission. I stepped back into the hall and shut the door just as the book hit the other side and the screaming started. I hurried for the stairs, listening to breaking glass and the sound of things hitting walls and floor. My gut hurt and my hands shook as I stumbled down the steps, holding the banisters, tripping and sliding. I'd won this battle, but it was a hollow victory when the war had been lost. Maybe she would kill me and that would be that. I wouldn't have to do it myself. Contemplating the long empty years in front of me was more than I could stand.

In my car, I wove down empty streets—wondering if a DWI might be in my future. Three cups of coffee couldn't put a dent in three days of non-stop morphine injections, though it did help. I imagined the flashing red lights in my rearview mirror and saw myself telling the cop everything. What she'd just done to me, what had gone on before, and please, Mr. Policeman, just take me to jail. It's safer there. She can't get to me there. And no such luck. The meandering path I'd taken through town was deserted. Even the two gas stations that stayed open all night held empty parking lots and silence.

She was right. I was a fucking wimp. No balls. No spine. She'd broken these vital parts of me. Crushed them to dust.

I considered driving my car off the new triple overpass they had yet to finish constructing west of town. A paved exit ramp climbed the slope and ended abruptly over empty space and the old highway beneath. My mind, still shocked and a little muzzy from the drug bounced from one suicide scene to another and back again until it returned, as it always did eventually, to Alice.

Surprised, I saw the grassy median and old-fashioned streetlamps of her neighborhood, and realized I'd driven here without thinking. Three years of hoping she would appear to me, beckoning like a siren from a dark corner, welcoming me back to her warmth and goodness. That thought had kept me going. The idea that I could look up some dark night and find her there, calling me back, kept me clinging to sanity and life.

I circled the block, rolled the tire up over the curb and back down as I tried to park, and cut the engine and lights. Blindly, I staggered around the corner, winded by even this much exertion, wondering if I'd just pass out for her to find on the porch in the morning like a bag of dog shit someone forgot to set on fire. Just another nasty joke gone awry.

God, I'd never needed her so badly in my life.

Forty-One:
Alice 1988

I'd just tucked Elyse in for the night. At almost three, she was prone to clever bedtime delaying tactics. After reading her the fourth and final storybook, I finally kissed her, pulled up the blanket beneath her sweetly rounded chin and turned out the light.

"'Night, Mommy," she said, as I paused with my hand on the doorknob. "I love you."

"I love you, too, darling. Sweet dreams." I closed the door behind me, pausing for a moment, because she sometimes just jumped up and followed me right out. I'd head her off at the pass and put her back in bed before she got too wound up and ready to play.

I listened intently, hearing only the sounds of an old house ticking and creaking, settling in for the night, and not the thump of my tiny daughter's feet hitting the floor. I smiled and headed to the kitchen for a glass of wine. As I made the turn into the hallway, I caught movement through the front windows and adrenaline shot through my system. A rapid, low knock sounded on the door and I hurried toward it. Without undoing the chain, I opened it a crack. "Who is it?"

"Alice, it's Henry. Can I please come in?"

My hand shook as I undid the chain and stepped back. He pushed open the door.

"Alice, I'm sorry to barge in on you like this..." He looked around. "Are you alone?"

I blinked. "Yes. Please come in and close the door." I shot a glance toward the end of the hall and prayed Elyse would go to sleep quickly. I didn't know if I could fake my way through that. I didn't want to explain. Didn't want a scene or...

He grabbed me. "Shit. I had to see you. Alice, I..." He hesitated, his black eyes shadowed beneath and the strained lines on his face made him nearly a stranger. The intervening years had not been kind to him. "Are you sure it's okay that I'm here? I know I shouldn't be here. I'm sorry. So sorry. But I just had to come."

"No, Henry. It's fine. I'm just… surprised. That's all." My heart fluttered in my chest, the old response to him still making itself known—that and the fear that Elyse might open her door at any moment and he would see her. He couldn't leave Sarah just because he had a child with me. He couldn't use that as a reason; he had to do it for himself alone. Obligation would not settle it. Ever. He had just enough of that old-fashioned chivalry in him that might cause him to act, when nothing else had. No. I couldn't let him see her. She looked just like him. There would be no mistaking whose seed had started her precious life.

Of all the things I'd done, thinking they were for myself, only to find that they were for him, I knew without a doubt that Elyse had been the exception. She was mine. I'd done that for myself. Me. Me alone. A fierce love for my baby nearly leveled me with its power. I shook myself and focused on him. "Are you all right?"

His face, miserable in the dim light told the truth before he'd opened his mouth. "No, I'm not. I can't. I don't. Ah, shit." He pinched the bridge of his nose and heartbreaking familiarity of that movement took me back. He was close to a breakdown.

"Come with me." I took his hand and pulled him down the hall in the opposite direction to my room. I didn't know what else to do with him. I closed the door and then held my arms open as I sat down on the bed. He fell to his knees between my legs and grabbed onto my waist for dear life. His tears began and I held him as he brokenly told me what Sarah had done. The Bishop had shown himself once more.

His warm scent enveloped me and all the feelings I'd put away, tried to forget, came flooding back, his pain knifing through me as though it were my own. I stroked his hair as he talked and cried, its dark, waving lengths like silk between my fingers. There were gray strands threaded now amongst the black, and it hurt my heart to see them. Our lives were passing us by. A death crawl most of the time, but then his graying hair reminded me that time here on earth was fleeting, too. My love for him was nearly as strong as my love for Elyse. Almost. And it was being tested right this minute. I prayed to the Goddess for the strength to do what I must.

I'd never once considered how a man might feel to be raped by a woman—never really thought it possible except at the hands of another man, but there it was. I doubted that he would've ever been able to tell this to anyone but me, so I was glad that at least I could be there for him. Perhaps now, he might be able to see his only course out of this nightmare. I was sorry for him, more than I could say, but then, I also knew very well that it would only get worse until he did what he needed to do to release us both from this enforced captivity. That is the way it worked. Had always worked. He would not be spared—nor would I. The years had changed me, too, it seemed.

Soon his pain turned to anger and he paced back and forth in front of me, cursing in a low voice and making what I hoped were empty threats against Sarah—though a part of me would've enjoyed watching it, had he meant any of them. My head came up at the word 'vasectomy,' and I realized just how close I'd cut it with Elyse. He'd said the last time that Sarah had pressured him about children and he'd taken measures to prevent that. He'd forgotten Branwen. Maybe it was for the best that he had.

Abruptly, he stopped, his eyes wild and hunted, locked onto mine as though seeing me for the first time. I hadn't interrupted him or commented, but let him rant until he had released the poison from his system. "I shouldn't be here. I shouldn't be dumping this on you. It's been three years. You have a life now and I can't just come barging into it because Sarah abused me. I'll leave now. I have no right to be here."

"No, but you could." I looked up at him, seeing the debauchery on his handsome face and thinking that he drank too much, too often and he'd be old before his time, or dead. His waist had thickened a little and in the lamplight, I could see pouches beneath his eyes, ones that before long would not go away with a good night's sleep. "Have the right to be here, I mean. I told you before what we could do..."

"Alice, did you hear any of what I just said? She's lost her fucking mind. She's dangerous."

A slow-burning anger rose up in me, something that had been simmering for a very long time, all those years I'd waited for him. Then the ones after, when I'd put him behind me. Seven of them all together and a good piece of the eighth already started. They lined up behind me like a granite wall, undeniable and solid.

"So just lay down, Henry. Lay down like the whipped dog you are and wallow in it."

His eyes flew wide and his face froze.

"That's right. You heard me. I offered you a way out. The chessboard is still set and all the men on the table, waiting for the next move. No one has died. Everyone is in place, waiting... waiting for *you* to make a *damned* move!"

He blinked rapidly, his mouth moved, but nothing came out.

"But no, torture is preferable to standing up to her. I get it. It took me years to understand it, but finally I do. Get out. Leave and don't darken my door again until you're ready to stay for good. Until you're ready to fight for what is right and good. *Do* the right thing. Own it, Henry!"

His eyes widened at that and I thought he might see it. I'd struck a nerve and the moment dragged on for an eternity as I waited.

He shook his head, and another protest formed on his lips.

I cut him off and pointed at the door. "The sight of you makes me sick. Get out. Now."

An impassive mask slipped over his face and without another word, he turned and left the room, like a ghost or a dream I'd had, the memory of which might never return or only come to me hazily and half-remembered.

His footsteps sounded in the hallway and faintly, I heard the soft click as he closed the door.

I let him go, knowing that unless he faced this now, in this lifetime, he'd be doomed to meet Sarah again, in like circumstances.

What I sincerely hoped was that I wouldn't be there with him. Making the break. Making it clear that I no longer wished to a part of this. Maybe that would finish it once and for all. The forgiveness part remained like a shadow upon my heart. How to forgive the unforgiveable?

Well, at nearly twenty-three, I supposed I had a few years to work that one out.

***

Three days later I opened my mailbox and found a small, plain-paper wrapped box. I knew what it held before I opened it. The iron crescent moon lay swaddled in cotton, its dull, beaten surface seeming to suck in the sunlight rather than reflect it. I pressed it to my lips, both relieved and dismayed to see it. Never had it been lost or in another's keeping for this long. He'd returned it to me and that act seemed so final—more so, even than the sound of the door closing when I'd told him to leave.

I turned with it in my hand, laying the box on the table inside the front door, not really surprised to find my eyes wet. Elyse looked up at me solemnly. She'd followed me through the foyer.

"Why are you crying, Alys?" Often she called me that instead of Mommy, understandable, because she'd known me far longer by that name, than this most recent title. She pronounced Alys with a perfect Welsh inflection. At three, the memories of who we'd been were much closer than who we'd become. This I understood all too well.

I smiled and held out the pendant on its blue satin cord. "Look, Elyse. Do you remember this?"

My smile broadened as I took in the look of pure delight on her sweet face and the little hand that stretched out to receive the iron Goddess token. I scooped her up and took her to my bedroom, then pulled the little stone mother figure from its place in my jewelry box. I sat down on the bed, her warm, solid weight on my lap, and my arms around her.

Elyse faced me, her bottom on my knees and her legs loose and trustingly splayed on either side of my hips. I watched her face as she stared, wide-eyed at the pendant in her right hand and the little statue in her left.

Finally, she nodded her curly dark head as though she'd decided something important. She held up the crescent moon. "Alys, this is yours."

"Yes, sweetie, that's right." She placed a little kiss on it, hugged it tight to her chest for the briefest second, and I bent down so she could place the cord around my neck.

"And this is *mine*!"

"Right again, love. Right again."

She rubbed the statuette against her pink cheek with a look of radiant happiness. I didn't bother to tell her not to lose it. She wouldn't.

Forty-Two:
Henry 1988

The sun was coming up when I pulled into the drive. Alice's words rang through my sodden brain, irremovable and on auto-play, as I twisted the cap off of a fresh fifth of Jack Daniels and stared dully at the overblown, ultra-modern house Charles Thurmond's money had built. *The sight of you makes me sick. Get out. Now.* Well, that made two of us, then. I couldn't blame her there. Not one bit.

Defeated, I lifted the bottle and saluted the house. "I know when I'm licked. I know when I'm mother-*fuckin'* licked. Well, lick this, bitch." I paused; shocked that I might be misunderstood, though I was alone in the car. "Not you, Alice. Her." I pointed to the house and giggled stupidly, gulping the whiskey, much of it running out the sides of my mouth and onto my shirt. I brushed at it. "Ooh, mommy won't like that much."

I jammed the whiskey bottle in my back pocket, then opened the door and fell out onto the drive, surprised when I woke up a little later half in and half out of the car. I dragged myself to my feet and staggered through the house's rear entrance. Sarah sat at the kitchen table.

"Sarah!" I slammed the door and she jumped. "So good t' see you! So nice t' be here. Hot damn. It's a bee-yoo-tee-ful day!" I felt the bottle in my back pocket and reached for it. I sat it on the table in front of me. The morning sun struck the whiskey and turned it to amber fire. Pretty. I uncapped it and took a swig. "How does it feel to taste defeat, shweetheart?" I pulled out a chair. It scraped loudly against the tiles. I fell into it.

Sarah stared out the patio doors and didn't look at me. "How does it feel? Huh? To have it all, right in the palm of your hand and bam!" I drove my fist into the table. "Gone. Gone like the wind." I laughed like a loon at that. "But you're not Scarlett O'Hara are you? You're more like Attila the Fucking Hun, aren't you baby?"

Finally she turned, her eyes blue ice chips in her doughy face. "Go to bed, Henry. You're drunk."

I fell back in the chair, aghast. "No, really? *Me?*"

She twisted in her seat and rose, obviously intending to leave.

"Where ya goin'? Don't you have more fun and games ready for me? Don't you want to tie me to the bed and fuck me?" I swayed as I stood and the chair crashed to the floor. I glanced at it. Maybe that chair was magnetized to the damned tiles. It always seemed to end up there. The red ink pen I'd used the year I taught high school came to mind the way random things often did when the only place I could really live was the past.

Sarah swished away, her silk kimono whispering as she exited the room.

I ricocheted off the doorframe, but caught her at the foot of the stairs. "Oh, I get it. It's no s'much fun when I'm not fightin' it. And oh yeah, almost forgot, I'm firing blanks now and *that*," I jabbed a finger at her, "doesn't fit your scam, Yosemite Sam!" I giggled at my rhyme and at the tiny, mean-tempered cartoon character that danced through my head. She'd taken a couple of steps away from me, a moue of disgust twisting her mouth.

"Well, here I am in all my glory. You win, *bitch*."

She fixed me with a scathing look and hurried up the stairs. I crawled on my hands and knees, determined not to pass out until I made it to the top. Careening wall to wall in the corridor, I aimed myself for her bedroom door and fell against it.

"Did you hear me, you ball-breaking cunt?" I slammed the door open against the wall and then wobbled my way to the bed. "I said, you *win*."

I fell onto her mattress and that was the last thing I knew.

Forty-Three:
Alice 2033

I opened my eyes upon the dawning of a mid-autumn day promising brilliance. The clouds had gone and the birds sang and chirped madly outside my windows. They didn't seem to care that winter was on its way, living only in the glory of the moment, which was lovely by any reckoning. Dew glistened on the grass and the fire bush I'd planted the first year I lived here blazed crimson glory on the border of my patio's flagstones.

My eyes drank in the colors, and I breathed deeply of the fresh breeze coming through the windows, taking note through the sliding glass doors that the squirrels were under no such illusion as the birds. They were busy picking up acorns, their little furry cheeks stuffed full as they ran madly back and forth beneath the rusty-leafed oak in the center of the yard. I'd long ago made my peace with oak trees and never thought of ropes or kicking feet when I looked upon it. This one I loved and had often, back when I was able, stretched myself beneath its sheltering branches, listening to the wind play its song through its rustling canopy. Beautiful.

I fervently hoped I would be well enough to sit in the chair outside today. That was sad. I remembered the bounding energy of my youth and middle age—its vibrant fountain flowing through my body even into my elder years, only just seeming to dry up in the last six months. It had gone slowly though, 'til it was just a trickle beneath the illness and exhaustion.

It pissed me off that all I could hope for now was enough energy to drag my damned carcass to a damned chair outside my own damned doors.

If I couldn't summon the happy buoyancy, then anger would do the job just as well, I guessed.

My stomach growled and the pain shot through my body as if on cue.

Well, at least I was hungry—that was a good sign. I shoved myself upright and shuffled to the kitchen for some toast, juice, and another damned pill. My sleep had not been restful—it never was when I took the pills. Dreams and endless traveling seemed to be the result of those high-powered tablets, banishing the pain as well as all my psychic defenses. They opened doors and lowered gates that I already knew stood ajar in my brain and soul, kicking me right on over the thresholds of the past, whether I willed it or no. I could no longer tell what I willed in that department and what belonged in the dominion of the pain meds. I supposed it didn't really matter. I was going on the trip anyway.

I knew without doubt that I would eat less than I wanted or needed, take a pill, maybe two, and head back for my bed. Time ran away from me. I couldn't help that. Maybe after I rested some more I'd feel better? Who knew?

As I limped slowly down the hallway to the kitchen with my hand trailing the plaster wall for support, I thought about the places I'd traveled with Azriel these last couple of days. Places that were mine and places that belonged only to Henry, but the pieces, like a jigsaw puzzle, interlocked and gave me some ownership over his stuff, too. That was all right. I'd never hesitated much to get in Henry's business. It was my *job*. I couldn't help but smile at that thought. Henry brought me joy, making me smile whether I liked it or not. I loved him, dammit.

You win, he'd said to Sarah. Henry's drunken voice echoed through my head. More significant than his words was the bed into which he fell. The symbolism of that gesture was dramatic and stark. Defeat at its lowest nadir. The ultimate surrender. My poor, poor Henry. But maybe it had been enough. I shook my head.

I thought long about that and wondered if my thinking wasn't just more of the wishful kind. He'd stayed with her for the next unimaginable forty years and how he survived that, I'd never know. But he did and that thought made my heart glad—well not exactly *glad*, but it did increase my hope that he might've released himself from her raptor-claw grip on him.

He'd met her requirement, though it had not been all she'd wanted, had it been enough? Could it have been?

His recent deathbed scene replayed in my mind. I'd forgiven him. I loved him. How could I not have forgiven him? It seemed preordained that I would. The knowledge of what I'd likely set myself up for in the next life, though I'd been determined not to do it, loomed before me and depressed what little good feeling I'd gained from the thought of Henry escaping Sarah.

Sarah. A sickness more powerful than the one currently eating me from the inside out sucked me downward into a black viscous, swamp and for a fleeting second, the connection between my illness and the hatred I felt for Sarah lit up my mind and soul and I saw that the two were intertwined like lovers. Yes, that was right. As usual, I'd done this to myself. Azriel had told me, warned me a long time ago. I'd refused his wisdom.

Oh well, I was old. Something had to kill me sooner or later. It wasn't all *that* bad. I barked out an abrupt laugh, suddenly reminded of my mom, who used to say such things when the very world threatened collapse over her head. Holy shit, I sounded just like her. This was *bad*. Who was I kidding? I felt like shit and it just grew worse with every passing day.

Despite my sudden epiphany, I knew I probably could not look upon Sarah and tell her I forgave her with any kind of sincerity. In that part, Henry had failed me and I couldn't do it without him. Azriel would be disappointed, but he'd get over it and help me through what would follow.

I remembered the look on Henry's face when I'd told him to get out. Stricken, hopeless, and completely shocked. I wondered if I'd done the right thing. Always second-guessing myself.

The things I'd forced myself to do for the sake of that love had nearly killed me. Turning him away had nearly vaporized me into a million particles of pure pain. Elyse had been the only thing that had kept me together afterwards. Branwen, even in a child's form had soothed me, her wisdom shining forth in simple childish words, but unflagging and dedicated to the two of us.

I stared at the bottle of pills in my hand and the toaster shot up two pieces of lightly toasted bread into the air with an exuberance that was surely a mechanical failure—but for some reason reminded me of sex. The toast hit the bottom of the cabinet and fell to the countertop. I glanced around, Henry on my mind, and wondered if he'd done it. Two pills, I decided. Just two.

I washed them down with o.j. and waited for the relief I hoped they'd bring.

Forty-Four:
Henry 2033

I turned away from the scene of my defeat.

"You surrendered," Azriel said, and shook his head.

"Alice told me point blank what to do and… I couldn't do it. Why?" I watched Sarah in the corner of the room watching Drunk Henry on her bed, her face unreadable. After a long while, she came to him, removed his shoes and belt, then pulled the blanket up over him, tucking it gently around his neck and shoulders. She touched a lock of his hair, bent down and whispered, "You should've done the right thing, Henry. It didn't have to be this way." She sighed and made her way to her side of the bed and lay down next to him. "I'm going to see it through this time, one way or the other."

I glanced at Azriel, his expression impassive and unreadable. "It was all so confusing, Azriel. Did she remember? Did she know?"

"Frightening, too, I would imagine," he said, thoughtfully. "I don't think so. She's not in my keeping, but I think she is like most humans. The truth comes out of her mouth unwittingly and oftentimes without understanding." He looked down on me with smiling blue eyes. "I think you are ready for the rest, Henry."

I looked at him in surprise. "There's more?"

He chuckled. "There always is. You would not see, refused to examine the pattern, when last we were together—come to think of it, you stubbornly refused to accept the entire truth the time before that, too." Azriel sighed. "You are an old soul, a veteran of the earth plane, and have earned a certain amount of control over your comings and goings. Your last incarnation, you rushed to the flesh to teach Alice a lesson. Perhaps had you allowed yourself to see, given yourself time to understand…" He shook his head, his long blond hair floating on invisible currents.

"It matters not because you will learn what you must and as I have said repeatedly, it is all the same to me, for I shall be here to guide you always, but Henry, this has become tiresome. You must face this and move on. You are strong enough to overcome it. There is nothing to fear. Surely you can see that now?"

I hung my head, knowing he was right, knowing pretty much what the point of Sarah's place in my life had been. I'd broken my vows, serious ones, and in the process, given Alice the shaft as well. I'd said it myself, I'd always loved her, but probably not the way she deserved. We hadn't always done this, but I couldn't quite grasp where it had all gone wrong. "Show me. I'm tired, too. I've gotta know the truth if I'm going to fix this mess."

Azriel beamed. "I am so glad you see it my way. It is *long* overdue."

"Smartass," I said with a smile, and liked him even better than I already did. Angels should have a sense of humor. He needed it with an idiot like me for a student.

"Next stop: the early 15th Century, my friend. They had just completed the new nave at Canterbury Cathedral. 1410, I believe."

"If you say so."

"I do." He held out his hand and I took it.

Sixteen years old, I knelt at the altar in that opulent, newly built nave at Canterbury, a small figure beneath the soaring Romanesque columns and vaulted arches. My benefactor, Bishop Stephanus de Bracy, stood before me, resplendent in his stole and chasuble, and placed his hands on my head, calling down the power of Jesus Christ to bless me in my new life as His priest. I raised my eyes to his when he finished and he smiled upon me with kindness and love. I smiled back.

He'd been my mentor and friend through the dark days when I'd come to him at twelve, a resentful and rebellious fourth son of a minor nobleman, with no other prospects but the clergy. He'd taken me under his protective wing, and I trusted him.

Though I had yet to feel a calling for this vocation, he had convinced me that it would come, in time. I believed him. His steadying hand on my shoulder and his warm, fatherly affection went a long way towards soothing my troubled soul.

Aleysia's sweet face in my mind tormented me, for I'd vowed celibacy and found I couldn't manage it—not with her around. She'd been my secret for nearly all of the past year before my ordination, and the one sin I would allow myself. After all I'd given up for my father's station in life, I could justify that one thing. That particular sin, I would confess and receive absolution for as many times as necessary without jeopardizing my immortal soul. I wanted to make my father and Stephanus proud of me and I would make the best of this vocation. Someday, maybe a cardinal's hat would be perched on my head. Maybe. I would try. Stephanus had said it could happen. He seemed to have my future all planned out for me.

I hadn't thought much past that point with Aleysia, only to the time and place of our next tryst, really, but had committed myself to the Church.

My cock did the thinking for me, I realized as I watched the scene unfold. I guess things really hadn't changed all that much in that department. I cut myself a break though, because it was Alice. She was the one person I'd never willingly deny. But I felt myself growing upset about it. That couldn't seem to be helped.

Azriel's golden presence calmed me, reminding me that I was an observer here and this was long past. He tugged my hand and we stood in the bishop's luxuriant rooms, not at Canterbury, but at his private estates on the Thames at Abingdon. We celebrated my ordination and the wine flowed freely. Refreshing, water-scented breezes came through the open porticos and dispelled the oppressive heat which had held the cities in its grasp all the long summer.

After a feast fit for the monarchy, though only the two of us had eaten at his long, over-laden table, Stephanus dismissed his servants for the evening and we sat before a cheering blaze in his private sitting rooms. The evening had turned cool and the fire felt good against my shins through the thin robe I wore. My head reeled and his image sometimes doubled, my mouth babbled, disconnected from my brain by the wine.

With a willful detachment from this undeniable version of myself, I looked to Azriel as Henry Sanfort drunkenly held forth to the bishop on Aleysia's many charms, her round breasts, and sweet bottom. His gestures were grandiose and his voice loud and bawdy. The bishop's eyes narrowed as Henry spilled his guts in the chair across from him, sloshing wine over the rim of his glass as he elaborated. The bishop listened intently, the knuckles of the hand gripping his wineglass turning white, his lips thinned to a tight gash in his face. Henry didn't notice, but continued on, giving intimate details of what they'd done together, his voice turning rapturous and wistful.

The heavenly hand gripped in mine held me tighter as I tensed, knowing suddenly what would follow. "Do not turn away, Henry. This is important."

The bishop stood, now simply clad in a plain dark robe, as was Henry Sanfort. An erection tented the bishop's gown, but Henry didn't notice. His head bobbed on his chest and Stephanus barely caught the wineglass as it slid from his fingers. He hoisted the drunken boy onto his shoulder and carried him through the heavy door through which only he possessed a key, which he turned in the lock. The tumblers clicked with a satisfying sound and Stephanus smiled.

I watched, sickened as Stephanus raped Henry Sanfort. I watched as Sarah took from me all that I was unable and unwilling to give her. The Bishop's thoughts, the twisted sickness that lived within him, were audible, as though no barriers stood between this timeless place and the one he occupied.

I didn't need to hear Henry's thoughts, his sodden, muffled screams and my own memories were almost more than I could handle.

Azriel said quietly, "Detachment, Henry. It is yours if you choose it. Feel what you must, but do not allow yourself to become him again."

I glanced over to the angel, whose solemn, vivid blues eyes met mine. I nodded. Having come this far, I would not turn from it. I survived Sarah's similar treatment. I could look at this. My future depended upon understanding.

"Shh, my darling. Shh! 'tis the sacrament of the brotherhood I, ah sweet God in Heaven! bestow upon you, uh," Stephanus grunted as Henry struggled beneath him, impaled like an insect on a hatpin.

"Marvelous, my boy! How quickly you learn." He grasped the slim hips and held him fast.

Henry bucked again, trying to scramble away, but Stephanus held him easily. Drunken boys never managed to thwart him. While Henry guzzled his wine, he had temperately sipped his throughout the long evening, letting the alcohol sharpen and hone his lust. Though no longer young, he was but five and thirty, and strong. He used that immense strength now, levering himself deeper into the writhing body beneath him.

It was wrong, oh God, how it was wrong and he'd be on his knees for hours over this—but it was an old sin, an aged stain on his conscience with which he'd lived a very long time. He'd risen through the ranks of priesthood like a shooting star, and would not stop until he wore the Archbishop's hat. This tender stripling under him, with his lineage and connections, just might make Cardinal with the right strings pulled—and he, Stephanus, knew which ones to pluck. He'd played those strings like a heavenly harp with all the right notes in his grasping hands.

"You are mine. You belong to God now and I will drive that filthy, devil-worshipping harlot from your mind. You must keep your vows."

He came with a muffled scream. Groaning, he gently and unwillingly pulled himself away. The boy was crying and needed comfort. He had that for him, more than enough. The love he felt for this lad was boundless. Waiting for him to grow up had been a torment he'd barely withstood. Long nights he'd spent, taking this neophyte or that one to his bed, pretending they all were sweet Henry, and never coming close to achieving the dream. The reality had been more beautiful than even he could've imagined.

Like a mother with a fractious infant, he turned the boy over and held him as he blubbered. Then, he lifted Henry's chin until the bloodshot, wine-glazed black eyes looked into his own.

"Henry, you have received a blessing which will protect you all of the days of your life, but you must quell your rebellious heart. Our Lord forgiveth, but he is a vengeful God who will send you straight to Hell if you refuse Him." Stephanus infused this last sentence with an unmistakable menace. He hoped Henry was not too drunk to comprehend the threat.

A hitching sob and more despairing tears were his answer.

Raped. The word echoed through my mind and all the pieces came together. This person had killed, tortured and plundered my soul as well as my body. Sarah had, too. How long would I suffer? How many more lifetimes before I could break myself from it?

Azriel showed me the months that followed in brief but merciless clips, his hand a steady, warm grip, leading me ever onward through the repeated assaults from the bishop, Henry's affair with Aleysia, her pregnancy and his attempts to hide it from Stephanus, all the way to Aleysia, tied to the stake, innocent and ignorant of his sins. Dying for him. Dying because she loved him and he couldn't break himself free.

When the brands sealed Henry Sanfort's eyes, he was grateful. When he died from his wounds, starvation, and thirst three days later, his gratitude knew no bounds. He didn't want to see anything ever again.

And that's where the trouble started. All of it. No wonder I'd run from it, refused to look at it. Sickened to the depths of my soul, I now understood, or thought I did. I couldn't begin to guess how to fix what had already been done.

I floated with Azriel in a warm, womblike void, comforting and dark. The angel's golden nimbus, subdued and protective, formed a barrier around the two of us. "How could I have withstood him, Azriel? He was powerful. He controlled me and everyone around him."

"Even a bishop answers to an archbishop and what Stephanus did to you and the other youngsters under his charge was against the laws of the Church—several of them, actually."

He seemed to drift for a moment, as though thinking of just how many laws rape might violate, but then turned to me, his voice brisk. "Your father was cousin to the king. Far enough down the succession to not be a threat but close enough that he still had influence. They were childhood companions as well as related by blood. Had you but reminded the Bishop of your own power and ordered him to desist..."

I shook my head. "No, Stephanus knew about Aleysia. Look what he did to her."

With a chuckle, Azriel said, "And do you suppose priests with mistresses were all that uncommon during those times? The archbishop himself kept an entire family—a mistress and six children—under the king's nose not a mile from London. No, it was not the affair that drove the bishop to murder and maim; it was jealousy.

"Moreover, the key to your release was your father. You had but to tell him and let him use his influence. Defrocking and excommunication may have been the least of his worries, for your father may well have killed him. But, alas! You bowed before him and both you and Alice paid the price for it. You broke your vows with her, true, but you had a choice. You could have been released from those vows, and well you knew it, for you had seen it happen with your own eyes."

"Why, Azriel? Why did this happen?"

Azriel smiled. "I know not why—only that humankind seems destined to inflict torment upon itself. Suffering has purpose, and without it, your kind cannot grow.

"So I do not know why this particular soul or why you required this particular teaching, I only know that it continues to happen because you have not yet confronted this person whom you have allowed to imprison you. Alice has faced violent, untimely physical death twice because of it. You yourself have suffered and ended your mortal existences prematurely. The one that has followed you will continue on her path until she is shown there are consequences to her cruelty. Running from her does not work. Allowing her to enslave you does not work. What is left, little one?"

"I have to do this again, don't I? I'll have to face her and I won't remember." A note of desperation came to my voice and I searched the angel's face, hoping for a sign that I might be wrong. It was too much to hope for and I knew it.

"Much can be accomplished in Spirit, Henry. Alice is a powerful priestess on the earth plane, and though she put that part of herself aside, *she* has not forgotten." Azriel looked past me, his eyes fastening upon something I could not see. He smiled, his sapphire eyes blazing in his ethereal face, and looked almost… happy. I could not fathom the ways of heavenly beings. Things seemed pretty bleak from where I stood.

"I didn't listen to her. I didn't let you help me, either. I… just couldn't deal with it." Like a child, I lay my head on his shoulder; the Monday morning quarterbacking had taken its toll. "I'm so tired, Az."

"I know Henry, I know. Rest for a bit and let your spirit heal. The best is yet to come."

Somehow, I doubted that, but I believed in Azriel. He'd never led me wrong, though I'd strayed aplenty under his watchful eyes. Something Alice once said came to me, "Free will and all that jazz." Free will had landed us both in trouble more than once. A double-edged sword, it would seem. But then, where would be the challenge if we never had to make a decision, were never allowed to screw up? Where would the pay off be in that? I shook my head. There surely had to be a better way, but damned if I could think of one.

I found myself back in bed with Alice, who still lay sleeping. I sighed. My sweet girl. I would do anything for her, though I didn't know what *could* be done now.

Gratefully, I settled into her warmth beneath the covers, molding myself to her. For the first time, I sensed the disease spreading through her body, the dark prince who would at long last release her to me. Her thinness and frailty took on new meaning. For some reason, I didn't feel the happiness I thought that long awaited reunion would bring. It bothered me in a way that Sarah's murky, ugly-hued aura had bothered me and I wondered if the two were somehow related.

I rose up, peering through the blankets, ignoring their fluffy substance, looking for her essence and breathed a little sigh of relief. Alice's colors were still that lovely shade of silver-white, though I could see just a tiny thin thread of black twisting through it, like an eel swimming below shallow, sunlit water. Not too bad, but bad enough.

I think I might've been partly responsible for that black ribbon weaving itself through the silver. Not all, but yes, I shared ownership of it just as surely as I owned my own soul.

Weariness descended me back to the bed and I tucked myself around her, giving her what healing I thought I might. She'd done it for me so many times, maybe I could help her somehow.

I slept.

Azriel smiled. I saw it through my eyelids.

Forty-Five:
Alice 2033

"*Much can be accomplished in Spirit, Henry. Alice is a powerful priestess on the earth plane, and though she put that part of herself aside,* she *has not forgotten.*" Azriel smiled at me as I stood behind Henry, his benevolent gaze loaded with meaning.

I understood my next task. Elation surged through my soul.

Henry had looked upon his dragon. I'd witnessed it myself. He'd done it from the safety of Azriel's embrace. I laughed and clapped my hands, so excited that I could barely contain myself. Almost free!

My nightgown and bathrobe disappeared and I stood clad only in my blue cloak, bathed in the silver radiance of an October moon. The iron crescent hung between my bared breasts, glinting dully beneath the luminous sky. I raised my arms to my Goddess's lunar face and laughed. This would be fun.

Unsurprised, I watched as the icon which had fascinated me since childhood, materialized. The old corn crib rode its earthen wave, the moonlight only enhancing the impression of a ship upon a tossing sea.

Entranced, I stood on the blacktop and drank in the night's beauty, dwelling for a moment as I usually did, on the utterly mind-bending fact of the old building's continued existence. The wind rustled through the trees and tall prairie grass swayed. About a half a mile away, Salt Creek murmured its purling song as it rushed along its growth entangled banks. I could hear it clearly, the breeze carrying the sound to where I stood. I considered making my way to it, for I needed water to scry, even on this plane, but knew the trees would block the moon. Besides, a rushing stream is too intent on its business to be still enough for that.

In the distance, clarified beneath the crystalline moonlight, I spied the mirrored surface of a gravel pit, now a small lake. Perfect.

I made my way toward it, breathing in the scent of the damp grass as it bent beneath my feet. The liquid notes of a night bird's song echoed from the trees and rose above the crickets' chirping concerto. As I drew nearer, bullfrogs added their basso tones to the symphony.

At last I stood at the pool's bank, nearly overwhelmed by the beauty of the moon upon the water. Ground mist had just begun to curl around the borders. I removed and then knelt upon my cloak as I gazed into the watery mirror, calling to the soul I must summon. The rippling reflection of the moon appeared as a light-driven streak across the nearly smooth surface.

Sarah's mental illness made this possible. I doubted I could have called to her, had she been in control of herself—well, I could've called all I wanted, but an answer would likely not have been forthcoming. A summoning usually only worked if the one being summoned resided in Spirit, or had characteristics like mine. As it was, she stood with one foot in this plane and the other in the worldly one. I would not go to her, oh no, never that. The balance of power had shifted. She would appear to me, on my terms, or not at all. It didn't matter much, I supposed, for all would come right in the end. I only asked for a fair fight. Nothing more.

Stephanus De Bracy. Sarah Holbert. Sarah Thurmond. I held all of them in my mind, all of the forms in which I'd known this soul and a latent shudder of revulsion passed through my body. I shivered again, resisting the urge to put on the cloak, and reminded myself that they could not hurt me now.

"Sarah, I summon thee. Come here to me now," I said, and felt the very air ripple all around me.

With my eyes closed, I sought the Way and opened the Paths for the command I had just issued. They appeared in my mind, shimmering with an inviting shade of cerulean blue. I would not walk them this night, but paid homage to the four elements of the earth and received their blessing. I opened my eyes and rose to my feet. The Paths lay all around me, a glimmering spider web of Life stretching in every direction, as far as the eye could see. I knew they had no end. Time is an illusion—but then again, so were these lovely Paths. A creature of flesh, a human being, I could only put any one thing in a frame I could visualize or comprehend. For Branwen, the Paths had always appeared a bright shade of lemon yellow. The natural world and the illusions we create…

Briskly, I shook away the thought; the intricacies of the astral plane could keep one occupied for an eternity. I should not be woolgathering at a time like this, and returned myself to the image of Sarah the Puritan girl. She seemed the easiest to recall, understandable, because she was the one with whom I'd had the most personal interaction. Camden had been a small, insulated, and social village, where all were dependent upon others. We couldn't have avoided each other had we tried. Her image appeared in the pool next to the rippling image of the moon.

Gradually, one of the trails glowed brighter than the rest, the others seeming to dim as another soul traversed the grid. Involuntarily, I took a step back as Stephanus De Bracy stepped from the mist. I'd expected one of the Sarahs, not… Well, why not him? Of the three, he was the most fearsome and no doubt chosen for that reason. Bastard.

Our eyes locked and I gathered power and energy around me like a shield. He towered over me by a foot or more and had we been on the physical plane, could've broken me like a twig between his hands—or worse. I glanced at the cloak on the ground at my feet but did not reach for it. I am as I am. Nothing more, nothing less. Screw him. He couldn't hurt me here. I stepped forward and stood my ground. "You have much to answer for, priest."

He smirked. "Was the fire and the rope not enough to teach you, witch?" His eyes traveled the length of my nude body and revulsion twisted his face. "You stand there as a whore with a prospective customer."

Before I could answer him, he turned on his heel and made for the Path on which he'd come. The way was blocked and he turned back to me. "What is the meaning of this? What evil sorcery have you done?"

"You will listen to me or you will not be free to leave. I have summoned you for a purpose."

"How dare you?" His gaze swept along the surface of the lake. "We never put you to the water test. Perhaps the time is nigh."

I hadn't come here to trade insults, though he sorely provoked me. "I summoned you to give you fair warning, de Bracy. Soon, Henry and I shall meet you on a field of my choosing. The time has come."

"And if I refuse?"

I'd expected this and also expected to stand here until hell froze over, or until he gave his consent to cooperate with me—whichever came first. But then, the air shimmered and a golden light split the shadows. I sensed Azriel standing behind me. Stephanus's eyes widened and I knew what he saw right then.

I gave him a sweet smile. "You have no choice," I said, breezily. "I shall see you shortly. Don't be late."

He tore his eyes from the heavenly entity behind me and bowed his head in acquiescence. "Be it so, then." Stole and chasuble belled out around him as he turned and stepped upon the Path. The mist swallowed him and he was gone.

The golden circle of light remained. I turned and smiled up into Azriel's beautiful face. "I am ready, old friend."

His blue eyes glinted with amusement. "Be it so, then."

I giggled.

Forty-Six:
Henry 2033

I dreamed or maybe I traveled. I don't know.

Alice stared at me through the dim shadows of her bedroom. Her face, still heartbreakingly young, had set itself in stubborn lines. She sat on her bed and I stood near the door. Her voice echoed and bounced off the Victorian, rose-strewn papered walls.

"That's right," she said. "You heard me. I offered you a way out. The chessboard is still set and all the men on the table, waiting for the next move. No one has died. Everyone is in place, waiting... waiting for *you* to make a *damned* move!"

"You're wrong, my sweetheart, everyone has died, but you and Sarah," I said. Our last chance had gone a long time ago. Couldn't she just give it up and face it?

Alice smiled that endearing, knowing smile I loved so much, and her tone changed to that of serene priestess, instructing a novitiate. I knew that tone, too, and welcomed it. I needed some help here. I trusted her, I realized.

"Much can be accomplished in Spirit, Henry. It is not too late."

My mouth dropped open. Azriel had said nearly the same thing to me.

"Death is an illusion. It is only another state of life and a departure from the physical world. Only our bodies die, darling, and that is a temporary thing. We always get new ones to begin with again. I've told you that over and over. You *know* it!"

"Pay attention, Professor!" She rose from the bed and swept a chiffon clad arm through the air, the sleeve trailing, long and wispy, with points at the end. I watched it part the lamplight in a fascinating swirl of dazzling white. "Watch closely now."

The walls fell away and I faced 1980 Sarah across a chessboard. Our eyes met coldly, like those of duelists at dawn right before the glove hits the ground, the backs are turned, and the pacing begins. I refused to drop my gaze or be the first to look away.

"You," I gritted out. "What are you doing here?"

"The same thing you are, imbecile. But why don't you ask your little whore? She's responsible for this stupidity."

I looked around, but couldn't find Alice. The scene seemed to be forming around us and the chessboard. With dizzying speed, the board expanded to enormous proportions and we were separated by the distance of a football field's length, a good hundred yards lay between us—which suited me just fine. To my amazement, goal posts rose in the end zones, which seemed to be the table edges. What the hell... then it hit me. Shouldn't a chessboard be square? I looked again and saw that it was. At my thought, it shrunk to half its former size. I glanced over to find teenaged Alice on the home team, my team's sideline. She shrugged and sheepishly grinned.

My eyes hungrily traveled over her, taking in every detail. Long white filmy skirts blew against her legs, a ridiculous pair of white and black pom-poms in her hands. Tall boots encased her slim legs and the wind trapped the skirt at the fork between them. Heaven lay in that triangle, I thought. She should've been in the end zone, I would've *Taken... It... All... The... Way.* John Madden's silly, overblown voice played over a loudspeaker.

I cupped my hands around my mouth and yelled above the strong wind that blew across the field. "What's going on here?"

She smiled and yelled back. "You'll see. Give me a sec." She pointed to the board.

Sarah paced at the other end. The stiff wind blew her coiled, long hair across her face. Seemingly annoyed, she shoved it back over her shoulder. Pink stiletto heels rapped a staccato beat on the table edge. She cupped her chin in the right hand as she stared at the board with intense concentration, her left arm crossed beneath her breasts, her hand clutching the crook of her right arm.

The sky roiled with fast-forward, time-lapse video speed, a special effect like the old MTV music videos in the 80s, when the technology was new. Stands appeared on both sides of the board, filled with cheering fans. Chess pieces materialized on each end, all in their standard starting positions. Mine wore white and Sarah's wore black.

All the pieces were in place, standing in red and black checks on the board. On their bases, they towered seven feet tall or better, with living faces on them. The faces shifted and changed as I gazed at them. Henry Sayre, Sanfort, and Spears, Aleysia, Alys, Alice, my mothers and fathers, hers, the Sarahs, her folks—the gang was all here, from every lifetime. And of course, no chess game would be complete without the Bishop. He stood on the black side of the board, dressed in his official finery, frosty eyes blazing out from Stephanus de Bracy's cruelly handsome face over the heads of the pawns in front of him.

The other three bishops seemed to be only carven images—the only faceless players on the table. In this present configuration, Stephanus faced my White Queen, the queen of my heart, my most precious love, Alice. When had they moved? This was a game already in progress, though they'd all been in starting position just a blink ago.

A severely sculpted dress molded the White Queen's fine curves. Lace and netting, sparkling with frosty diamonds, swathed her bare shoulders. At her slender throat lay a large, flat ruby in the shape of a heart, the only spot of color on her, except for her lips, which were painted a luscious, soft red. Okay, her eyes were brown and her upswept hair and skin the right color, but the white effect was overwhelming.

White Queen Alice smiled at me, demurely, flirtatiously dropping her gaze as she curtsied upon her stand. Her slender leg, encased in a white lacy stocking—the leg of a ballerina, showed from a deep slit down the dress's side. At the top of that sculpted, dainty leg, I glimpsed lace-edged white garters running up her thigh, my imagination tracing it up that delectable length to a belt that surely held up that stocking beneath the dress. Something huge inside me turned over then tightened my balls. She'd better stand up or I was going to come in my pants, or take her right off that base and do her on a red square right in front of God, the Bishop, and everybody.

To my relief, she straightened, looked the Bishop in the eye, and with a sweet smile, flipped him off, the slender middle finger of her right hand erect and defiant, which sent me into gales of whooping laughter that laid me out on the ground, pounding the grass, tears squirting from my eyes in hilarity. The look on the Bishop's face as he moved diagonally back across the board, made me whoop harder.

John Madden loomed over the crowd on an enormous viewing screen, an old fashioned microphone on an unseen desk in front of him. Excitement lit his hooded eyes and his mobile, rubbery features turned comical with a giant-sized grin. "She did it! Big score for the White Team!" He winced theatrically, bushy eyebrows meeting over his large nose. "But oh *ouch*! The Bish is gonna feel *that* one in the morning, fellas!"

White Queen Alice grinned at me, her brown eyes snapping mischief beneath her silver-white crown, and gave me the bird, too. God I loved that woman.

The home team went wild. We didn't lose any points over it, either.

Insanely, and with complete appropriateness, the familiar opening notes of an old progressive rock song by Yes, a two-parter which began with a intro sub-song called, "Your Move" that eventually segued into, "I've Seen All Good People," played over the sound system. I listened carefully to Jon Anderson, the lead vocalist, who now stood on an elevated glass platform with no visible supports. It hovered just a little above the field, close enough he could've beaned me with the microphone on its cord if he'd wanted. Masterfully, he laid out his lyrical abstraction for me with a doom beat keeping time like a slow motion metronome behind his high, angelic voice.

Was it half-time already?

"Take a straight and stronger course, to the corner of your life…" He continued with what might've just been abstract lyricism describing a white queen who ran from a suitor with a speed that made matrimony impossible. Just like on the radio, he drew out the word 'wife' and his veddy British, narrow face, looked somberly upon the scene below him as he sang. He was young, I noticed, as were we all in this dream.

I glanced back up to him with a puzzled look on my face at the white queen line and he shrugged as if to say, "Hey man, I wrote the lyrics, it's *your* dream, dude." I laughed again. Maybe I *had* made the white queen run so fast she hadn't had…time…to be…my wife. She'd run from me several times, come to think of it—straight into the path of disaster. Son of a *bitch*.

Anderson nodded wisely as he continued his song, crooning into the mic about time and captured news that a Queen could use. My god, the lyrics to this song were freaking me out. Illicit photographs taken covertly. Captured news seemed a good description for blackmail.

Christ on a cracker. Look at that, why dontcha? Sarah over there, all done up in a queen's garb, but hers was pure black, the dress a dark twin to the one Alice wore. She waggled her stubby, shiny black-tipped fingers at me and lasciviously licked her ebony-lacquered lips. Her ample bosom nearly overflowed the gown's décolletage, and she filled the rest it of like Mae West. Her hair, too, was upswept in a fancy do. Black diamonds glittered over every inch of her.

Black Queen Sarah bowed her head and a haughty smile twisted her mouth, a painted black slash in her dead-white face. She took her due as any royal Black Queen should.

She'd used the news against us, to its fullest, most psychotic extent, leaving no stone unturned. She moved across the board to face the White Queen, who smiled at the sight of her and nodded as though unsurprised at her approach. The look on Alice's face said she wanted that move, welcomed it. The light of battle shone in her dark eyes as they locked onto the pale blue ones in front of her. That would be my Alice and I began to laugh again and wondered why I wasn't afraid. Shouldn't I be shitting myself with fear about now?

It then occurred to me that they were equals here—both queens with no age or social advantage, and no difference in power. Alice, I thought, might even have the better chance with those encumbrances stripped away. I knew her; she could do things no one else could. Not even Sarah. Hope soared in my heart and soul.

I wondered how and when the change had occurred. Sarah had always seemed to outrank Alice—at least she had in the lifetimes where our paths had crossed.

"Don't surround yourself with yourself. Move on back two squares…"

I shivered in the wind, Anderson's voice sending chills rippling over me. I did as he said and gained a new perspective on the game laid out in front of me. Interesting.

Don't surround yourself with yourself.

My gaze swept the board, and realized that I'd listened to him. All of us were there, not just the Henrys, but everyone who mattered in this game. Copies and multiples stood on each side of the board, dressed in black and white. I was as much an enemy to myself as any of them were. That seemed clear.

The music stopped right at the wall of signature sound for which *Yes* had been known, Anderson dramatically drawing out the word 'captured' until it wobbled and echoed on into eternity. I waited for the happy, ditty-bop guitar intro to "*I've Seen All Good People*" but it didn't happen. Silence followed the echoing voice, spreading itself like a cloak over the chessboard field.

I looked up and Jon Anderson lay on the platform just above me, on his side, with his head propped on his hand, his elbow on the glass, completely at ease. He pointed at me. "Your move, old chap." His clipped, upper-class posh accent caressed the words.

I smiled. It certainly was and high time, I'd say.

I'd just turned to the board, intent on a new strategy, when a whistle blew and several penalty flags hit the turf. A short, skinny ref marched from the sideline as though he had a major case of the small man syndrome, stalking purposefully onto the board and I followed his path through the tall pieces. The wind plastered his black and white striped shirt against his concave chest as he pointed and then held up his arms in ref sign language. I didn't understand the penalties in this game. Or maybe I did, his gestures looked familiar, but this zebra-striped banty rooster with the whistle in his mouth looked excited to the point of outrage.

I stepped around a White Knight with my father's face. Behind him, knelt 1980 Sarah with a yellow nylon rope in her hands, tying Henry Spears the White Pawn to his square. She didn't look up from the task of using her high heeled shoe to pound in the anchoring stakes, but only reached for another loose end to secure.

Henry the White Pawn's eyes darted fearfully and looked down upon Sarah in abject terror, unable to move. Trussed up like a Christmas pig, all he lacked was the apple in his mouth. This made me angry. It was too close to what she'd done in reality. At least he still had on his clothes.

The ref shook his head at her and waggled a finger, then pointed to the ropes and stakes. Sarah didn't look up, so he blew the whistle again and yelled in a nasal, Tennessee twang, "Il*legal Pro*-cee-*dure!*" He jumped up and down in indignation, then pointed to a pawn on the black side. "You're outta here! And take those two varmits with ya." The black pawn hung his head and then hustled two others off the board.

"Holding!" Again the ref's finger pointed and another group of black chessman left the board. The crowd on the black side booed, while the white side held their breath, eagerly waiting.

"Now wait just a pea pickin' second," the ref said, as Sarah stomped away from him in a huff, leaving poor White Pawn Henry hopelessly pegged to the board. "I ain't done yet. Stand fast, missy!" He hitched up his white ref pants, his skinny legs planted far apart.

Sarah turned around with her hands on her hips and opened her mouth.

"I'd be quiet if I were you, girlie. There's a penalty for cussin' the ref, too."

She clamped her shiny pink lips together and rolled her eyes.

"Undo him. Now!" The ref's fists were now on *his* hips and Sarah yanked the stakes out of the board and untangled the ropes slung around the base. White Pawn Henry smiled and looked relieved. He flexed his fingers and bent his knees, then stood upright.

Too bad this guy hadn't been there when she tied me to the bed. The ref glanced over at me and said, "I *was*, young feller. But *you* had to make your move before I could make *mine*."

My eyes widened and I looked over to find Alice jumping up and down on the sideline, waving her pompoms. "Go Team!"

My attention was abruptly brought back to the ref when he blew a single, sharp note, obviously enjoying both the sound and the attention. "*Il*legal Contact!" His eyes fastened on Sarah's. "*And* Delay of the dad-burned *Game*!" Several more black pieces left the board.

The two queens still faced each other; Queen Alice glanced at the ref with a question in her eyes. He nodded. She smiled, blew him a kiss, which pinkened his cheeks, then turned to the Black Queen.

"You will leave this board at my command," Alice said in an uncompromising tone.

Black Queen Sarah's chin came up. "I refuse."

Queen Alice's leg flashed so quickly from the slit in her dress I nearly missed it. With a swinging karate kick Bruce Lee would've enjoyed, her high-heeled foot connected squarely with the Black Queen's chest and toppled her from the pedestal.

Sarah, her skirts jumbled and her legs akimbo, rolled to a stop on a black square and sat up, huffing. "Well, I never! Ref! Ref! Penalty! *Pen-al-ty!*"

The ref stared benevolently at the White Queen for a moment, as though bemused, but then turned hard eyes on Black Queen Sarah, and removed his cap. "That there, yer highness, was league-sanctioned zone *de*fense and a righteously executed free kick." He jammed the hat back on his head, blew his whistle, and pointed to the sideline.

White Queen Alice smiled; her face a portrait of amused sarcasm. "I said leave. Your time here is done. You did this to yourself." She rolled her eyes and twitched a shoulder in 1980 Sarah's direction. "Quite. Obviously."

Two black pawns helped the Black Queen to her feet. She stood between them and said, "You'll pay for this, bitch."

Alice blew another kiss in her direction and made shooing motions with her hands. "I already have. Be gone!"

And the Black Queen was gone, which set the fans on both sides into a frenzy.

Suddenly the ref's whistle blew an ear-splitting shriek and all eyes returned to him, a restless babble spreading through the crowd.

"I ain't done yet, dag-nabbit!" His eyes swept both stands. "Quiet! Or I'll eject all of yous from this here game. I will!"

The crowd hushed, seemingly cowed by his wrath.

With a decisive, approving nod, he continued, "And, last but not the least! And it's got me purty riled up and ready to open up a fresh canna whoop-ass!"

His little wrinkled-apple doll face scanned the crowd and he looked even more put out than before. "Y'all payin' attention to this here game?"

"Yes!" they roared back at him.

"Well, okay that's more like it! Last of them violations I saw with my own two Tennessee eyes! This ain't Missouri, but she showed me like a jumped-up-ever-lovin' Mazurah rattler and I hates them damned things." He stared balefully over the chessboard and no one doubted him, I could see that. He turned back to 1980 Sarah.

"*Un*sportsmanlike Con*duct*!" He blew the whistle and pointed at me. "When the players have departed the field, it's your move, White." He strutted back to his position on the sideline, his eyes alert for any further shenanigans.

The black knight put his heels to his enameled horse's sides, saluted the ref with his lance and left the board, leading a small group of other pieces trailing in his wake, his twin knight bringing up the rear.

Alice & Henry

The crowd on the black bleacher side groaned and booed. The Bishop stood alone, a black blot in a sea of white pieces. There was no where for him to go. His teammates were off on the sidelines looking upon the board with grim, expectant faces—chess-piece football players in the last seconds of a game when their third string kicker is going for the field goal and they know, just *know* he's going to drop it, muff it, or otherwise fuck it up royally.

The Bishop's eyes darted to the white chess players surrounding him, his peaked hat wobbling, the scepter of office clenched in his beefy hand, which he shook at me menacingly. "I own you, Henry. Just remember that." He smirked. "But I love you. You have the sweetest cornhole in the entire *world!*" It was Sarah's voice that mocked me from his mouth.

Pompoms wildly waving caught my eye and I glanced around his broad back to see Alice smiling at me from the sideline. She shook her pompoms once more, then dropped them and put her hands to her mouth, shouting, "Henry! It's your move, darling! Go for it!" She clapped her hands, her excitement plain.

I yelled at her, "I will if you will, honey!"

She gave me two thumbs up.

I knew my next move. My giant hand reached down and with a forefinger, I flicked the tiny bishop off the board. "Check and mate, asswipe." I picked him up and looked into his tiny face. "I'm sorry it came to this. But you are not going to win this one, dingleberry. I am."

I stuffed him in my shirt pocket and as the cloth closed over his head, his tiny voice said, "It's about damned time."

I laughed again.

Forty-Seven:
Alice 2033

I arose from my bed, stiff and feeling my age. The sickness that had been coiled inside me, peeling the flesh from my bones little by little seemed to have taken a break for the moment. I hadn't wanted to know what it was, had no interest in fighting it—though I'd been aware of it for quite some time. Feeling punk, I'd gone to the doctor a year ago and my elevated white cell count had started him talking things like chemo and radiation. I smiled, thanked him for his trouble, and asked him for enough prescription painkillers to get me through the rest of it. He'd known me long enough to know when "no" meant "no." He ponied up on the pain meds like a good boy should.

My journeys of late had been all of the spiritual kind, and the long rest I'd taken after Henry's funeral perked me up a bit. There was enough fire left in me to do this one last thing, surely.

Finally, I understood and believed I could say the words and mean them, now. Henry had done what needed doing and I was proud of him. He was here in this room with me, as surely as I was, and if I looked just right, I could see him from the corner of my eye. Azriel's golden light was a vagrant shimmer, an arcing refraction, just outside my line of vision.

I reached for my clothes, not wanting to waste a second of this brief surge of wellness. I couldn't be sure how long it would last.

As I pushed open the nursing home door, I felt the last bit of my resentment drain away as my time grew short here and this most recent chapter drew to a close. When at last I stood at Sarah's bedside, I felt only pity for her, and yes, at long last, forgiveness. She had played her part as a stern, relentless teacher of a lesson for Henry and me both. It was the Way of It, how we learned and grew. Despite the many things I remembered and all the Paths I knew, the one to forgiveness was something I'd been unable to walk—I couldn't do it by myself, not without Henry.

He'd turned the rusty key in the lock imprisoning my soul. I enjoyed the sound and the feel of freedom beckoning. I felt pretty good, really.

As I took her hand, I sensed a gathering around me and glanced up to find Abby and Charles Thurmond gazing severely upon me from the foot of the bed. I quailed a bit in my resolve and dropped Sarah's pudgy, liver-spotted hand onto the bed.

Next to them, stood my mother and father, long dead these many years, and the sight of them brought a tremulous smile to my lips. I'd missed them so. Mom smiled, her eyes spilling over as usual, glossy and such a fine shade of aquamarine I almost lost myself in them for a moment. She made the 'ok' sign with her thumb and forefinger and courage blasted over me like a warm heat wave from an over-stoked kiln. Dad only looked a bit puzzled to be there—much as he'd always seemed to me whenever he stepped too far from the cab of his beloved trucks. That was all right, too. I wiped a tear.

On the other side of the bed, Henry stood bracketed by his mother and father. I wondered who would speak first in this strange place that mere seconds before, had only been a standard private room in a nursing home. The room expanded, the walls shimmered and became insubstantial. I glanced at Sarah and she sat cross-legged on the bed, twirling her hair around her finger and cracking her gum, oblivious to the old, dying woman who lay beneath her.

"Well? You're all here. Is it time, now?" She glanced eagerly to all the faces around her.

Her father nodded and stepped away to reveal a long ago scene, a place in time where a young Puritan girl accused another of witchcraft. Sparing me nothing, my own lack of respect for the contract already written and signed was shown as I lay with Henry in the meadow. The tip of my nose stung with unshed tears and I jerked when I felt Sarah take my hand. A quick glance told me she'd done the same with Henry on the other side of the bed.

Henry watched the scenes unfold with an air of modest acceptance about him—not humiliation. He held up his head and stared clear-eyed at all that was revealed. Good. He owned his part of it. Though it had all begun in an earlier time, this part had been the one that had truly trapped him. A blood oath broken and a binding contract that could only be dissolved by the people who'd witnessed it. His first vows as a priest had only been a foreshadowing to the ones he would make next.

Rapidly the scenes played forward to our drama in this life. The old tape I'd seen in Henry's apartment filled an entire wall, that and all that had followed showed in merciless detail. Still the hand gripping mine did not let go. When it was done, I looked Sarah straight in the eye and said, "Sarah. I am sorry and you are forgiven."

I bowed my head as Henry echoed my words and sentiment, with an addition. "I do not wish to be married to you, Sarah. I am sorry for my part of this and I acted dishonorably. I apologize for that, too."

Sarah nodded, an open, sunny grin upon her face competed with what I judged might be relief. "I really asked for it, didn't I?" She giggled and shook her head. "Well, at least this time, I didn't physically hurt or maim either one of you."

Henry's eyes met mine above her head. This much, was true. She'd gained some control over herself and that was an improvement, a slight one, but a step up, nonetheless. I had the distinct feeling that of all the things that had passed between the three of us, the most telling was the scene taking place here and now. Sarah would make a huge jump in her personal growth. I certainly hoped so. It had cost her plenty.

A slight, cynical smile touched Henry's mouth as his eyes met Sarah's. "I'll give you that much," he said. "You didn't and you could've, many, many times over."

I resisted the urge to shudder as I thought of him tied to his bed, helpless. She could've hurt him much worse than she had. She could've done most anything, really—after all she had done far worse before.

Sarah turned sober. "I didn't harm myself that way, this time, either. I mean, the scourge or hair shirt, or the cutting… burning my skin." She seemed to look inward, absorbed in this thought for a moment. "What I did was bad enough without all that, though…" She looked to me, puzzled. "I couldn't seem to stop myself."

I looked down upon her, my sympathy doubled as I understood so well that sentiment. Her release from her role had been as contingent upon Henry as mine. "It is the way it is, Sarah. The way it works."

She turned to Henry. "I am sorry for my part of this—and I mean that truly. I have hurt others and myself, over and over, but now I can heal. I will take this forgiveness with me to the next place and the next life. I will trouble you no further. You are absolved of your obligation; at least by me."

I watched as her eyes followed a slender silver bridge that appeared above our heads connecting Henry and me—and immediately the image of the Disney prince facing the evil queen in Sleeping Beauty jumped into my head. That poor, blasted bridge seemed restored. Whole. I myself had never witnessed this particular imagery that so clearly joined the two of us together. In the way that humans will follow another's glance, Henry gazed at the bridge in wonderment. Sarah turned to me. "Alice, I forgive you and understand. I am sorry." Still she held our hands and I was okay with that.

The three of us looked then to the faces ringing the bed. One thing remained. Henry's blood upon a parchment must be undone. Freedom from the vow could only be given under the terms it had been written and by the witnesses to that binding contract. I thought about the Bishop, and figured Henry'd squared that one on the chessboard field. It just didn't come up, and it would've, because this seemed to be the reckoning time.

Charles Thurmond held the up the contract in his hand, showing it to all. "I hold here a marriage contract signed and witnessed, a legal, binding document, the terms of which have not been met." His chilly blue gaze fell on Bill Spears. "As Magistrate, William, what say you on this?"

Bill nodded. "It has been repeatedly shown that this couple is not compatible. No issue, no children came from their union, nor will they. That is a duty neither of them can fulfill. They seem willing to dissolve the bonds. I approve of its dissolution." Mary Spears, whom I'd never met, echoed her husband's sentiment. Puritan marriage depended upon the producing of children. Grounds for divorce in those hard-scrabble times.

Charles Thurmond turned to my parents. "Though you were not signed witnesses to this original contract, your presence here indicates that you were, in fact, part of my congregation and did approve the original, though your signatures do not appear on it. I would ask you then, as parents of the girl with whom Henry broke his vows, who bore him illegitimate issue, do you approve of the dissolution of this contract?"

Mom seemed unable to contain herself and didn't even glance at my dad. "Hell yes, we do!"

Dad, mincing no words, said, "We do." He met Thurmond's eyes, though it appeared he sincerely wished to be elsewhere, and guessing just where that might be wasn't hard. I couldn't blame him, really, but this needed doing. He'd never shirked what needed to be done. It had been his personal creed.

Finally, Charles turned to his wife, Abby. "My dear, you have a vested interest in this document and its fate, what say you?"

Abby's face looked rebellious and my heart fell. "I only wanted Sarah to be happy. I'd thought Henry a good choice. I love my daughter and would give her anything."

Sarah said, "Mom, give it up. I don't want him anymore. It was stupid and you let me have my way, way too much. Don't make this harder than it has to be. Let go of it, okay?"

Abby hesitated, her eyes locked onto her daughter's with almost a pleading look in them. Finally, she turned to Charles. "All right then. So be it."

He turned to the three of us holding hands. "As the elders in this meeting, we are in agreement that the tenets of this contract may now be dissolved." He tore it in two with a satisfying ripping sound. I let go of the breath I'd not realized I held.

Azriel appeared in glowing, golden splendor, blotting out the artificial light in the room and I had to close my eyes. When I opened them, I stood alone at Sarah's bedside with my bony hand tucked inside her gnarled, fleshy one. Gently, I removed my hand and laid it back on the blanket. "Be at peace, Sarah."

I made my way back down the corridor, my old sneakers barely making a whisper on the shiny tile floor, feeling lighter and less connected to this earth with each passing second. I tossed my well-used visitor's badge on the main desk as I passed. I wouldn't be needing that anymore. With relief and an awareness that my disease was rallying, sucking the last of my energy and life, I sank into the front seat of my car and stabbed the code that would take me home. As usual, I'd cut it pretty damned close. My death would not be halted by our actions today, and that was all right with me. I'd done what I'd come here to do and I was ready to move on. That thought brought a weak wave of eagerness washing over the illness. Yes, I was ready. More than ready.

***

"Branwen," I said into the phone. So close was the otherworld, I'd forgotten the name I'd given her. "Elyse, it is time."

My daughter paused on the other end of the line. "Mother, I shall come."

A similar pause came to me. "I am ready and Henry is with me. All will be well. I've left..."

My eyes were drawn to the end of the room where my daughter now stood. Always much quicker than me at the Paths, she made it in record time. Silver streaked her hair, nearly as much as it did mine. I dropped the phone, rose from my bed, and went to her. "My baby. I love you so. I will come to you whenever you call me."

Words were not necessary. We had done this for each other many times... In a flash, I saw myself, ageless and timeless, in that eternal space between earthly existences, performing this same task for her twenty-two years, seventy-three days, ten hours and forty-three minutes from this very moment. To my relief, she would be ready when she summoned me and no violence would force the calling.

My gaze found the beaten iron crescent moon that hung between her bared breasts, which showed, glinting dully between the parted edges of the cloak she wore. She'd taken the earth mother statue with her when she'd left my home and married Arthur. I would find them together, as I always did—this time in a forgotten panel in the attic of this house, vacant but still standing in 2113. Sisters next time—I think I liked that configuration best of all, because then we'd likely spend our lives on a parallel, not having to miss each other much before death would claim the one in the parent role.

All was right and good with the world then.

I stood holding her hand and Henry's. Azriel blanketed the three of us with his protective, soft light. Elyse pulled a silver dagger from within the folds of her cloak, kissed first me, and then her father of this lifetime—with whom she shared a long, searching look and a smile.

"You did well, Henry. We shall meet again."

He nodded and kissed her again. "I love you, you know."

Her eyes shone in the dim light and I wasn't surprised to hear the words I'd used myself when he'd once told me I was something special. "I know." But without the flippancy of my own reply, in an eerie echo of *his* words, she added, "You are special, my father and old friend. This I've always known. It's not the first time, nor will it be the last and I return your love a thousand-fold."

Her smiling eyes came to rest on me, knowing and wise, their black depths reflecting every available particle of light. No question remained between us. I nodded. With a decisive swipe, Elyse cut the silver cord holding me to the used-up body on the bed.

I stepped into the warm circle of Henry's arms and sighed. All would be well.